# FOREVER FRIDAY

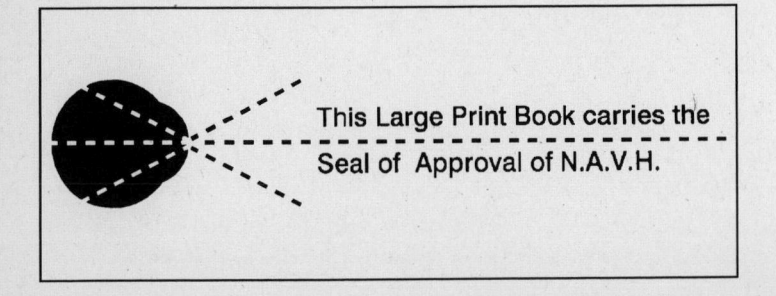

This Large Print Book carries the
Seal of Approval of N.A.V.H.

# FOREVER FRIDAY

# TIMOTHY LEWIS

**THORNDIKE PRESS**
*A part of Gale, Cengage Learning*

Farmington Hills, Mich • San Francisco • New York • Waterville, Maine
Meriden, Conn • Mason, Ohio • Chicago

GALE
CENGAGE Learning®

Thorndike Press® Large Print Clean Reads.
The text of this Large Print edition is unabridged.
Other aspects of the book may vary from the original edition.
Set in 16 pt. Plantin.

**LIBRARY OF CONGRESS CATALOGING-IN-PUBLICATION DATA**

Lewis, Timothy, 1954–
　　Forever Friday / by Timothy Lewis. — Large print edition.
　　　pages ; cm. — (Thorndike Press large print clean reads)
　　ISBN-13: 978-1-4104-6741-6 (hardcover)
　　ISBN-10: 1-4104-6741-4 (hardcover)
　　1. Divorced men—Fiction. 2. Married people—Fiction. 3. Relationship quality—Fiction. 4. Large type books. I. Title.
PS3612.E987F67 2014
813'.6—dc23　　　　　　　　　　　　　　　　　　2013047809

Published in 2014 by arrangement with WaterBrook Press, an imprint of Crown Publishing Group, a division of Random House LLC

Printed in Mexico
2 3 4 5 6 7 18 17 16 15 14

*For Dinah:*
*my wife, my soul mate, my Forever Girl*

Hope is not a granted wish or a favor performed; no, it is far greater than that. It is a zany, unpredictable dependence on a God who loves to surprise us out of our socks.

— Max Lucado, *God Came Near*

# PROLOGUE

*Summer 2006*
*Adam Colby*

Some great romances worth the telling are never told, their lovers slipping silently between life's timeworn cracks only to be pitched with yesterday's trash. As owner of a small estate-sale business, I'd witnessed evidence over the years of various couples' love lives. So I'd learned to sift through the piles of forgotten memories. Learned to appreciate a second look . . . and perhaps ease my pain.

That was how I discovered the postcards.

Bargain hounds and treasure hunters pushed through the heavy front door of Gabe and Pearl Alexander's beloved home early before rushing away to their next classified find. Antique buyers, who were more savvy, missed the cards because they were camouflaged among several dozen identical photo albums. Inside their vinyl maroon

covers, these albums held not the usual faded family snapshots, but hundreds of colorful postcards revealing six decades of married passion recorded in rhyme beside canceled postage stamps.

Surprised to find postcard poems instead of photos, I began reading them in between my dealings with customers. As a thirty-eight-year-old man who had once committed to "forever," I was intrigued. What was this couple's secret? In a fast-food world of abbreviated relationships, what supernatural love potion kept Gabe and Pearl enamored with each other for more than half a century?

So I continued reading through lunch and into the sale's afternoon lull. I'm not sure I believed in love anymore, especially married love, but found myself becoming more entranced as each minute passed. Even though the Alexanders had lived together in the same house, the postcards were sent over the years from Gabe to Pearl, beginning in 1926. Each unique card was signed "Forever, Gabe," the poem connecting an episode of their love to the picture on the front.

My guess was Gabe died in the mid-1980s, because that's when the cards stopped.

One of the earliest cards was dated September 4, 1927. On the front was a picture of two colorful seashells. On the back, this poem:

```
Two tiny shells, together side
  by side
Wandering to and fro about the
  morning tide.
Two tiny shells, now picked up
  by a man
Who sets them out to dry upon
  the glistening sand.
Two tiny shells, how delicate,
  how proud
To be created by the One whose
  throne's above the clouds.
And these two tiny shells are
  sent to you by me
Because I know you understand
  God's wonders by the sea.
                    Forever, Gabe
```

I was curious if he'd mailed Pearl two actual seashells along with the postcard and, if so, what had happened to them. Surely she'd have treasured them, but the only seashells in their belongings were large and obviously store-bought. The ocean must have played a significant role in their mar-

riage because there were several cards with sailboats and beach scenes, and with Galveston so close by.

"What kind of man invests this much time in his marriage?" I said aloud, feeling a little betrayed by a guy I'd never met. Love wasn't a competition, but Gabe had left me floundering in the dust, and most other men as well. Men who loved their wives, or *said* they did, even though many times their actions proved otherwise.

At least I wasn't a hypocrite.

Or was I?

Just before the sale ended, a customer declared himself the Alexanders' next-door neighbor, so I discreetly asked about their interest in the sea.

"Wouldn't know," he said, then shrugged. "Gabe died shortly after I bought my place. Pearl would speak to me from across the yard, but she wasn't keen on in-depth conversations."

"Why?"

"Valued her privacy, I guess." He shrugged again. "Spent the last year of her life confused and in an extended-care facility."

"Can you tell me anything else?" I asked.

"Pearl had an unusual nickname."

"Nickname?"

"Yeah, like a man's, but I can't remember

12

it." The neighbor paused. "Do you know what happened to their car? A big 1940s model Oldsmobile. Mint condition."

I shook my head, wondering if the postcards contained Pearl's nickname.

"The old gal probably needed the money and sold it," the man continued. "Shame. I'd have bought it." He rubbed his chin. "Any tools left?"

"Out in the garage," I replied.

"The Alexanders were nice folks," the man added before walking away. "Too bad you never met them."

The neighbor was correct. I'd never met them, but had heard from the attorney who hired me that they had no children and were donating the bulk of their estate to charity. However, their will included detailed instructions that certain sentimental items be delivered to various relatives still living in the Houston, Texas, area. I usually contracted that job to a moving company, but since the Alexanders' home was only a few miles from mine, and the items were small, I elected to deliver them myself. After reading the postcards, I felt strangely invested in Gabe and Pearl and was more than happy to oblige.

Over the next few weeks I made deliveries and asked questions. Some thought it odd

that a total stranger would take such an interest in their kin. Others spilled all they knew to me, even digging up yellowed newsy letters. I selfishly decided not to mention the postcard albums unless someone asked about them, and no one did. So I concluded they were kept secret. In some ways, it even seemed the postcards had been written for me. But I couldn't keep them, not in good conscience anyway. At the end of my quest, I'd take them to an Alexander relative as "accidentally overlooked."

Gabe's typewriter went to their niece, Alice Davis. Alice recently had knee replacement surgery and was, in her words, "convalescing nicely." I spent a rainy afternoon wrapped up in her thoughtful recollections. She also told me about the Alexanders' deceased longtime housekeeper, Priscilla Galloway, whose daughter, Yevette, looked after Pearl during that final year. I contacted Yevette and scheduled an appointment to meet with her the following week.

I suppose my obsession with the postcards was as much a matter of timing as anything. The stinging loneliness of my divorce still lingered, the blunt ache of a failed marriage. As I sent a confirmation e-mail to a somewhat reluctant Yevette, my eyes settled on a folder I'd saved with messages from my ex-

wife. I opened it and clicked on her final e-mail. Even though it was dated approximately two years prior, devastation washed over me as though I were reading it for the first time.

Adam,
Today we're officially over. Thanks for respecting my wishes. If you're still hoping I'll change my mind, don't. I need my own life. You need to move on. So please, no more questions. When did I stop loving you? I'm not sure. Is there someone else? Yes. That's why I didn't contest the house. I never intended to hurt you.

Haley

The words "someone else" were, unsurprisingly, still the most painful.
Someone else?
In twelve years of marriage we'd had our share of difficulties, but hadn't everyone? I had never doubted our love, nor envisioned a life without her. Other than what couldn't have been helped, where had we gone wrong? What could we have done to prevent disaster?
For each hour I pored over the Alexanders' postcards, I wondered if I could ever

love another woman. Worse, after striking out in my first marriage, did I deserve a second chance?

I didn't know. I thought I should have the best that life offered until the woman I loved walked away. At first I blamed her. Then I blamed myself. But one thing was clear: Pearl and Gabe knew something Haley and I'd missed. So I'd seek the source of the Alexanders' wisdom. And learn from past mistakes. My gut told me that time was my friend *and* my enemy. If I bogged in my quest, despair could scar into bitterness.

Years ago I discovered that jotting my thoughts on paper, then punching them into a computer, helped me organize. Helped me process. So by recording the Alexanders' story, I hoped to uncover their secret. I suspected that something Gabe called "The Long Division" in the poems was key to their marital longevity. But I still had many postcards to contemplate, along with a few loaned letters and whatever I might glean from Yevette. If feeling bold, I'd fill any remaining blanks in the Alexanders' story with my own interpretations . . . or longings.

Could a man turn an about-face after marching in the wrong direction for more

than a dozen years?

At this point, I could only hope.

# ONE

Mrs. Alexander lay in her hospital bed at Bayshore Extended Care and daydreamed of being anywhere but there. She despised the bland food, her beige room, and the incessant talk-show tripe from a television across the hall. Living in the same building with a bunch of elderly people was taxing at best.

To make matters worse, the patient roster listed her as Pearl Garnet Alexander. She'd hated the name for most of her ninety-nine years. Not the Alexander part. Alexander was her married name and had been since 1926. Before that she'd been a Huckabee.

Pearl Garnet Huckabee.

One jewel-encrusted name was bad enough, but she'd had to endure two. That was until her seventh summer birthday when she decided her family must call her Huck.

19

Huck Huckabee.

Her mother, Annise, refused at first, saying she'd spent many precious hours considering a fancy name for each of her thirteen children. And now her youngest daughter insisted on a plain name like Huck. A boy's name. It would remind folks of that poor orphan in Mark Twain's novel who smoked, drank, and caroused up and down the Mississippi with a runaway slave.

But Pearl argued that slavery, thank goodness, had ended during the last century and borrowing a name from a grand tale like *Huckleberry Finn* only made one appear just as grand.

So at age seven and a half, the name Huck stuck.

Stuck like globs of grammar school paste, gently smoothed, then hardened over time. Somewhere in that half year, the glorious transition occurred. Family first, then friends. By Thanksgiving, using her given name was unthinkable.

Huck sat up in her bed. She adored the name Huck; its carefree, adventuresome aura defined her. Lamar, her good-natured twin brother who was six minutes older, had wanted a nickname too, but nothing caught on until they were in high school. He was a natural at baseball, especially when it came

to hitting well-placed grounders. And since a fast ground ball was labeled a *daisy cutter,* Huck had immediately dubbed him Cutter. A few of their classmates had mischievously tried to call him Daisy, but without success. He carried the name Cutter for the rest of his life. After Huck married Gabe Alexander, they'd ardently followed Cutter's career from the minor leagues into the majors.

So just where was Mr. Gabe Alexander? It was Friday. He would leave work soon and she should be ready. The nurses had lied about last week's postcard. Said there was no mail, even though she'd later heard snippets of truth sprinkled among condescending little whispers. And here it was Friday again. There would be a new card with a lovely picture on the front. On back, a wonderful verse composed just for her. Over the years Gabe had missed only one Friday . . . that dreadful week he'd slept alone in intensive care.

Huck peered out the window. A budding mixture of pink and white azaleas signaled the end of the mild Houston winter. She smiled, recalling a glorious spring day from long ago. She'd boarded a Main Street trolley engaged to Clark Richards and disembarked enamored with Gabe, falling heart-

long in love that night on a deserted Galveston beach. Each time he breathed her name his eyes twinkled. Even after sixty years when he could barely catch his breath.

She refocused her attention back inside the room and reached for the phone, thankful to have it back. The nurses had removed it until she'd promised them — and Yevette — that any future calls would be made in a responsible manner. It was embarrassing to have bothered that sweet child with such trivial matters. But an entire month without a trip to her own hairdresser had been a true emergency. A lady's hair style and color set her image.

The current postcard situation was equally dire and Yevette must agree. Hiding someone's private mail was the same as stealing. It was a federal offense, and there was only one responsible thing left to do.

For the second time within a week, Huck Alexander dialed 911.

It took only minutes for the wail of sirens to reach her ears. She lay back and smiled . . . remembering the first time she saw Gabe.

# Two

When our eyes met,
Your beauty blazed
Desire's slow burn, and yet
Love's embers ever yearn
The brilliant glow
Of hearts who know.

                    Forever, Gabe

*March 1926*
*Houston, Texas*
*Huck*

"Pardon me, sir. Do you have oysters?"

The young man behind the counter sported an easy grin in response. "Oysters? Of course. With or without pearls?"

"Without," Huck replied, never having liked pearls because of her name.

"Too difficult to chew?"

She nodded. "Harder to swallow."

"It's a good thing oysters don't grow diamonds." He glanced at her ring finger.

23

"Not that you need, or even want . . . um . . ." He cleared his throat.

She suppressed a giggle at the glass intentions of men. The clerk's clean-shaven smile and quick wit intrigued her, even though the remark was a bit too friendly. As an English teacher for the prestigious new Sidney Lanier Junior High School, her reputation was fragile. And even though she wore no diamond, she *was* engaged.

Then she noticed his eyes. Horizon eyes. Heaven-brushing-the-sea colored eyes.

She should have bolted out the open door of Cecil's Fish Market & Seafood Emporium. Run to the Market Square streetcar stop and never looked back. Should have, but didn't. Could have, but wouldn't.

His easy grin returned, now adorably crooked. "My name's Gabe Alexander."

"Well, Gabe Alexander, I'd like a small amount of your freshest oysters, please."

The sea-sky eyes moved closer. "I've never seen you in here before, Miss . . . ?"

"Shucked."

"A pint of oysters for Miss Shucked," Gabe called to a snickering clerk.

"I dare say someone's hooked a tiny humor fish," Huck replied. "What's your clever bait?"

"The most beautiful lure." Caught in her

24

gaze, he placed the jar in a paper bag and pushed it slowly across an enamel-top counter.

Huck's cheeks warmed. "What do I owe you?"

"Your name. Then we'll haggle price."

She opened her purse to buy a little time. What was the harm in an innocent nibble? It would be their first and final flirtation. "It's Huck. Huck Huckabee."

"How about I treat you to dinner tonight, Miss Huck Huckabee?"

Closing her purse, she clutched the bag, then smiled a calculated smile. "Why, Mr. Gabe Alexander, you already have."

Over the next few weeks, as the cool bluster of early spring warmed into April rain, the memory of Gabe Alexander intruded upon Huck's private thoughts. His smooth, fair forehead, slightly receding into boyish sandy curls. His gentle face supported by a strong jaw. But it was Gabe's eyes that pierced her most, invading her dreams. More than mere color was an infusion of honesty and kindness. A "Mister Jack" depth of vision, she recalled, where heart met heart and soul met soul.

At age ten, she'd encountered Mister Jack a few weeks after discovering a secret glen

along the banks of a thickly wooded creek that flowed between her parents' property and the woodland home of Texas hero General Sam Houston. Bathed in crisp blue sunlight, the glen became her private Shakespearean stage, its circular floor covered with soft Bermuda. Here, she would act out scenes from *A Midsummer Night's Dream* or *Romeo and Juliet.*

One day, after a particularly spirited rendition of Juliet's death speech, she spied a small bush at the glen's edge covered with pale pink blossoms. She approached the bush slowly, never having noticed it before, its simple beauty stark and intriguing.

"Those is orchids," offered a sudden pleasant voice from the opposite side.

Startled, Huck spun to face shirtless bib overalls hanging below a trustworthy face with clear eyes. Her opened mouth met only air.

The stranger removed a weathered widebrimmed straw hat and laughed. "Guess all your sound got lost in reciting them fancy words of Mister Shakespeare."

"It's *those* fancy words," Huck replied, knowing better than to correct an elder but being unable to help herself. "And those *are* orchids."

"Ain't that what I said?" He barefooted

across the glen and eased down beside the orchids. "They's Anacacho orchids. Just in case you was wondering."

He toted a hand-smoothed cane with diamonds, clubs, hearts, and spades carved on the handle, but he didn't limp. Sweat glistened on his bare scalp like thick dewdrops.

Especially because she was a girl, Huck had been sternly warned about talking with strangers. Each year, her father was hired on as a mounted guard at the nearby state penitentiary when his crops were laid by. "A man you don't know could be an escaped convict," he'd said. "Some convicts are killers, some have mental problems, some are rapists." When she asked him to explain "rapist," he grunted, then mumbled, "A bullet's the best cure for them." Huck chose not to inquire further. However, she soon relayed the conversation to her twin. "I probably shouldn't tell you," Cutter had whispered, "but a rapist is a man who doesn't wear clothes."

Since the stranger wore overalls, Huck didn't have to worry about that. But there had been recent gossip of an odd character loitering about. Descriptions were vague and no one could pinpoint his exact location.

27

The stranger pulled a red bandana from the crown of his hat. "When I was your age, I had a head full of curly hair." He mopped his scalp. "Wasn't the same color as my eyes, though. Your hair and eyes is a perfect match."

Huck frowned. Not only was her hair straight, it was dark-brown-boring. Plus, she'd have given anything for blue eyes. "Who are you?"

"Reckon I'm a teacher, of sorts."

"A professor?"

"Maybe. Depends on what you want me to profess." His swath of friendly teeth widened into a chuckle.

"Do you have a name?" Huck asked the stranger.

"Name?"

"What do people call you?"

Again the grin. "Folks call me all sorts of names. Most ain't polite enough to travel past a young lady's ears."

"That's not what I mean and you know it." Huck inched closer. "What name follows Mister?"

"Oh that." He thought for a moment. "I s'pose the name following Mister is Jack. I'm Mister Jack."

Huck eyed the cane. It looked suspiciously prison-made, being fashioned from the

same yellow pine an inmate had used to carve a rolling pin for her mother. "Why the playing card suits?"

"Thought you'd never ask." Mister Jack studied the carvings. "This here cane reminds me to be content with my own hand. To hold my best card as long as possible and not blame the dealer if my game goes sour, though it can be a little tricky deciding which card's best. Question is . . . how does you know what to keep and what to throw away?"

Again, her open mouth was accompanied by silence. Huck knew Mister Jack wasn't talking poker and prided herself at deciphering adult riddles spoken in the presence of children. So instead of feigning ignorance, which she nearly always followed with suppressed laughter, she returned the question to its giver . . . a strategy her father employed when discussing business. "Back that ornery mule up," Ethan, her father, once told her. "The tail end may not be pretty, but it gets folks moving a lot faster."

"So how do you know what to keep and what to throw away?" Huck asked.

Mister Jack fished a slender pine straw from the emerald bevy in his front pocket and picked his grin. "Look deep into a man's eyes and you'll see his hopes and

29

dreams. Woman's eyes too. Look deep enough and long enough and you'll know their future, along with all the bad things they done."

"The bad things?"

"Oh they's there all right. Sneaking 'round and hiding behind the good. Everybody's guilty of something. Even you."

"Then what's my future?" Huck asked, deciding her father's mule analogy wasn't appropriate in every situation.

"Hmm." Mister Jack rubbed his chin.

It was a question she'd asked the fortune-teller each year at the county fair, knowing the answer would be bogus from the get-go. No one could predict the future, at least no one *human.*

"Your future," Mister Jack said finally, "has to do with this here Anacacho orchid bush. Fact is, this bush and your future is kin. Just as this bush shares itself with youngsters like you, you will share yourself with your children."

"You'd better look deeper because I don't want any children." With so many bossy siblings, except for Cutter perhaps, she'd dreamed of being an only child. A house full of grimy urchins was the last thing she wanted, even if they were her own offspring.

Mister Jack examined a fallen Anacacho

30

blossom and gently stuffed it into his pine needle pocket. "Your future is also about hope, 'cause nobody stays on this earth forever, which is backwards to the way originally intended."

"Like children who die before their parents," Huck shot back, then immediately wished she'd never broached the subject. Death was something she'd rather not discuss.

"You know there ain't no guarantees about living long," Mister Jack answered, then added softly, "even for children."

He was right, and it was the primary reason she didn't want kids. One of her brothers died a few weeks after his birth, and a sister at age eight from a ruptured appendix. Her mother still cried from time to time, always on their birthdays.

Mister Jack continued. "Most young'uns become adults, but not before causing their folks to grow a peck of wrinkles." He grinned again.

"Or a bushel," Huck replied, picturing her own parents and an array of prune-skinned kinfolk. Wrinkles meant "old" and she wanted no part of that. "Then the only way I'll ever have a child is to birth one already grown."

The grin vibrated into a booming laugh.

31

"Now what will your future husband think about that?"

For the third time in her ten years of life, and during the same afternoon, Huck Huckabee was speechless. Dreaming of a future husband was her most private endeavor and Mister Jack knew that too.

"Ain't nothing unusual in a little wishful planning 'bout your soul mate." Mister Jack fingered the symbols on his cane. "Look deep and you'll find that best card. Grab hope and never let go. And don't forget what I said about the dealer and the game." The laugh boomed again. "Now close your mouth before Mister and Mizz housefly change address."

In her bed that night, hours after the laugh had dissipated, Huck stared out her open window and reasoned final thoughts concerning Mister Jack. No killer she'd ever heard about valued eyes, Shakespeare, and flowers. And someone with mental problems probably wouldn't be savvy enough to compare life to a card game and God to the dealer, although she wasn't quite sure how the Almighty felt about that.

What intrigued her most, however, was the term *soul mate.* It was new to her, and she instantly adored the obvious implication. So after referring to the enormous

32

family dictionary, dubbed "The Un-abridged," she decreed it part of her vocabulary and came to a logical conclusion: Since Mister Jack knew so many secret things about her — including her most private dream — he wasn't human. Therefore, he must be an angel. Her guardian angel. She'd never considered angels being teachers, carrying playing-card canes, wearing bib overalls, or speaking with incorrect grammar. And since angels — at least the good ones anyway — always told the truth, she could stop worrying about being an old maid like her older sister Molly Beninna. It was common knowledge that most husbands wanted children, and Huck still felt adamant about never having any. But if Mister Jack was really who she believed him to be, he'd somehow change her mind. At least, that's what she hoped. Perhaps that was the "hope" he wanted her to grab.

As Huck drifted into slumber, she again heard Mister Jack's unusual laugh, this time floating high atop the night breeze. Her mother swore God created chickens because he had a sense of humor. If God laughed, then so might his angels. But Huck and Mister Jack had discussed subjects far more compelling than funny-looking birds. Perhaps his laughter possessed a deeper, more

fearless meaning: a heavenly grin meant to destroy the smirk of evil.

For the next two years, she returned often to her secret glen but never saw Mister Jack or the Anacacho orchids. As a rule, she eagerly shared the events in her life with Cutter. Girlfriends were too wishy-washy emotional, and sisters couldn't be trusted. But what if her twin thought she was being silly or, worse, wouldn't believe her? The encounter with her guardian angel had been much too personal to risk belittlement or disbelief. So Huck vowed to save the story for her soul mate, which made finding him a priority.

She kept her vow, but as each green summer ripened into autumn gold, her life matured in different directions, blurring the lines between adolescent reality and childhood belief.

At age sixteen, Huck fell from the rumble seat of a moving car and suffered a broken collarbone, along with possible internal injuries. Because of a modern x-ray machine, she was rushed to Houston's Baptist Sanitarium and Hospital. The hospital had six floors and 115 beds. On top of the sixth floor was a combination garden area and "baby camp" equipped to care for fifty babies. Part of her recovery was to relax in

the fresh air and sunshine of the roof garden; however, the constant giggles, gurgles, and cries transported her thoughts back to the Anacacho orchids and Mister Jack's words of hope: "You will share yourself with your children."

The day before Huck's discharge, Molly Beninna broke the news. "The doctor says you'll never conceive," she said softly, her eyes brimmed with tears.

"Don't cry, sweet sister," Huck replied, determined to remain strong. "Mother's conceived enough for us both."

As soon as Molly Beninna left, Huck rolled over in her hospital bed and wept.

After meeting Mister Jack, she'd grown somewhat inclined to the possibility of parenthood, which kept his words of hope alive. Kept her guardian angel real.

Until the accident.

Why had she been so irresponsible? Celebrating the last day of her junior year atop the rumble seat of a speeding roadster. Dancing like a daring wing-walker on a high flying biplane.

On a breezeless morning two days later, Huck set out to revisit her secret glen. As the lazy summer sun peaked above tree line, she reached the glen, its far side partially hidden behind a vanishing mixture of dark

shade and humid haze. "For your information, Mister 'Teacher of Sorts,' " she whispered sarcastically, "there won't be any children." Then started to add, "Nor probably any future husband either," when she spied the familiar pale pink blossoms. It was the first time she'd seen them since meeting Mister Jack. While rushing toward the delicate flowers, her mind immediately flashed to his words: "They's Anacacho orchids, just in case you was wondering."

Reaching out, she then carefully plucked a perfect bloom and supported it with both hands. Several moments passed, timeless, with understanding. She took a deep breath and slowly spoke. "Just as this orchid I'm holding shares itself with me, I will share myself with my children." The answer from her angelic "teacher of sorts" had been there all along. She'd share herself with her children by becoming a teacher. Would study hard and make education her profession.

And hope?

Hope her sadness over being barren wouldn't last forever.

Hope to meet a man who would understand.

So with the childbearing dilemma solved, Huck Huckabee returned to her favorite

pastime. A young woman's soul mate search, known only to herself and Mister Jack.

# THREE

```
Your woman-smile
Is the lure of men,
But to this man's delight
Its soft imprint, a gift
Heaven-sent. . . .
For soon our lips ignite
The smoldering fires
Within.
                    Forever, Gabe
```

*March 1926*
*Houston, Texas*
*Gabe*

Gabriel Robert Alexander untied a fish-spattered apron and watched the most striking woman he'd ever met walk out the door of Cecil's Fish Market & Seafood Emporium. He took a deep breath, savoring her scent. If a man was lucky, a woman's perfume would linger behind her for a second or two. Huck Huckabee's did, reminding

him of spring's first blossoms. It was an al-
luring fragrance he'd never forget.

"You let her leave without paying," an
anxious young clerk said. "If old man Cecil
wasn't in Dallas, he'd —"

"He'd dock your pay and well he should."
Gabe pitched the apron to the disheveled
clerk. Fish scales floated to the floor. "You
let me do it."

"But —"

"Don't worry, Louie. Cecil's much more
interested in attending his grandson's wedding than monitoring your imprudence."
Gabe patted the clerk's bony shoulder and
grinned. "I'll ask the bookkeeper to fix it.
He won't mind."

"Mr. Alexander, you are the bookkeeper."

"Thanks for the apron, Louie. You might
consider washing it sometime."

Gabe headed for his upstairs office as the
big clock atop Market Square bonged
Houstonians home from another work
week. "No need to waste good money on a
fancy timepiece," Cecil would say. "You can
hear that confounded ticker all the way to
San Antonio."

Old Man Cecil, otherwise known as Cecil
Laborde, had begun his career hawking
fresh fish out of a rented grocer's stall
located inside Houston's city hall on Market

39

Square. After hoarding every penny, he and his wife, Norma, had bought and remodeled a ramshackle brick building two blocks north at the corner of Main and Commerce on Buffalo Bayou. It wasn't long before Buffalo Bayou was dredged into the Houston Ship Channel and Cecil suddenly found his business thriving at the center of port activity. The old man put on a miserly front but was one of the most generous men Gabe knew. A portion of each week's inventory was earmarked to be given away.

Before climbing the stairs to his office, Gabe passed a stocky man heaving the last of a shipment of red snapper into a large walk-in cooler. It was Friday and Cecil liked to be well stocked for the Saturday morning rush.

"Afternoon, Gabe."

"Hello, Charlie." Gabe grinned. "Looks like the snapper are running."

"They're running all right. Running me ragged." He slammed the thick wooden door before mopping his face with a handkerchief. "Hauled more of them slippery rascals than's healthy for a landlubber."

"Take a couple of fat ones home for dinner. On the house."

Charlie nodded thanks, then reached into his shirt pocket and offered Gabe a hand-

rolled cigarette. "What are you so happy about?"

Conversation paused as the men lit up and retreated outside to the loading platform. The honk and rattle of downtown automobiles blended with the nearby chug of ship channel tugboats. Gabe spoke into the cool March breeze. "Ever thought much about a woman's smile, Charlie?"

"Just her smile?"

"That's what I asked."

"Which woman?"

"Any woman." Gabe blew smoke, watching it spiral skyward.

"Can't say that I have . . . just her smile, that is."

"A woman's smile is a gift, Charlie. The most beautiful gift a man can ever receive."

Charlie thought for a moment, then thumped ash from his cigarette. "Every time my wife smiles, she cooks me a big dinner and we have another kid."

Gabe chuckled softly. Charlie's wife, Chloe, loved food and children, bearing a brood of husky curly-headed boys to show for it. The woman didn't look normal unless she was pregnant. Cecil had employed both Gabe and Charlie as clerks when they were sixteen. Even though Charlie's urban background was different from Gabe's rural

one, the two young men shared a similar work ethic and had become fast friends. Two years later America entered The Great War, and they'd fought side by side in the gas-filled trenches of France, with Charlie bringing home a French wife.

Both men had decided to enlist after public outrage over the Zimmermann Telegram. By use of a coded telegram, Arthur Zimmermann, Germany's secretary of foreign affairs, proposed that if America entered the war, Mexico should ally with the Germans and take back the southwestern U.S., including Texas. The message hit American newspapers after being decoded by the British and incited a quick U.S. response. Gabe's maternal great-grandfather had sacrificed his life at the Alamo. Any army under the illusion of conquering the Lone Star State, or the rest of the forty-eight, could be accursed and march straight through the gates of hell. So while most eligible males in Texas had enlisted immediately, Gabe and Charlie had to wait over a year until they turned eighteen.

After the war, Gabe returned to Cecil's and advanced to bookkeeper. Charlie began driving for a wholesale fishery that delivered daily Gulf Coast catch. The two friends had

been exchanging smokes and conversation for almost a decade.

"So . . . ?" Charlie asked. "Does Miss Any Woman have a name and number?"

Gabe gazed skyward and breathed a final drag. "It's Huck Huckabee," he replied, her name flowing out effortlessly with the smoke. "I didn't ask about a phone."

Charlie rolled his cigarette between his thumb and forefinger. "Unusual name for a woman. But I like it."

"Me too," Gabe replied.

"And just how long have you known Miss Huckabee?"

"Met her about twenty minutes ago when she came in to buy oysters." Gabe flicked the butt off the edge of the platform and faced his friend. "But I've known her my entire life."

"Knowing her phone number your entire life would be better."

Gabe pulled two smokes from his pack of Lucky Strike. "Remember how over in France I always knew we'd make it home?"

Charlie nodded.

"This is the same gut level instinct. I *will* see Huck Huckabee again . . . and soon."

"When you do, get her number."

The men lit their smokes and the topic changed to weather. Unless it was Prohibi-

tion scuttlebutt or an election year, their talk snuffed with the second cigarette. So after discussing the cooler than normal spring, Charlie grabbed his supper and drove away.

Gabe climbed his office stairs to tally the day's receipts. The small room was nothing fancy, just bare plaster walls surrounding two hard swivel chairs, some oak filing cabinets, and a hand-me-down desk. However, it did have a large window that overlooked the store below. A window he'd glanced through after checking his pocket watch at exactly 4:46 p.m., spying this remarkable woman perusing the aisles. That was when he'd leapt down the stairs and literally jerked the apron off poor startled Louie.

When Gabe closed the store at six, it was his habit to eat supper at the café across the street, then catch a trolley for the two-mile trip home. Tonight, though, he wasn't particularly hungry and decided the weather was more suited for walking than riding the crowded streetcar. Besides, he loved the pulse of city sidewalks and enjoyed window shopping.

At the corner of Main and Franklin, he passed First National Bank. It had been there since he could remember and was

where his parents borrowed against their "cattle dreams." John and Maggie Alexander had operated a small ranch in Fort Bend County on the flat coastal plain just southwest of Houston. They'd envisioned buying several sections, building an enormous herd, and passing the wealth along to their only child. As a youngster, Gabe learned to rope, ride, and even cook chuckwagon fare. From the first through eighth grades, he attended a one-room schoolhouse, excelling in writing and arithmetic. He strove to please his parents but found baby-sitting cows monotonous, being much more interested in poetry and numbers than sourdough and yearlings.

When Gabe was fifteen, John was gored through his right lung by a surly bull. He never fully recovered and died the following winter from pneumonia. Fearing for the health of his exhausted mother, Gabe convinced her to lease the ranch and move to the city. He'd only been at Cecil's Fish Market for a month when Maggie died. A few hours before her death, she'd removed her gold wedding band and placed it in her son's hand. "Keep this in a pocket close to your heart," she'd whispered, barely audible. "Give it to the girl of your dreams. The man of my dreams gave it to me." Gabe had

45

swallowed hard. He'd carried the ring each day since.

Continuing his walk down Main Street, Gabe glimpsed a newsstand photo that shot an excited shiver the length of his spine. On the front page of the *Houston Chronicle* was a picture of a local female tennis champion. For an instant he thought it might be Huck, then realized it wasn't.

Their brief conversation had resembled a tennis match, he thought. When he'd served his oyster comment — which was almost out of bounds — she'd returned it without stammer or blush, pacing the volley of their conversation with her intelligent wit. Advantage — Huck. And just when he thought he'd charmed her out to dinner, she'd slammed him with an ace. Game — Set — Match. He chuckled. Tennis was the only game scored with "love."

In the distance, Gabe could see the enormous Rice Hotel. One sultry night, he'd taken a date to a dinner dance there because the Rice Café was the only air-conditioned public room in the city. When he proudly informed her that the hotel was built on the same exact spot as the historic capitol of the Texas Republic, she'd merely yawned and said, "Gabe dear, our state capitol is in Austin," then complained she was cold and

asked him to collect her wrap. He didn't bother to explain the difference between a republic and a state. He also didn't bother to ask her for another date.

A bit farther down Main, in the window at Foley Brothers department store, Gabe glimpsed several mannequins dressed in the latest flapper fashions. Houston was a city known for beautiful women, and at age twenty-six, he now preferred courting the marrying kind. Most of his female acquaintances were "surprises" initiated by well-meaning married friends. They'd invite him over for dinner, only to have Miss Available drop by with a dessert she'd expertly prepared from an old family recipe. Occasionally, one of these girls would attract his further attention, but it would never last. In the end, they all wanted the same thing. A family. And family meant children. He saw nothing wrong with populating the earth, but fatherhood was not a priority. At least not yet.

Gabe leaned against a lamppost and watched a young couple stroll past. They paused in front of a bridal gown display and briefly kissed before moving on. He lit a Lucky. First and foremost, he sought lasting romance. The kind of sensuous in-love-ness lacking in most of the married couples he

knew. Couples who began as intimate lovers, exploring every curve and valley on the great matrimonial highway, but after numerous detours of children and career, limped along as platonic road-weary travelers. It was a phenomenon he called "The Long Division." In arithmetic, long division required many dutiful steps that continually divided and then multiplied further divisions into the lowest possible dividend. Likewise, far as he could tell, a marriage was filled with numerous obligations that divided time spent together. If over the years those divisions were allowed to multiply, then the once-shared passions slowly separated into single-minded interests.

The Long Division.

Gabe wasn't quite sure how he would do it, but he refused to ever let this phenomenon happen to him. He'd rather not be married at all.

At the next corner, he paused for a street-car to pass. Painted on the side was Lucky Strike's new ad campaign for women: "Reach for a Lucky instead of a sweet." He smiled. Cigarettes had never appealed to him until he'd stumbled into love with a woman who smoked. Amelia Addison was the reason he'd started, even adopting her brand. They'd met at the Iris Movie Theater

two months before he shipped out for The Great War. It was a bitterly cold Saturday afternoon, unusual for Houston. He'd been running errands and slipped into the crowded theater to get out of the icy north wind. Showing was *The Accidental Honeymoon,* a romantic comedy he'd wanted to see. The suggestive plot entailed the chance meeting of a man and woman, perfect strangers who were mistaken as honeymooners, then forced by hilarious circumstance to spend the night together. After allowing his eyes to adjust, Gabe finally located an empty seat in the back row of the balcony in the smoking section. He barely noticed the girl sitting next to him, until she offered him a cigarette.

"Want a Lucky?" she whispered.

"No thank you." He'd never seen a more attractive blonde and found himself wishing he smoked.

"Love stories make me cry, even the funny ones. It's embarrassing. Helps if I smoke. Sure you don't want one?"

"My hands are so cold, I'd probably drop it."

The woman laughed. "Bet I'll change your mind before the movie gets to the sad part."

By the time the film ended, Gabe knew her name was Amelia, she was a legal

secretary and five years older than he. He'd also tried his first cigarette, right after she'd warmed his hand underneath one of her shapely legs. Hot and nervous, he sweated and coughed through the sad part while Amelia cried. Then for the next eight weeks, Gabe and Amelia spent every nonworking hour involved in their own accidental plot: talking, smoking, kissing.

When Gabe embarked for France, cigarettes kept neither of them from tears. The war days were hard, the frightening nights hellish. So he smoked to taste Amelia's sweet lips, feel the fire of her soft caress. Tobacco was his sanity. When the doughboys returned home almost a year later, Cecil met him at the train station with a note. Amelia had married a lawyer from New York and wished Gabe the best.

A screech of tires forced Gabe's thoughts back to Main Street. "Hey, buddy!" yelled a motorist. "You gonna stand in the road or cross it?"

Gabe waved an apology and shuffled to the curb. He sighed. The hurt over Amelia had long since passed, and he no longer missed her. But he still thought about her from time to time and wondered if he'd ever find another woman to love.

Until today.

His gut instinct about seeing Huck again was merely the next scene of a wonderful new story unfolding in his life. Gabe patted his shirt pocket, thankful he'd not given his mother's ring to Amelia.

He strolled another block and ducked into Benny's Diner, a popular spot he normally frequented for breakfast. There were several empty booths, so he chose a clean one by the window. Most of the supper crowd had filled their bellies and parted. He lit another Lucky and plunked down a nickel for a cup of joe.

"Special's corned beef and cabbage," said an unfamiliar waitress with red puffy eyes. "That's about all that's left."

"Just coffee, please."

"Got some brewing, so it will be a minute."

Gabe watched as the waitress worked. She was about his age, attractive, and seemed to have been crying. He wasn't sure why, but his instinct was to rescue tearful women from whatever or whomever had wronged them. He'd attempted it twice, recently, and failed both times. The first girl wasn't crying, just suffered from hay fever and produced more tears because he'd noticed. The second girl was crying. Worse, she was "expecting" and wailed even louder at

Gabe's generosity. After that, he'd sworn to mind his own business, if possible, and *always* check for a ring. The waitress wore a thin gold band. Huck Huckabee's ring finger had been delightfully bare.

The waitress returned with a strong cup and a weak smile. "Let me know if you change your mind about the special."

Gabe inhaled the rich steam. Before he was old enough to walk, he'd sucked thick cowboy coffee dribbled onto a teaspoon of sugar. One of his favorite boyhood memories was traveling with his parents to the Galveston wharves. If the wind was right, he could smell the grainy aroma of raw coffee beans before the trade ships docked. By the time his father died, he was downing several cups a day, roasting the beans to perfection in an iron skillet and grinding them one pot at a time. Long before cigarettes, coffee helped make life worth all the trouble. And today, he'd met a girl whose hair and eyes matched the brew's exotic color.

Taking a sip, he glanced out the window . . . almost dusk. Across the street he could see foundation work for the massive new Gulf Building. When complete, it would be an Art Deco masterpiece of castle-like Gothic design, boasting the tallest and

most commanding skyscraper west of the Mississippi. Rumor was that Gulf Oil Corporation would be hiring a horde of entry-level bookkeepers. Since he'd advanced as far as possible at Cecil's, he'd filled out an application. Working for a major oil company had never been his passion, but Gulf paid top dollar. Any sensible man should be willing to expand his financial future. Especially a man who wanted to provide nice things for a woman like Huck.

"Gulf Building's gonna be quite a spectacle, ain't it," croaked a voice that resembled a bullfrog with gravel stuck in its throat. A middle-aged potbellied cook plopped down opposite the table from Gabe. "Saw the architect's drawing in yesterday's *Chronicle*. Looked like some runaway medieval birthday cake."

"Have a seat, Benny."

"Already got one. Wish it was big enough to hold up my britches." He laughed.

A different waitress appeared, coffeepot in hand. "Ready for a warm-up?" Without waiting for a reply, she topped Gabe's coffee, poured a cup for Benny, and disappeared.

"See you're still scaring off the ladies." Benny pulled a half-smoked stogie from behind his ear and lit it. "Where you been,

Gabe? Find a gal to cook breakfast for you?"

"I've been working double duty. Cecil's away in Dallas since last weekend. His grandson's getting married."

Benny frowned. "Happens to the best of us . . . and the worst."

"Looks like you've hired some new girls. What happened to my first waitress?"

"Got a picture postcard last week from her husband. Rascal up and dumped her after eight years. Ran off to the Caribbean with another woman."

Gabe nodded. "I thought she'd been crying."

"Wouldn't you?" Benny slurped coffee with the cigar still clamped between his teeth. "Worked her first shift today. Kept staring at her wedding band. Wouldn't take it off. Finally told her to go home early. Never worked outside the home till now and got three kids."

The second waitress returned. "A delivery boy is here with eggs for tomorrow. Where do you want them?"

Benny stood and hiked his britches. "Where they won't get cracked this time. All I get around here is busted eggs and broken hearts." He shook Gabe's hand. "Don't be a stranger."

Outside Benny's Diner, the Friday evening

traffic was thickening. In another thirty minutes, Main Street would be an unbroken line of honking headlights looking for a parking space — cars plodding impatiently along like bawling cattle in search of bedding ground. Gabe finished his coffee and headed out the door. Potent exhaust fumes blended with the pungent odor of electric trolleys. Streetlamps glowed white beneath colorful restaurant signs and movie marquees. Stores stayed open late to accommodate the throng of money-spending Houstonians.

Remembering he needed a new typewriter ribbon, Gabe entered a stationery shop. He preferred to type, although he'd been told more than once he had excellent handwriting. Passing a display of picture postcards, he recalled Benny's comment about the waitress and her husband. Ending an eight-year marriage with a postcard was cruel. The man was a gutless coward. He'd probably mailed her a photo of some deserted beach to symbolize his own desertion. Odds were that their broken marriage was just another casualty of The Long Division.

One particular postcard caught his eye. A pretty young woman, her face teeming with anticipation, was reaching into a mailbox. The caption read, "Could there be a note

from my sweetheart?" Gabe chuckled. Of course there would be a note, unless this gal's man was blind and stupid. Any woman's most treasured possessions were her love letters. After Gabe's mother died, he discovered a small bundle tied with a ribbon and safely tucked near the bottom of her cedar chest. He'd felt a little guilty about reading them, even though they were mostly concerned with his parents' ranching plans. It was obvious she'd read one letter more than the others because it was the most faded and contained a poem composed by his father. Gabe had no idea his father ever wrote poetry and could only remember the last two lines:

Out where the coyotes and doggies roam
Our work and love will build a home.

He smiled. The man who rarely showed his soft side had created one simple love poem, which his wife cherished for decades. What if he'd written her a poem each year? If the waitress's husband had sent a few romantic postcards early in their marriage, he might have felt close enough to look the other way when tempted. It made sense. A man whose thoughts about his mate lingered into beautiful prose would be less

likely to stray.

What if the waitress's husband had sent her a card each month?

What if *her* was Huck Huckabee, and *he,* Gabe, was the card-sending husband?

A sudden tingle surged, warming the depths of Gabe Alexander's lonely soul. He'd safeguard their relationship with postcards *and* poetry. The Long Division would lie in ruins at Huck Huckabee's feet. He began to imagine it. Beginning the first week of their marriage, he'd compose a short verse about their love on the back of a meaningful postcard, then mail it in time to arrive for the weekend. With fifty-two Fridays each year, their bond would multiply into a million unbreakable connections.

After some digging, Gabe found a postcard with a man and woman gazing into each other's eyes. Perfect. He'd made up his mind.

"Are you finding what you need?" a salesclerk asked.

"Absolutely. Unless you have a postcard with oysters."

"Oysters, sir? What's the occasion?"

Gabe smiled. "I'm getting married."

# FOUR

Huck slowly raised the lid on her jewelry box and peeked inside. Her engagement ring was still there, of course.

Waiting.

Patiently.

She listened to the ticking alarm clock atop her dresser and sighed at the folly of her own annoyance.

"How long must I wait for an answer?" Huck whispered. She'd not returned to Cecil's Fish Market that wet Houston April, purposely avoiding Gabe while seeking divine guidance about marrying her fiancé, Clark Richards. She hadn't expected to see Mister Jack again, but had offered several prayers each day for wisdom, then focused her thoughts on the pleasant times she and Clark had shared. After all, it was his ring

58

that *sometimes* encircled her finger.

*Sometimes* because she wrote left-handed and it scraped the chalkboard at Sidney Lanier. *Sometimes* because of her daily chores. It would be silly to wash dishes or perform cleaning duties while wearing a one-carat diamond. She might lose it. So the ring resided in her room at Mrs. Thompson's boardinghouse, except on days when Clark came to call. Unexpected days like today, or rather evenings.

It was Monday and she'd stayed after school tutoring students and grading papers. She still had to enter the marks into her grade book before bedtime, as well as make her lunch for the following day. On top of that, she'd looked forward to spending part of the evening soaking in a hot bath and washing her hair. It was almost waist-length and took forever to dry. However, the moment she'd arrived back at Mrs. Thompson's, she found a note thumbtacked to her door. Clark was in town on business and would swing by and pick her up at eight p.m. He was dying to try the city's finest new restaurant, Pickwicks.

"I'll have to wait to wash my hair on another day," Huck muttered regretfully.

She reached inside the jewelry box. The ring felt heavy, even larger than on the

afternoon Clark gave it to her. She held it up to the light and studied the stone's multifaceted brilliance. It *was* beautiful. And even though she knew it was impossible for a diamond to grow in size, everything else about their relationship had shrunk, especially her feelings. Clark constantly boasted about owning the biggest and the best. Sometimes he acted as if he owned *her.*

Huck slipped the ring on her finger. Her fiancé's materialistic ideas were frustrating indeed. But in the Richards family, expensive gifts measured the depth of one's love and devotion. Clark would've never given her such an exquisite diamond if he didn't love her with all his heart.

She glanced at the clock. Thirty-three minutes to spare. So she lay back on her bed and propped her legs up on two pillows. Perhaps Clark would be different this time. He'd not always behaved in such a serious manner. In fact, she'd never known anyone as delightfully funny. Moreover, he could read her better than anyone in the entire Huckabee household, even Cutter. She sighed. Clark knew immediately when she was being honest, or not *entirely truthful.* Even so, she'd never had the courage to tell him about her guardian angel.

60

Huck closed her eyes. After her encounter with Mister Jack, she'd wondered if Clark might be her soul mate. But thoughts of her chance encounter with Gabe still swirled through her mind. Had she been mistaken?

Both Huck and Clark had grown up seventy miles north in the piney East Texas community of Huntsville. Started first grade together and even attended the same church. Throughout their public education, Clark penned and passed dozens of love notes, but never did anything wildly romantic until seventh grade Sunday school. It was Bible Memorization Day, and girls paired with girls and boys with boys. The gender was uneven, so Clark suggested he and Huck partner. Instead of memorizing the Twenty-Third Psalm, he whispered an especially daring passage out of the Song of Solomon, inserting both their names and emphasizing descriptive words. If she hadn't gasped at the word "breasts," old Mrs. Hudge — dubbed Methuselah's Grandmother — would never have known. Until then, everyone thought her ears had played out around the turn of the century. So instead of Sunday's tasty fried chicken dinner, Clark suffered a nasty helping of lye soap with razor strap sting for dessert,

spending the rest of the day standing outside the privy between soap-related bouts. Huck had never heard of anyone in Walker County being punished for reciting Holy Scripture and had no idea God even knew the word "breasts" or that married folks carried on that way. So she read the entire Song by moonlight after the family had gone to bed.

During high school, Clark was an all-state linebacker with gladiator good looks and voted most handsome. She was captain of the cheer squad, naturally stunning, and chosen most beautiful. And he was a friend as much as a beau: carefree, daring, and always interesting. When the slow freight trains would steam through town, she and Clark would occasionally hop an empty boxcar and pretend they were hobos. They'd sit leisurely in the open doorway, and Clark would steal a kiss or two. When the train began to pick up speed, they'd hold hands and jump off. Once, a man saw them and threatened to inform the railroad authorities. So they concocted a wild tale about how they'd ridden all the way from Tampa, Florida, in search of their lost family. The man handed them a dollar and wished them luck. For days afterward, Clark would whisper "Tampa" in Huck's ear, and then they'd laugh themselves silly.

At Sam Houston Normal Institute — SHNI, the local college — Huck majored in education and Clark was an all-American. They attended the same postgame parties and other collegiate functions, soon evolving into a "likely couple," which sometimes pleased Huck as much as it displeased her. Clark could be debonair one minute and crude the next. Somehow, he always shadowed her, even at church. When she finally consented to a formal courtship during their senior year, it gratified her mother immensely.

"He's a well-educated boy," Annise had said one evening while putting away the supper dishes.

"I know, Mother." Huck stacked several plates and handed them over. "But there are lots of educated men."

"And — missed a spot on this one — and he's a member of our local congregation. Brother Ralph Leggett says Clark hasn't been absent from a service since he can remember."

Huck inspected the plate. "The same Brother Leggett who can't remember to button his suspenders, so he paid the price last Sunday during 'Stand Up for Jesus'?"

Annise ignored the remark. "You know what I mean. Heaven forbid you marry

someone from a different denomination. Remember your brother."

"Cutter's still single, Mother. Is there something about him I should know?" Huck smiled and glanced at her mother, who remained expressionless.

"I mean your oldest brother's wife, Helen, my only daughter-in-law who refused to change her church affiliation once she knew the truth."

Huck slid the plate underneath the final stack. It wasn't dirty, just a bit different in design. Helen was probably closer to God than anyone in the entire Huckabee clan.

It wasn't long before Clark began hinting at marriage, planning each moment of time together. To Huck their relationship reeked of predictability. As college graduation neared, he'd become businesslike with their relationship, even domineering. To complicate matters, she'd begun doubting that he was her soul mate, so evaded all proposal attempts.

When they graduated from SHNI and Huck landed the job at Sidney Lanier, Clark wanted to follow. However, his father was president of Huntsville's First National Bank and quickly offered his son a junior vice-president's income and prestige. That's when Clark purchased the big diamond.

Huck never really intended to accept it, but he asked her in the middle of the Huckabee Christmas afternoon domino game. Ethan was in the process of skunking several sons, their wives, and a number of grandkids when Clark suddenly dropped to his knees, slipped the ring on Huck's finger, and offered his eternal fidelity. Before she could answer, her mother and most of the others welcomed Clark into the family, dragging him into the kitchen for his pick of celebratory dessert. Her father dropped his final domino and grunted. Then jammed a chaw of tobacco between his teeth and retreated outside to chew and spit off the gallery. Cutter followed.

Huck watched the front door slam. Her father and twin brother would eventually accept Clark into the family. It would just take time, and perhaps a few hundred domino games. Someone called Huck's name from the kitchen. She stood, glancing at her father's empty chair. His last domino lay facedown. How did he always know what to keep and what to throw away? As if on cue, her mind flooded with thoughts of Mister Jack. She'd asked him the same question. And suddenly, his answer made her uncomfortable. "Look deep into a man's eyes and you'll see his hopes and

dreams."

Huck shuddered. Clark was constantly spouting about his hopes and dreams. Somehow, she'd never seen them in his eyes.

Clark arrived at Mrs. Thompson's boardinghouse at eight o'clock sharp to take Huck to dinner. They drove to a refurbished downtown building and pulled up out front. "Redoing these old dinosaurs into elite restaurants is all the rage," he stated proudly as the valet opened Huck's door. "And talk about a good investment."

Pickwicks' elaborate entryway reminded Huck of pictures she'd seen in travelogues of Elizabethan mansions. And instead of one large dining room, there were several smaller ones, all hearth and candlelit cozy, each one elegantly furnished.

"This is lovely," Huck said as soon as they were seated. And then the restaurant's name suddenly made sense. *The Pickwick Papers* was Charles Dickens's first novel. She breathed deeply. Perhaps the evening would turn out better than expected.

A white-gloved busboy served ice water, while another placed an embroidered napkin in Huck's lap. A waiter appeared with menus, his movements as starched as his uniform. "Please take your time," the waiter

said. "Prime rib is our house specialty. I'll return momentarily for your order."

Clark fixed his gaze on Huck's left hand. "I love coming to Houston to see my diamond ring," he said casually.

Huck glanced down, having considered it *hers.* "Just the ring?" She repositioned the napkin in her lap.

"You know what I mean. I also love seeing who's attached to it." He laughed and studied his menu.

"An extremely tired woman is attached," Huck said. "I'll be recording grades in my sleep tonight. My classes have been diagramming sentences for the past two weeks. I've tried to make it interesting to them, but —"

"How about that prime rib?" Clark interrupted. "It's served with new potatoes in a white wine sauce."

"I'd rather have a small beefsteak, well done. And a salad."

"That's what you always order."

"Prime rib's too rare for my taste. You know that."

Clark raised his chin and leaned forward. "I think since I went to all the trouble of escorting you here, you'd want to honor my suggestion."

"Fine." Huck was too tired to argue. And

after the day she'd had, she'd rather talk than eat anyway.

The waiter returned, took their order, then spun on a heel and marched away. Huck continued her story. "As I said earlier, I've been teaching my classes how to properly diagram sentences."

"That's nice, not that they'll find it useful in a career."

"And what do mean by that?"

"Oh, Huck, don't come undone. This is the age of science and industry. Do you think the Wright brothers invented flight by defining subjects and predicates?"

"Of course not, but they had to succinctly write about their discovery." She paused. "And since we're on the subject, what does banking have to do with our modern age?"

He laughed. "Finance controls everything. Without the proper backing, no great invention would ever make it out of the laboratory. Successful industry depends not only upon investors who believe in science but us banking wizards who are savvy enough to make a profit for all concerned."

Huck stared past Clark and considered the great author who had inspired the restaurant's name. His brilliant prose still lived, unhindered by the boundaries of the modern industrial age, while encompassing

the heart and soul of all mankind.

"Speaking of banks," Clark said beneath raised eyebrows, "guess what happened at work today?"

Huck frowned. "It got robbed and there's no more money for science and industry?"

"Absolutely not." Clark glanced about the room and lowered his voice. "Please consider the ramifications of your words before speaking. That's how rumors get started."

"Clark, dear. I wasn't being serious."

"Obviously." He cleared his throat. "You weren't being smart either. Don't turn around and look, but I think one of our shareholders just walked in. He's liable to recognize me and drop by our table."

"You've nothing to worry about." Huck smiled sweetly. "I'll make sure to speak on his level of understanding."

"See that you do." Clark paused, then sighed and wagged his head.

When the man didn't appear, Clark frowned. "You insist on being facetious when I've got monumental news to share."

Huck leaned forward. "News?"

"Well . . ." He grinned. "I'm being promoted to senior vice-president."

"Oh, Clark. That's wonderful."

"My salary will double, plus I'll be vested. Naturally there'll be added responsibilities,"

he continued, explaining each one in great detail until the food came.

"Which means we can get married sooner than planned," he finished as soon as they were alone again.

Huck stared down at her plate and felt slightly nauseous. "I didn't think we'd set an exact date."

"Correct. Now we can." He began eating.

A definitive date was the last thing Huck wanted to discuss, but Clark seemed intent, which was probably the main reason he'd insisted upon dinner. Perhaps she could redirect their conversation.

"So?" he said between bites. "How about —"

Huck spoke up. "Before the wedding, I was thinking about cutting my hair."

He swallowed. "Your hair?"

"Into the latest flapper bob. It's all the rage."

Clark turned redder than the beef. "I forbid you to snip a single strand," he said abruptly.

"You what?" In all her growing-up years, she had never heard her father "forbid" her mother to do anything. He might strongly disagree, citing various reasons, but ultimately the decision was her mother's.

Clark continued. "My future wife will not

look like a floozy. I won't allow it."

Huck slowly stood and undid her bun, letting her hair fall down her back. People stared.

"What are you doing?" he whispered. "You're embarrassing me. I demand you sit at once."

"I wouldn't dream of embarrassing you, Clark dear." Huck shook her hair out, making herself resemble a wild, windblown woman. "See? Now there won't be any question about what you allow or your future wife's status as a short-haired floozy."

"You're acting ridiculous. I demand you sit and keep your voice down."

"And one more thing . . ." Huck grabbed a few strands of hair. Holding them at arm's length, she separated a single hair between her thumb and forefinger. "Is this the one you forbid me to cut? Or is it one of the others?"

Clark glanced about the room, stood, and spoke in a distinct hushed tone. "I will pull out your chair and you will calmly sit." Reaching for Huck's chair, he grasped her wrist instead.

"You're hurting me. Let go."

"Let go of your hair first," he replied in a tone indifferent to her pain.

With her free hand, Huck seized her meat

knife and slashed the strands in a single whack. Clark reacted with a jerk, providing Huck a chance to pull free. He stepped back.

"Your future wife doesn't like being ordered what she may or may not do." Huck set down the knife and inched toward the astounded Clark. "As far as *we're* concerned, future is a noun that depends upon how *you* invest in the present. An unwise investment means eating the profits. Any good banker knows that." She released the strands. "Diagram these, *dear.*"

Everyone in the room watched them float onto his plate.

Huck strode outside. By the time Clark had called the waiter and settled the dinner tab, she'd be riding a streetcar back to Mrs. Thompson's boardinghouse.

# FIVE

*Summer 2006*
*Adam Colby*

"Have a great evening, Mr. Colby." A wide-eyed carhop handed me a soda and a grease-spattered sack. "See you again tomorrow and thanks for the tip."

I cranked my SUV's engine, then glanced at my side mirror and watched her skate back inside the burger joint. "A great evening?" I muttered. "Someday, maybe."

It had been a grueling week, but the Gruver Estate Sale was finally over. At least I had a few days before pricing began on the next one.

That's what took the most time.

Pricing.

It was a tedious chore Haley had loved . . . back when she loved me.

Instead of shifting into reverse, I killed the motor, reached into the bag, and selected a scrawny french fry. "Looks as pathetic as

73

my life," I said blankly to the car parked next to me.

I thumped the fry back into the sack with its burgerless buddies, took a sip of my soda, and checked my cell phone. No calls from Yevette; no messages either. She'd already canceled two of our scheduled meetings, so I didn't hold much hope for number three, even though it was supposed to be a charmed digit.

In the message I'd left Yevette concerning our first meeting, I didn't go into much detail; I just explained I'd handled the Alexanders' estate sale and had some questions. In scheduling meeting number two, I was a little more desperate and mentioned finding the postcard albums. I figured the woman who'd cared for Mrs. Alexander during her final days would be eager to talk. Either Yevette didn't know about the postcards or didn't want them found.

"I have to cancel" was what she'd recorded on my voice mail both times. No reason, or even a sympathetic "I'm sorry." Just four words as cold as my nightly junk-food supper. It was as if she knew exactly when to call. Exactly when I was busy with a customer and couldn't answer.

Turning the key, I restarted the engine and listened to it idle. I'd tried to move on,

as Haley, and now others, had suggested. But two years was an eternity for a lost man. Besides, it was still hard to imagine not being married anymore . . . almost unthinkable.

Sometimes I'd be paralyzed at the thought, though I continued to mimic the motions of running my estate-sale business. Throughout each gloomy day, I'd pore over the postcards every spare minute, searching for the precious secret to Huck and Gabe Alexander's happiness. Evenings were spent punching their story into the computer in my study — I even slept there, merely passing through our bedroom as quickly as possible on the way to my closet. Occasionally, I'd type something about how the Alexanders were reminiscent of Haley and me, and then pay the price as fresh tears burned my cheeks.

Many lonely questions still plagued my restless nights, dragging them into unanswered days. And no matter how meaningful, the piecing together of each postcard's beautiful verse into Huck and Gabe's life story proved difficult to impossible. There were so many private things the cards alluded to that I didn't understand. So many unexplained connections I couldn't make.

As I took another sip, my cell phone rang.

"Hello. This is Adam."

"It's Yevette Galloway."

"Hey. Great to finally talk."

"How about meeting at Starbucks?"

"Which one?"

"Are you familiar with the one at The Town Square in Sugar Land?"

"Of course. When?"

"Tomorrow. Ten a.m.?"

"Sure thing. Should I —"

"See you then." Yevette hung up.

"— bring some of the postcards?" I finished, then looked at myself in the rearview mirror. "Well," I whispered. "I guess I'm finally meeting Yevette."

# Six

*Bayshore Extended Care Facility, 2004*
*Yevette Galloway*

Yevette strode through the etched-glass entryway at Bayshore Extended Care and into the plush lobby. She swallowed. Even the expensive places for the elderly smelled of antiseptic and a few trace odors she chose not to think about. After passing the gift shop, she continued through a set of automatic doors leading to the nurses' station, then smiled at the nurse on duty. "Good morning, Judy. I got your message."

"Hi, Yevette. It's bound to be a good Saturday morning somewhere."

A nearby medical student thumbing through patient charts offered a slight chuckle.

Judy continued. "Mrs. Alexander wasn't happy with us yesterday because we removed her phone. It was another three-ring circus."

"Will she get it back?" Yevette asked.

"Not this time."

It annoyed Yevette that Huck had called 911 again, especially after they'd talked about the consequences. "I'm sorry."

"This morning she's forgotten about her phone but is accusing Bayshore of theft."

"The old lady's got spunk," the student said. "I like that."

"And I'd like you to address our patients with a little more respect and finish those charts." Judy turned to Yevette and lowered her voice. "Mrs. Alexander swears that some of her mail's been stolen and blames our staff. Do you have any idea what she's talking about?"

"It's a long story, but she believes her deceased husband is still sending her postcards."

"Really? Do people even send those anymore?"

Yevette shrugged.

Judy looked thoughtful. "Would you assure Mrs. Alexander that no one working at Bayshore would ever steal from her, especially her mail?"

"Sure. Thanks, Judy." Yevette headed down the long corridor. She'd not known about Gabe's beautiful postcard poems until Huck had asked her to help place them

into albums, which they'd done on Fridays for the past several months. Yevette had learned more about Huck and Gabe's extraordinary relationship than she'd ever dreamed possible, but they'd completed the job and there were no more cards. On some Fridays, they'd laughed themselves silly. On others, fought back tears. And two Fridays ago, they'd closed the final album and wept. "We mustn't be sad," Huck had bravely stated. "Gabe's promised another card, with a poem more beautiful than any of the others."

Feeling tearful, Yevette entered an empty sitting area just off the hallway to gather her emotions, pausing in front of a large aquarium. She'd been only twelve years old when Gabe died, and found herself still missing his grandfatherly humor and thoughtfulness. She couldn't fathom how Huck felt. And even though Huck's favorite furniture pieces — a love seat and marble-top dresser — were in her room, she'd made it clear that this *place* wasn't home and never would be.

Yevette took a deep breath and slowly released it. She'd planned a visit to Bayshore today anyway because her head was full of questions. Questions about her mother. Specific questions Yevette finally

had the courage to ask. As close as she and Huck were, some issues were best left for another day. But Huck's health was slowly declining, and Yevette couldn't delay asking any longer. Hopefully, Huck's dementia would cooperate.

Before Priscilla's untimely death, she'd been Huck and Gabe's housekeeper for twenty-six years. Her initial dream was to attend college and start her own business. Instead of doing either, she'd married Rob Galloway, an air force pilot who, two months after their wedding, crashed on a training mission over South Vietnam. He could've ejected and lived, but chose to steer his jet away from a populated area. Then it was too late.

"If he'd survived and been my real father," Yevette whispered, "I wouldn't be me."

She gazed into the peaceful aquarium. The angelfish were Huck's favorite, which made perfect sense after she'd explained meeting Mister Jack. Yevette had never met her own guardian angel, but that didn't matter. Through the years Huck and Gabe had shared their rich faith in God, not only in conversation but in the way they'd loved her and cherished each other.

"I just wish I could trust a man, as Huck did Gabe," Yevette said to the most beauti-

ful angelfish. She'd been engaged twice and neither relationship had lasted, which made her think the failure was somehow linked to her mother's distrust of men after Rob died. From as far back as Yevette could remember, Priscilla had warned her daughter to trust only what was genuine, what was real. "Most men aren't," she'd said at least a thousand times. "Men like your birth father. You're not old enough to understand, but I didn't even know his name."

When Yevette reached Huck's room, the door was partially open. Tapping lightly, she peeked inside. Dressed in an emerald robe, Huck sat on the love seat, sleeping. Since she couldn't get out of bed without help, someone had already been tending to her needs. However, her breakfast remained on the serving tray within arm's length, untouched.

"Huck?" Yevette tapped louder.

"Gabe? Is that you?"

"It's Yevette."

"Oh, come in dear, I was waiting to tell Gabe about the stolen postcard and must have dozed off." She smiled. "He'll call out an entire posse of Texas Rangers."

"Nothing's been stolen."

"Did *they* instruct you to say that?" Huck's smile disappeared.

"We placed his last postcard in an album two weeks ago, and then I hid them."

"At our home?"

"Just as you suggested. In Gabe's study among the photo collection."

"And you won't forget what to do if I never leave this wretched place?"

"I'll remember."

Yevette cocked her head to one side. Huck had been adamant about finishing the albums before Gabe returned. But since Yevette's schedule prevented her from working on the project every week, Huck's adamancy evolved into pettiness and gloom. So a few weeks back, Yevette had gently reminded Huck that Gabe was deceased.

"He promised to come back, and I believe him," Huck said sternly. "If he doesn't, then the cards must be destroyed."

"Is that what Gabe would want?" Yevette asked, surprised Huck would even suggest it.

"We discussed it on our wedding night. Neither one of us wants them falling into the wrong hands."

What *hands*? Yevette had wanted to ask. She knew Huck wasn't in her right mind that day to make such an outrageous claim, but also knew better than to push the issue.

Yevette focused on the current situation.

"So why haven't you eaten your breakfast?"

Huck patted the seat beside her. "Come sit, dear."

"Not until you drink your orange juice."

"The food here is inedible."

"Not the juice." Yevette handed her the glass. "Looks freshly squeezed."

"You're as persistent as Priscilla." Huck took a sip and handed it back. "It's delicious, but that's all I want. Have Priscilla squeeze you a glass too."

"Mother's no longer with us," Yevette said softly, then sat beside Huck. "Remember?"

"Yes," Huck said. "She's dead, you know. Priscilla."

"I know."

"So, so tragic. Her car hit by a drunk driver not long after Gabe died. Do you recall how badly I wanted to adopt you, promising you we'd stay together *from now on*?"

"I do." *From now on* had become their special catch phrase.

"But since Priscilla's sister Cynthia demanded to raise you, I was denied."

"We've discussed it many times." Yevette paused. She'd lived in Dallas with her aunt and uncle until she was of legal age, then moved back to Houston. "I have a question about something else."

"Ask me anything, dear."

"Before I was born, did Mother travel?"

"I suppose. We gave her a paid month off every summer."

"Did she go out to Big Spring?"

"Big Spring?" Huck thought for a moment. "I believe she had friends there."

"Was one of her friends . . . a man?"

Huck frowned. "Priscilla was much too friendly, much too trusting."

"She never took me there with her. Why?"

"It was more convenient for you to stay with Gabe and me. My, didn't we have fun."

"More convenient? Or did she go to Big Spring because of the state mental hospital?"

"Hand me my juice, dear. I'm afraid my mouth is dry."

"You're avoiding my question, but I know the answer. Last week I was going through some of Mother's papers and found her history of admittance and discharge forms."

"Grief affects some more deeply than others. Even though your father died a hero, Priscilla suffered serious spells of depression. Gabe insisted we pay for her annual evaluation and treatment."

"Rob Galloway wasn't my natural father. Mother told me, remember?"

"That was far too much information for a

child," Huck said sharply. "Priscilla wasn't good at keeping secrets." Huck sipped the orange juice and stared out a large picture window.

Yevette continued. "Was my father a one-night affair?"

"It makes little difference, dear, because we have you." Huck yawned and patted Yevette's hand. "Priscilla had a weak moment indeed, but God blessed her anyway."

*And then took her from me,* Yevette thought, *as well as Gabe.* She glanced at Huck's wrinkled face and swallowed hard.

A staff member knocked and entered. "It's time for your bath, Mrs. Alexander."

Yevette hugged Huck, then stood. "I'll be on the road for a month. Don't forget I'll love you —"

*"From now on,"* Huck finished, then grinned. "Perhaps when you return, Gabe will join us?"

"You never know." Yevette waved good-bye. As she walked toward the lobby, she pictured her mother and the last time they'd been together, the memory still clear.

*"Promise me you'll trust only what's genuine,"* Priscilla had said, *"only what's real."*

"I promise." Yevette smiled at the memory. From now on.

85

# SEVEN

```
That magic May Day,
On a Main Street trolley
The Eternal Hand strummed
  destiny
And heartstrings sang sweet
  symphony
To celebrate
The you . . .
Of me.
                    Forever, Gabe
```

*May 1926*
*Houston, Texas*

The first day of May dawned cloud-clear, riding the crest of a late spring cool front that drove every drop of humidity back out to sea. Huck Huckabee slid out of bed, closed her eyes, and raised the window shade in her private quarters at Mrs. Thompson's boardinghouse. Fresh sunlight bathed her face. It was Saturday and she

didn't have to teach school. She breathed deeply, filling her lungs with the sweet fragrance of magnolia blossoms. It was also May Day . . . the mystical day of *lovers.*

Yesterday, her students at Sidney Lanier held a pre–May Day festival, crowning a king and queen, then dancing around a Maypole while twisting colorful ribbons. She'd assigned her honors class to research "little known traditions" about the day. One tradition happened on the night before. A man would place a Maypole outside his sweetheart's window, then perform a sunrise dance to celebrate love's madness.

Huck opened her eyes. No madness. Nothing but the magnolia tree.

Even if Clark Richards had known about the tradition, he wouldn't have gone to all the trouble. Shortly after the big diamond appeared last Christmas, romance vanished . . . at least the wildly spontaneous kind. Clark might finance the largest Maypole in the city, but he'd never dance around it.

Balancing on her tiptoes, Huck twirled about the room, watching her nightgown billow.

There was something joyous about dancing barefoot in the soft dawn air. It held a fresh excitement that made her feel pretty.

Made her feel free. The same excitement and freedom she'd experienced in that fleeting moment with Gabe Alexander.

Gabe Alexander. His eyes still haunted her heart.

Huck spun to a stop in front of the window. A cool shiver hunched her shoulders forward. It wasn't proper for an engaged woman to entertain such daring thoughts about another man. And she knew better. After all, she'd barely met Gabe. Besides, she'd convinced herself countless times that their brief encounter was meaningless.

"I'm marrying Clark," she whispered to herself. Even after what had happened last month at Pickwicks. She shivered again. "It's only right."

Huck tried to continue her dance, but her legs suddenly felt heavy, awkward. So she leaned against the windowsill to clear her mind.

But what if marriage to him wasn't right? Not even her mother or father was agreed on the matter.

Because of what had happened at Pickwicks, there was still no wedding date.

The evening had left a bitter taste, even though Clark showed up later that night apologizing profusely — Mrs. Thompson letting him into the parlor an hour after

house curfew because he held a dozen red roses in one hand and two solid gold earrings in the other. He'd thought it over and would allow Huck to cut her hair because he loved her, but might they compromise on, say, shoulder length?

Closing her eyes, she determined to think no further about the incident, so immediately pictured Gabe. And in fairness to her father and twin brother, allowed herself a moment to ponder why she desired to know Gabe better. The moment passed, and Huck concluded that during their brief encounter, their spirits had somehow touched.

She opened her eyes. Under different circumstances, Gabe might have placed twenty Maypoles outside her window and danced love's madness around each one of them.

Ignoring her tug-of-war conscience, she smiled at the dizzying thought and gave herself permission to ponder further, this time an extended moment. When it passed, she'd turn her thoughts toward the day at hand.

Actually, she'd awakened early to go "a-maying," a medieval tradition of spending the day in search of flowers and tree branches to use for home decoration. Even though she couldn't carry much and would

be going alone, she'd made the decision after reading the words of William Shakespeare to her classes:

Away before me to sweet beds of flowers:
Love-thoughts lie rich when canopied with
   bowers.

Huck laughed again, picturing Gabe and herself picking flowers and sawing off tree branches in front of Houston's City Hall . . . a daring imagining she'd never even considered with Clark. She whispered Shakespeare's words, wondering what she still saw in her fiancé. In his last letter, he'd mentioned coming for another visit. He'd purchased an elegant new sedan called the 1926 Vertical Eight. It was a luxurious upgrade of the Stutz Bearcat, and he couldn't wait for her to see it. At first she thought he'd intended to drive down for May Day, but after a dull and detailed explanation of a hunting trip he'd be on with his father, she realized he meant coming the following Saturday. Huck was relieved. Now the entire day belonged to her.

The aroma of brewed coffee wafted from Mrs. Thompson's kitchen down the hall. On weekends, the girls were allowed to do their own cooking; however, all the board-

ers but Huck were away until Sunday night. Even Mrs. Thompson would be leaving shortly for an overnight visit to an ailing sister.

Huck turned her head in the direction of the kitchen. She was too excited to prepare and eat breakfast. Market Square would be crowded with food vendors offering free samples. She enjoyed browsing the colorful booths, sniffing appetizing aromas, and munching on a bite of whatever intrigued her. And since she'd be in the neighborhood of Cecil's Fish Market & Seafood Emporium, it might be interesting to pick up some canned anchovies to have on hand. See if Gabe worked on Saturday. See if he'd still remember her. It had been over a month since she'd playfully turned down his dinner invitation. She'd heard her housemates gossip about how some men viewed female rejection as a challenge, begging for dates over and over. How these men were usually insecure, arrogant pests. Other males, they said, developed prideful amnesia, conveniently forgetting a girl's name and pretending they'd never asked.

"Those types of men," Huck said aloud, "are *not* Gabe." At least, that's what her intuition said. Her mother had taught that a woman of conviction must have a faith

courageous enough to act on her God-given insight. It was only proper. Huck nodded now in respectful agreement. This was one instance where they concurred one hundred percent. And even when they disagreed, Huck admired her mother's passion and overall good sense. If any woman could stand tall on her own experience, it was Annise Huckabee.

After putting on a robe, Huck grabbed a washcloth and her toothbrush. The bathroom was directly across the hall. Since she'd bathed the night before, it wouldn't take long to wash her face and brush her teeth.

Back in her own room, she chose a lightweight dress of pastel yellow with a waistline that dropped to the hip. Most women she knew who were middle-aged and older considered the low waistline brazen. Huck smiled. Poor old-fashioned ladies. If they only realized that a sleek modern slip must be worn underneath instead of a drab underskirt. She removed her gown and dropped the dress over her head. It fit perfectly and would match her new shoes and handbag.

Sitting at her vanity, Huck gathered her hair into a tidy bun and pinned it into place. She studied her reflection and added one

more hairpin. The whole unpleasant hair-cutting affair came to mind again and made her frown. Clark would *allow* her to cut her hair shoulder length because he loved her? She'd grow it down to her heels before she'd agree to a controlling compromise.

And what about makeup and perfume? Clark had already voiced disapproval with the exciting new colors and the mysterious Oriental scents. She flung open a drawer and applied ruby lipstick, bold rouge, and a hint of jasmine perfume — her new favorite. The final touch came from her jewelry box. A fashionable long necklace of sparkling glass beads.

In less than five minutes, it would be eight a.m. Shops around Market Square were already open, including one that specialized in native flowers and greenery, but it usually sold out in a few hours. If she hurried, she could board the next Bissonnet Street trolley to Montrose Boulevard, then walk one block east and catch a Main Street trolley all the way to the business district.

The Bissonnet Street trolley was half full, and she had no trouble finding a place to sit. The Main Street trolley was a different matter. Eager passengers pushed and shoved into any available space. Women balanced children on their laps, while men stood in

the aisle or crowded upon the steps and rear platform to smoke. Huck shared a seat with a woman holding a baby girl and twin toddler boys. The baby fidgeted, drooling a steady stream, while the toddlers tried to unwrap a smashed chocolate bar. The mother looked tired and seemed oblivious to her surroundings. Shopping with this energetic brood probably meant she couldn't afford a sitter. Huck sighed. It was a problem she'd never have the opportunity to worry about.

An image of Mister Jack filtered into her thoughts. Meeting him seemed eons ago. Each year, it became harder to distinguish between what had actually happened and what she'd conjured in her childhood imagination. Experience and maturity reasoned he was probably some kind of deranged drifter instead of her guardian angel. But her heart and soul begged to differ.

Her secret glen, where she and Mister Jack talked that day, was destroyed shortly after her revelation to teach. Huntsville and the State of Texas bulldozed and rerouted the creek in order to develop a park surrounding Sam Houston's woodland home. Unable to revisit the glen, she'd had two vivid dreams about Mister Jack and the Anacacho orchids. In the first, he stood in the

center with arms stretched in opposite directions and hands cupped, an Anacacho blossom resting on each palm. The second dream happened the night after she'd met Gabe. It was the same scenario as the first, but this time Mister Jack pulled his hands together so that the blossoms touched. He never spoke, his face a blur except for a wide white grin.

"Tommy, Jimmy, no!"

The exhausted mother's consternation whirled Huck's thoughts back into the streetcar, but it was too late. The toddlers had smeared chocolate all over her new dress.

"I'm so sorry," the woman said. "They were just trying to share. I dug the bar out of my handbag to keep them busy. The wrapper was stuck to the chocolate, and I didn't think they'd get it off." She pulled a spit rag from her shoulder, and the baby began to wail. "If we found some water, I could —"

"It's all right," Huck managed to reply as the streetcar bumped to a stop. "You need it worse than I." She nodded to one of the little boys. "Tommy's painted his brother."

"You mean Jimmy," the mother said.

"Of course." When Huck disembarked at the corner of Main and Preston, all three

children were crying.

She fought back a frustrated groan and scampered across Main to the trolley stop on the opposite side, hiding the worst of the chocolate smears under her purse. The dress was her May Day outfit and she'd wanted Gabe to see her in it, that is, if she happened to run into him. Now she'd have to rush all the way back home and soak it, even though the stains had probably set. A better choice, although impossible, would be to drop it off at the nearest laundry. That would mean parading down Main afterward in her slip, and Clark thought short hair was the definition of a floozy. Strolling through the city scantily clad was a daring imagining she wasn't quite ready for. She managed a slight smile. It would almost be worth telling Clark her scandalous musings and watching the horror erode his face. But then, after the hair-cutting episode and the way he'd hurt her wrist . . .

She shivered.

Perhaps she'd just keep such additional thoughts to herself.

Huck joined the anxious throng awaiting the next streetcar. In the future she'd be more careful where she sat. Even though it was rare for ladies to stand in the aisle or on the rear platform, it would be preferable

to sitting with sticky children. She took a deep breath and slowly released it. By the time she could get home, soak her dress, wash it, hang it out to dry — not to mention ironing — the greenery shop would be long closed. May Day had started so full of promise. Dancing and imagining. The chance to see Gabe the most daring dance of all. She peeked beneath her purse at the chocolate handprints. At least he wouldn't see her in this embarrassing condition.

She managed to squeeze onto the next streetcar, several passengers behind a matronly woman carrying a large shopping bag and a stack of hatboxes. The woman plunked into the last available seat. Huck couldn't see very well, but she heard the woman order a man standing in the aisle to hold her boxes while she dug something out of the bag. As the streetcar began rolling, Huck decided the rear platform would be better than the stuffy aisle, so she moved in that direction. It was awkward to keep her purse over the handprints and steady herself at the same time.

"Pardon me," Huck said, maneuvering along the crowded aisle.

The man holding the hatboxes, his face hidden, was just a few feet ahead, blocking her path.

"Pardon me," Huck said again. The matronly woman, still digging, was blabbering too loudly for anyone else to hear.

As they picked up speed, the man shifted slightly toward Huck. Suddenly, the streetcar swayed, then jerked, and she lost her balance. Dropping her purse, she turned to grab the nearest seat and slipped, falling backward into the man. The next thing Huck knew, she sat in the aisle amid crushed hatboxes . . . in the lap of a total stranger.

"My hats!" screamed the woman. "You've ruined my new hats."

Someone helped Huck to her feet. "I'm so sorry," she said to the woman. Then turning toward the stranger she asked, "Are you all right?" Huck looked down. The man's sea-sky eyes and crooked grin met her gaze.

"Nice dress," Gabe Alexander said casually. "I have a passion for . . . um . . . chocolate."

Earlier that Saturday morning, Gabe awakened in the bedroom of his small garage apartment and couldn't go back to sleep. He glanced at the bedside clock. Four a.m. Usually he woke early due to worry, and he'd wrestle the sheets for hours in anxiety. If he tried hard enough and didn't allow his mind to become too anxious, he could

refocus his thoughts on something pleasant, eventually drifting back into slumber. But this time, the "something" pleasant was a "someone" — Miss Huck Huckabee to be exact. So he lay there a wide-eyed-while longer, tapping his fingers to the clock's tick, finally deciding to get up. Since he had the day off, it might be wise to spend some nonworking time at his office watching for Huck. Most women shopped early, and this was the most popular errand day of the week.

Gabe threw back the covers, sat on the edge of the bed, and scratched the stubble on his chin. He wasn't in the mood but had promised to meet his friend Charlie downtown for a late breakfast. He rubbed his eyes and sighed. He'd much rather be meeting Huck.

After stumbling into the kitchen, Gabe put some water on to boil while he showered, shaved, and brushed his teeth, all the while concocting sequel scenarios about why Huck had never returned to Cecil's. He slapped on a little aftershave and remembered it had been over a month since they'd met. After donning clean boxers, socks, and a freshly laundered dress shirt, he dripped a pot of coffee, then sulked through two cups, the first black and the

second with cream. Between sips, he wondered not for the first time if his oyster comment had offended her. She might already have a diamond . . . and a fellow to go along with it.

He rinsed out the coffeepot and cup, then slipped into a gray linen suit. Standing before his dressing table, he faced the mirror and picked up a bottle he'd purchased the previous day. Wildroot Hair Tonic promised to help "if your romance hung by a hair."

"What romance?" Gabe mumbled at his reflection. He rubbed a sprinkle of Wildroot through his hair and combed it into place.

His hat and suit jacket felt good in the cool morning breeze as he exited down the stairs of his apartment a little before seven. Mr. Blane, his landlord, was already up, tinkering with the engine of a rusty Model T Ford. The Model T lived in the garage below and would backfire when cranked, shaking the entire structure. The apartment was an okay place to live and had met his needs and those of his mother. However, his plans were to eventually sell his parents' small ranch and buy a nice house in one of Houston's newer residential neighborhoods.

Gabe stepped softly, hoping Mr. Blane wouldn't hear him leave. The man was a

talker with spider-like characteristics, capturing innocent victims in his web of words, then boring them to death with the same stale stories.

Making a clean getaway, Gabe then walked down the street to the nearest trolley stop. As predicted, the Model T cranked, then backfired. He'd considered buying his own car, but decided that public transportation was adequate until he met the right woman. Now, he imagined providing Huck with some of the finer things life had to offer. That is, if he ever saw her again.

When Gabe disembarked the streetcar at Market Square, the vendor booths were already bustling with activity, which lifted his spirits. He walked a block to Cecil's, entered from the rear, and climbed the stairs to his office unnoticed. He usually didn't smoke before breakfast, but lit a Lucky and peered out his window into the store below. "There's not a *single* woman down there who even resembles her," he said aloud. "Nor a *married* one either." He grimaced at his own bad joke, the renewed hope from a few minutes prior escaping like air from a child's poorly knotted balloon. It was foolish to think he'd see Huck today, especially from his office window. He knew better than to try to recapture a magic mo-

ment. Life just didn't work that way. But this was where he'd first been drawn to her wit and obvious intellect, not to mention electrified by her beauty. Perhaps she was like lightning and never struck the same place twice.

At eight o'clock, Gabe gave up and walked down Main toward Benny's Diner. Yesterday evening, after he and Charlie had finished their smokes on the loading platform, Charlie suggested they meet the next morning for breakfast. He didn't say why, never did; probably just wanted some time away from his hectic home life that didn't involve work. Every now and then, the two men would get together on a Saturday morning for biscuits and gravy, which usually meant discussing something interesting in last evening's *Chronicle*.

A block away from Benny's, Gabe could smell bacon frying. Just like sourdough biscuits browning in a dutch oven, it was a comforting aroma that normally meant everything was right in his world. But that was before he'd lost contact with the woman of his dreams. For that matter, he'd never even established contact. A man pitiful enough to not ask for a phone number didn't deserve someone like Huck.

He stepped into the diner's smoky hub-

bub, located Charlie at a corner booth, and hung his hat. The waitress whose husband left her was nowhere in sight, and he wondered if she'd ever returned to work. He couldn't see Benny but could hear him barking orders from somewhere in the back.

"Hey. Wait until you see this." Charlie looked up from the newspaper with a sly smile as Gabe slid onto the opposite bench. "What's the matter?"

"What do you mean?" Gabe righted an upside-down coffee cup and pushed it to the edge of the table.

"You look lost."

"I couldn't sleep last night, that's all." It frustrated him that he couldn't shake his obsession with Huck and move on, at least long enough to enjoy breakfast with his best friend. But not seeing her again was like losing a twenty-dollar gold piece in an ocean of pennies.

An attractive waitress appeared with a pot of steaming coffee. "You boys need a menu?" She filled Gabe's cup and topped Charlie's off.

"Nope. Already know what we want," Charlie replied. "Two eggs over easy, sausage, biscuits, and gravy."

She looked at Gabe. "And you, sir?"

Silence.

"Sir? Do you know what you want?"

"I thought I knew."

"Don't listen to lost boy." Charlie winked at the waitress. "He's read that menu a thousand times, knows the plot and the ending. Bring him what I'm having, except bacon instead of sausage."

The waitress glanced back at Gabe.

He nodded.

Charlie watched the waitress walk away. "Ain't it a beautiful day?" he whispered. "Don't you agree?"

"Agree to what?"

"Okay." Charlie leaned forward. "What's the matter? I know something's happened."

"Nothing's happened. It's been an entire month and *nothing's* happened."

"Oh, I get it. You're still bellyaching over Miss Huckabee. I thought we'd already fixed that situation . . . several times."

Gabe scowled. They hadn't *fixed* anything, but had discussed Huck out on the loading platform at Cecil's until Gabe grew weary of hearing Charlie's pat answer. Why did married men always think there were hundreds of extraordinary women waiting to replace any single man's girl who didn't work out?

"So, what did you want me to see?" Gabe asked, changing the subject. He raised the

coffee to his lips and tasted the captivating color of Huck's hair and eyes.

"Oh yeah. Wait till you read this." Charlie pitched the paper across the table. "Editorial section, 'bout middle of the page. Written by some bishop."

"I'm really not in the mood to discuss Prohibition."

"That's not what it's about." Charlie grinned. "It'll take your mind off what's bothering you. Guaranteed."

"Then read it to me." Gabe slid the newspaper back, suddenly in no hurry to forget his obsession. "I didn't get much sleep, remember."

Charlie lowered his voice. "Guess what today is."

"I know what today is."

"Ever hear of the International Pageant of Pulchritude?"

"When did you start speaking Latin?"

"Just answer the question."

Gabe shook his head. "Never heard of it."

"Me neither. That's 'cause they changed the pageant's name this year."

"Who is 'they'?"

"Folks in cahoots with my jealous wife."

"Why should Chloe care about a beauty contest?"

"Because this one," Charlie said mock-

ingly, "has become an evil tradition that destroys a woman's sense of modesty."

"Are you talking about the Bathing Girl Review in Galveston?"

Charlie nodded big. "And the opening of beach season, Splash Day, gorgeous dames."

"I went one time, way back, because of all the flak about it then." Gabe set down his coffee cup. "Nothing to see but a few local girls in the latest swimming attire. You'd think with all the gambling and bootlegging down there, folks wouldn't notice a little beauty contest."

"Well this year, the flak returns with a vengeance."

"How's that?"

" 'Cause it won't be just local gals competing anymore." Charlie cleared his throat. "And there's a lot less attire, if you catch my meaning. There's gonna be parades and fireworks and . . ." Charlie paused, a huge grin lifting his cheeks.

"And . . . ?" Gabe asked.

Charlie picked up the editorial and lowered his voice even more. "This bishop fellow is trying to talk women out of strutting their God-given goods. He says, and I quote" — he looked down at the paper, reading — " 'If you come here, you will be asked to parade only in a bathing suit before

a motley crowd who will scrutinize you at close range.' " Charlie's eyes grew round. "Know what that means?"

"The tradition becomes even more evil?"

"That means from only a few yards away, a man can witness world-class cleavage. And some of them gals will be wearing those new French bathing suits that reveal an entire leg."

"What about the other leg?" Gabe chuckled.

"Joke all you want, but the winner gets $2,500 in cash. That's gonna be one expensive pair of thighs decorating the Galveston seawall."

"Are you suggesting we go?"

Charlie smirked. "Right. I'll just ring up Chloe and tell her I won't be home this afternoon because I'm helping forty half-naked young women destroy their modesty. Don't you remember what happened the last time I helped a female?"

"Destroyed her modesty?"

"Very funny. You know all I did was take her to a mechanic's garage."

Gabe sipped his coffee. Charlie had an eye for skirts but would never cheat on Chloe. Several years ago, she'd accused him of having an affair and threatened to make him sleep in his delivery truck — the scene

of the crime — until he could convince her of his innocence. In truth, he'd done nothing more than give a stranded young woman a ride after her car broke down. To show her appreciation, the woman blindsided him with a kiss, smearing lipstick on his collar.

The sly smile reappeared as Charlie thrust the newspaper back across the table. "Doesn't mean *you* can't go, then tell me about each fine feminine detail. So don't be late. Starts at two."

Gabe sighed. "Wish I could go, but I've got some things back at the office that need my undivided —"

"Forget the stinkin' office," Charlie interrupted. "Go buy a straw hat and spend your day off at Galveston Beach. That's where the beautiful women are."

"Yeah," Gabe replied thoughtfully. "Where the beautiful women are." He repeated the phrase again, as if hearing the words for the first time, allowing them space to slip in between his troubled thoughts. "Where the beautiful women are," he said a third time. As a fan of numbers, he'd always been fascinated with the law of probability. When flipping a coin, there was a fifty-fifty chance of guessing the outcome. Not a great percentage. But betting on a relatively sure thing, like a good poker hand, was a differ-

ent matter. The chance of winning multiplied.

And then it hit him. A new plan. One with much better odds, steeped in tradition. Instead of trying to recapture a magic moment, he'd make a new one.

Finding Huck meant looking where he'd see the most women. Watching from his office window had been like flipping a coin. Main Street would be like holding a royal flush.

The waitress appeared with a tray, unloading several hot plates and refilling coffee.

"Benny says he'll join you two outlaws directly." She smiled. "Y'all holler if you need anything else."

When she moved to the next booth, Gabe stood and dropped several coins onto the table.

"Ain't you going to eat?" Charlie asked.

"Give my plate to Benny."

"Then you're off to . . . ?"

"Where the beautiful women are," Gabe interjected. "It's a tradition." He retrieved his hat and headed for the door.

"I want details," Charlie called. "And remember the straw hat. A wide brim will keep the sun out of your eyes so you can see."

The bongs from the clock on Market

Square echoed nine o'clock as Gabe paced toward the nearest streetcar stop. That very morning he'd convinced himself to go to his office and watch for Huck because Saturday was the traditional day most women ran their errands.

*Where the beautiful women are,* he kept repeating, imagining every detail of Huck's essence. Her smooth oval face. The fullness of her lips. Her exotic scent. With hundreds of stores on Main, the odds of eventually spotting her walking somewhere along that street were good. She'd be smartly dressed, loaded down with shopping bags, and would hopefully accept his offer to help.

So he'd ride the streetcar up and down Houston's busiest thoroughfare until he found her. Ride it all day if he had to. And if he didn't see her, he'd do it again the next Saturday. And the next. And even the one after that. The winning cards were in his hand, and it was no time to fold.

Gabe boarded a streetcar at the corner of Main and Rusk, paid his token, and shuffled through the crowd toward the rear platform. From that vantage point, he'd be able to smoke and watch both sides of the street with ease. Midway up the crowded aisle, an elderly gentleman dropped a hand-carved cane, and Gabe paused to retrieve it. He

handed the cane back to the man as a large woman struggling to carry a shopping bag and stack of hatboxes plopped into a nearby seat. Before Gabe could move, the woman thrust the boxes in his direction.

"Take . . . my hats . . . young man," the woman demanded, quite out of breath. "They're expensive . . . so don't drop them."

"Yes ma'am," Gabe replied, holding the boxes high enough to not interfere with any of the seated passengers.

The woman regained her wind and began rummaging through the shopping bag. "I really must find my receipt for those hats," she announced. "I fear I've been over-charged. The clerk said they were each discounted twenty percent. But now that I think about it, the one I bought to wear tomorrow was full price. Cheating a woman on her Sunday best is as bad as cheating the Good Lord Himself and that clerk should be . . ."

The streetcar eased forward and Gabe wondered how long he'd be stuck in the aisle, his face full of cardboard, listening to the ravings of a mad woman. "Just my luck," he muttered. Huck could've been standing on the next corner and he'd never know.

It was an older model trolley, swaying and groaning as it picked up speed. Gabe repo-

sitioned his feet for better balance and wished he was out on the platform. Even before he began smoking, he preferred to stand at the rear and watch the city slide by. The interesting people, the pleasing cackle of laughter, the humid breeze cooling his face.

Without warning, the streetcar dipped with a metallic scrape, then jolted. There was a sudden girlish yelp. In an instant, Gabe found himself sitting in the aisle with a shapely young woman pressed upon his lap. Instead of cold cardboard, his face was smashed against the nape of her delicate neck, the spring-like scent of her softness . . .

Overwhelming.

Familiar.

Captivating.

He placed his hands around her dainty waist as someone helped her stand. And before she ever turned to look at him, he knew . . .

He'd finally found his Forever Girl.

# EIGHT

Beneath midnight stars
Caressed by spring's pure breeze
Two lovers strolled
Hand in hand
While waves lapped moonlit sand
Connecting souls.

Forever, Gabe

*May 1926*
*Houston, Texas*
After picking up hats and reassuring the woman that only her boxes had been crushed, Huck and Gabe quickly exited the streetcar. Gabe offered his arm as they stepped up to the curb.

"I thought you'd be . . ."

"I hoped you were . . ."

They both spoke at the same time, then laughed, pausing to meet each other's gaze.

"Working," Huck continued. "I thought you'd be working." She realized she was no

longer holding her purse over the stains, but still grasped Gabe's arm, feeling a muscled tenderness she'd never noticed with any other man. She held on a full second longer before releasing.

"I have weekends off," Gabe replied.

"That's too bad."

"It is?"

"Because I was planning to stop by Cecil's and pick up some anchovies."

"You were?"

"Unless the oysters ate them."

They both laughed again.

Another streetcar stopped to empty passengers. "Let's walk," Gabe said. "This corner's getting a little crowded."

Huck held her purse over the stains as they strolled the busy sidewalk, with Gabe positioning himself closer to the street. Including the day they'd met, she'd known this man for mere moments, yet was comfortable walking next to him. She guessed he was over six feet tall, with long solid legs like the Huckabee men, but he matched her abbreviated stride with an unhurried ease. Clark was several inches shorter than Gabe and had no patience when it came to traveling by foot, almost dragging her along.

She glanced at Gabe. "I thought you'd be working and you hoped I was . . . ?"

"Running errands." He grinned. "Anything else on your schedule besides anchovies?"

"I had big plans until a child on the streetcar decided to become a fashion designer." She peeked at the stains and sighed. "By the time I get home and remove the chocolate, my plans will be ruined."

"That's wonderful."

"Wonderful?" Huck stopped in her tracks. "Wouldn't *lousy* be a much better adjective?"

"Not as good as *marvelous.*" Gabe turned and faced her, his grin lopsided and lovable. "I think it's marvelous we're getting to spend this beautiful day together, that is, if you want to."

"Then, you know about today? The tradition?"

"Y-yes I believe so," Gabe stuttered. "It was a popular topic at breakfast, although a bit controversial."

"Controversial? Why?" Huck knew people who were indifferent, but never dreamed anyone would have a problem with May Day.

Gabe laughed. "Perhaps *debatable* is a better word choice. Whatever the case, my friend Charlie was so excited, he could hardly eat."

Huck giggled. "I look forward to it every year."

"You do?" The grin returned, more inquisitive than crooked. "Do you take part in the tradition or just prefer to watch?"

"I take part, naturally." She frowned. "So who wants to debate?"

"Some bishop," Gabe said with a shrug, "but he probably argues about everything. Let's keep walking."

They passed a street repair crew, the roar of heavy trucks competing with the ringing thud of pickaxes making it impossible to talk. A dizzying excitement propelled Huck's every step. Spending time with one man while engaged to another was the controversial issue, not May Day. But even the dour bishop would have to agree that engagement wasn't bound by marriage vows. A woman's prerogative was to change her mind about whomever, whenever she wished — which was both wonderful and marvelous. So for the moment, she'd consider taking Gabe up on his offer to spend the day together. Especially after the hair-cutting episode with Clark.

When they paused for traffic at the next corner, the noise faded and Huck made up her mind. She moved the purse away from the chocolate stains, revealing them. "I

couldn't possibly wear this dress all day. And if it's ruined, I'll have to buy a new one."

"Brilliant idea," Gabe said, shoving his hands into his pockets. "Foley Brothers isn't far and I was headed there anyway to buy a new hat. You could select another dress, then ask the store to deliver the chocolate one to Burkhart's Laundry. They might be able to save it."

Huck felt her cheeks redden. She hadn't meant buying another dress *today*. "Why, Mr. Alexander . . . I've never purchased a dress with a man along."

Gabe laughed. "Don't worry. We'll be in different departments." Then he leaned toward her and lowered his voice. "Miss Huckabee, you might consider calling me Gabe since . . ." He halted in midsentence, his eyes drawing her closer.

"Yes?"

"Since we're buying clothes in the same store, someone might mistake us as married."

"Oh dear," Huck said, then swallowed. "That would be a mistake."

"It would?"

"Wouldn't it? Unless . . ." Her words drifted into an infinite number of unspoken

117

thoughts, each held captive by his sea-sky gaze.

"You were saying?"

"Unless . . . you call me Huck."

They both smiled. Huck purposely slid her arm through Gabe's and they continued walking. Clark was getting exactly what he deserved.

"Look at it this way, Huck. Being a bystander may not be exactly what you'd planned, but we'll be the best dressed couple on Galveston Island."

"A bystander on Galveston Island?"

"Tradition, remember? Splash Day? The International Pageant of Pulchritude?"

She gave his arm a squeeze and laughed. "Why, Gabe, it appears you've tricked me into traveling to Galveston and attending some kind of a beauty pageant."

"Actually it's a bathing beauty contest, but we don't have to go. There are all sorts of other activities there, and dances that go on until midnight."

"Not go see the latest swimwear on an island my mother refers to as a den of wickedness?" She gave his arm a playful pat. "I wouldn't miss it for the world. And dancing until midnight would be such a daring way to celebrate May Day. Most men don't even know the day exists."

Gabe cleared his throat. "I'm ashamed to admit you're right, but we're learning."

It was only a ten-minute walk to Foley Brothers department store. They had a delightful visit along the way, asking each other the requisite vanilla job and family questions one might inquire about at a dinner party. Huck told how she was an English teacher at Sidney Lanier, lived in a boardinghouse for career-minded women, and grew up in Huntsville. Gabe asked if she'd attended Huntsville's major institution. When she answered yes, she knew he was teasing because he acted shocked.

"I didn't realize the penitentiary allowed female inmates," he added.

She patted his arm again, more spirited than before, and chattered about her father being a farmer and prison guard. How her parents' land was adjacent to Sam Houston's historic home and how she and a twin brother were the youngest of thirteen children.

Inside Foley Brothers, Gabe escorted Huck to the entrance of the women's department. A mannequin advertised a modern waistless dress, the sleek material dyed in a dramatic color combination of pure pastels.

"What about this one?" Gabe asked,

directing her toward the mannequin.

"Look, it's a shift dress." Huck giggled. "I love the new styles." She released his arm to stroke the fabric. "And the beautiful colors. A perfect match for my purse and shoes."

"May I help you?" An eager salesgirl appeared wearing a summer business suit and a broad smile.

"She'd like to try on this shift dress," Gabe said casually. "In my opinion, it would be a perfect match for her purse and shoes."

Before Huck could reply, the salesgirl turned to her and asked, "Does your husband have any single brothers?"

"Pardon me?"

The salesgirl laughed, then continued. "I don't mean to pry, but most men wouldn't come near the women's department, much less know about style and color."

"No brothers," Huck said, shooting Gabe a lighthearted glare. "Thankfully, he was an only child."

"I need to . . . um . . . go find a hat," Gabe managed.

An hour later, Huck, Gabe, and thirty other passengers were seated aboard the Galveston–Houston Interurban, speeding to Splash Day and the controversial International Pageant of Pulchritude. Gabe donned

a new straw hat, and Huck wore the colorful shift, her soiled dress in the hands of Burkhart's Laundry. For the most part, she'd left all thoughts of Clark behind as well. But an occasional pang of guilt still invaded what had become a delightful morning.

"That's Dickinson Bayou," Gabe said, pointing out the window. "It flows near our ranch. When I was a kid, I built a one-man sailboat. Fished and explored that body of brackish water whenever I had the chance."

"I didn't realize I was seated next to a sea captain." Huck glanced at Gabe's strong profile. He did seem a little sea-captain-ish, with his immaculate gray suit and easy confidence.

"More like a cowboy/bayou captain," Gabe replied. "Each year, a few of our cattle would wander off our land along the water's edge and I'd have to find them." He laughed. "I think my father knew I found sailing more exciting than being stuck in a saddle all day."

"Sounds intriguing. Herding cattle from a sailboat."

"They were tame as porch dogs, the way my mother babied them. All I had to do was wave my arms and shout. They'd lumber back home the way they came."

"I'd love a real sailing adventure," Huck said after a tiny sigh, then wondered what it would be like as Captain Gabe's first mate. She giggled softly, suddenly remembering Mister Jack and the term she'd adopted so many years ago: soul mate.

"So the lady wants an ocean adventure?" Gabe scooted closer. "Then one day we'll sail the seven seas, or at least the shallows of Galveston Bay, in a boat named *Cleopatra.*"

"*Cleopatra?*"

He laughed. "The Egyptians invented sailing. It would only be proper."

"Aye, aye Captain!" Huck playfully saluted.

"And we'll drink rum from the bottle and eat hardtack and mutineers will walk the plank."

"But, Captain . . . What about pirates?"

"Pirates?" Gabe's eyes twinkled. "Well, matey, 'twould be the ghost ship of Jean Lafitte, no doubt. Some say he still haunts the bay in search of his lost treasure."

"And what if we find it and he captures me?"

"I'd die first," Gabe said, loud enough for people to stare.

"You would?" Huck asked softly, then realized their legs were touching.

"I'll never let you go." He gently grasped her hand. As their fingers entwined, her body tingled with warmth. A glowing warmth mixed with happiness she'd never felt before.

The Galveston terminal was located on Twenty-First Street, only blocks from the beach. As they disembarked, the salty sea breeze carried every delightful aroma of carnival fare: succulent smoked meats, roasted nuts, buttery popcorn. Even the sugary smells of cotton candy and saltwater taffy refused to waft by Huck unannounced.

"There's a parade starting over on Broadway," someone called as Huck and Gabe exited the station into the throng of excited Splash Day revelers. "The grand marshal is King Neptune!"

"Look at the people," Huck voiced above the joyful roar as they scampered across a busy intersection, then strolled hand in hand down a less crowded side street. "There must be thousands here."

"According to a source, there should be several hundred thousand altogether. Since we're headed toward Broadway, how 'bout we catch the parade? That is, if we can find a place to sit. The bleachers will be packed."

"You're the cowboy captain. And didn't

you mention a beauty pageant?"

"I did." Gabe stopped walking and faced her. "But we really don't have to go."

"Why not? I've never been to one. It'll be interesting."

Gabe cleared his throat. "Are you aware that this town has a reputation for —"

"A wide variety of entertainment?"

He nodded.

Clark's forbidding expression flashed before Huck's eyes. "The pageant sounds fabulous."

Gabe laughed. "You're a fascinating girl, Huck. Is there anything that doesn't interest you?"

"Closed minds and hearts," she answered thoughtfully. "Anything else you want to know?"

"Does the lady always speak the truth?"

"Of course." She gave his hand a squeeze. "Unless it benefits me otherwise."

They strolled another block until the brassy blare of a marching band quickened their pace. "Let's hurry," Huck said, her voice brimming with excitement. "The parade's starting."

Pulling Gabe's hand, she led him into the thick crowd. As he'd predicted, the bleachers were full, but Huck smiled sweetly to a stout old gentleman, who let them sit in an

area reserved for the yacht club.

"Besides telling the truth, does the lady always get what she wants?" Gabe asked as soon as they were seated.

"Of course. But the appropriate smile helps."

"Unless it benefits you otherwise?" he finished.

"Let's just call it a woman's prerogative." With an impish grin, she surrendered once again to his sea-sky gaze, thinking her present engagement to Clark Richards a mistake and unexpectedly wanting to tell Gabe everything. She'd eventually have to tell her mother, but Annise Huckabee could be handled.

Huck studied the passing parade and shivered. Breaking up with Clark would be ugly. He'd really frightened her during the hair-cutting incident. And it was more than just the fact he'd grabbed and hurt her arm. It was something else. At first, her brain wrestled with her heart, refusing to admit the truth. But each time she reminisced, the scene became clearer, her mind always focusing upon Clark's eyes. At the height of their argument, something dark had washed over his pupils. Something opaque and ominous. Then it was gone.

"What happened to that appropriate

smile?" Gabe's mellow tone soothed Huck's worries, transporting her thoughts back to the present.

"The smile's still here, ready to charm its next victim."

Gabe spoke in a weakened tone. "I think it already has."

When the parade ended they headed toward the beach, after thanking the portly gentleman, who clasped Huck's hand as if she were his long-lost daughter. The International Pageant of Pulchritude was to begin promptly at two, with several hundred bystanders and a few policemen lining the seventeen-foot-high seawall. A wooden stage had been erected on the wide sandy beach below, with five folding chairs shaded by an awning for the judges. To the right of the stage was a large yellow striped tent with a banner that read, Dressing Area — Contestants Only. To the left a small band shell, complete with an upright piano and five musicians in black tie playing Dixieland jazz.

"I'm definitely not the only female in the audience." Huck eyed the other spectators as she and Gabe jockeyed for prime viewing space atop the seawall. She'd heard of bathing beauty contests and was intrigued by the idea. "In fact, there are lots of interested

women."

"Like you, they appreciate beauty." Gabe positioned himself behind her, gently resting his hands on her waist. He leaned forward. "Because beauty deserves attention."

She turned her head slightly, then giggled. "Did you notice the dozen or so women grouped right behind us? They don't appear to be the type who would . . ." She paused, caught off guard by his clean smell.

Gabe whispered close. "The type who would what?"

His warm breath upon her neck made her shiver. "The type who'd appreciate being here. They look angry about something. Especially the oldest one. She seems to be their leader."

Before Gabe could reply, the band crescendoed into a lively fanfare. The master of ceremonies, a lanky man wearing a lavender pinstriped suit, climbed onto the stage and shouted through a megaphone. "Ladies and gentlemen! Welcome to the first annual International Pageant of Pulchritude!" The crowd burst into applause as a line of bathing beauties paraded out of the tent and onto the stage.

"Harlots!" screamed one of the women from the group behind.

"Jezebels!" yelled some others.

The verbal protests continued no longer than thirty seconds as the emcee quickly motioned for three policemen to escort the dissenters out of earshot. "My apologies, folks. I'll ask our lovely contestants to remain on stage while we try this again." He turned toward the band. "Gentlemen, the fanfare please!" After the second fanfare and welcome, the crowd burst into an even bigger round of applause.

"What was that all about?" Huck whispered.

"Everyone's clapping because the contest is ready to begin."

She wrinkled her nose. "That's not what I mean and you know it."

Gabe leaned closer than before, his lips almost brushing her ear. "There seems to be some opposing views about a woman's sense of modesty."

"That's silly," Huck replied. "A woman's modesty is her own business, unless she's breaking the law."

The band segued into a soft medley of popular tunes as the emcee explained how the girls were judged by beauty *and* poise. He then introduced each of the thirty-nine contestants, all between the ages of eighteen and twenty-five, wearing the latest bathing

attire. The sleeveless swimsuits were colorful and form-fitting, some with short skirts that could be removed for greater mobility in the water. Many of the girls were Texans, while others hailed from various states as far away as California and New York. There was also a contestant from Cuba, two from Canada, and even a girl from France. The judges chose ten finalists, then to the delight of the crowd, had the contestants present poses from various angles. As the band played a final number, the judges tallied their scores and chose a winner . . . a slender southern belle from Mississippi. After the emcee awarded her the cash prize, he placed a crown on her head, and she marched across the stage holding an American flag.

A few minutes later, Gabe and Huck sauntered along the seawall in the warm afternoon sun. What excited him most was that she'd voluntarily grasped his arm once again. A few hours ago he'd been on the floor of a trolley, tangled helplessly in her presence. And now they strolled atop the immense, concrete barrier where land met sea. It was one of his favorite places on earth.

"Mother says that the prettiest women

come from the Deep South," Huck said. "But that's because she was born in Alabama." There had been no more protests and most of the audience had dispersed, ending the controversial International Pageant of Pulchritude until next year.

Gabe studied the delightful girl holding his arm. He'd been right about her, and she grew more perfect for him with each passing moment. "Your mother sounds like a smart woman, but I have to disagree. The most beautiful girl I know is walking beside me . . . and she's from Texas."

"Oh no," Huck replied. "Now we have a problem."

"We do?" Gabe began to perspire and slowed them to a stop. As far as he could tell she wasn't upset, but perhaps he should have been more discreet with the compliments. The last thing he wanted was to scare her away. He reached for a Lucky, then paused, realizing he'd never asked if she'd mind. The smell of tobacco, the smoke, or both bothered some people. Besides, he'd have to turn away from her to light it and she might release his arm.

"There's something you should know," Huck said. "Before we spend another minute together, I want to be honest."

"Because the lady always speaks the

truth?" Gabe pulled a handkerchief from his back pocket and mopped his brow.

"I guess it's a Huckabee curse." She laughed. "Just now, you said that you disagreed with my mother?"

"I prefer to call it a friendly difference of opinion."

"Gabe, dear. This is the problem: no one ever successfully disagrees with Mother, unless they know the secret."

"Thanks for the warning." He smiled and returned the handkerchief to his pocket. Huck had just called him "dear."

"Don't you want to know the secret?"

"Unless it benefits me otherwise."

"Very funny, Mr. Clever. For your information, I'm the only one of her children who knows the secret and it's saved me enormous grief. I learned it from watching Papa."

Gabe started them walking again, relieved that she was comfortable enough to joke about her family. It also meant that she might be planning for him to meet them.

Huck continued. "Mother's very opinionated about certain topics, especially education and religion. So when she asks you a question and you don't see eye to eye, avoid falling into her trap. Lightly broach your answer, then coax the truth toward your

own advantage — like an honest politician — making your point while gradually changing the subject. It's fun."

"Hmm," Gabe replied. "Never heard of an *honest* politician, but I'll try your method." He made a spectacle of clearing his throat, then spoke in a deeper, more distinguished tone. "My dear Miss Huckabee. Isn't it amazing how even in Texas, the most beautiful women have roots from the Deep South, especially Alabama . . . a state known for feminine charm and fine southern cuisine." He grinned, returning to his normal voice. "So how 'bout we get a bite to eat?"

Huck laced her fingers around Gabe's arm, resting her head on his shoulder. "We think so much alike, it's scary."

"Are you saying we're predictable?"

"Never." Huck frowned. "Predictable is an adjective that doesn't pertain to us."

*Us.* Gabe savored the word before he spoke again. "So what adjective does pertain to us, Miss English teacher?"

"Hungry," Huck said. "I haven't eaten all day."

They ate under a large umbrella at Mermaids, an outdoor restaurant at the end of a long pier whose sign boasted Dine Out

Over The Deep. A fussy waiter informed them that since it was midafternoon and lunch was over, they could only order shrimp cocktail or crab gumbo. But the bar was open, and he'd be right back to take their drink order.

"What about Prohibition?" Huck asked, as soon as the waiter disappeared. The only liquor she'd ever seen was the amber whiskey her father drank at Christmas. She knew where he hid it — up in the hayloft underneath a loose floor plank. As a child, she'd sneak out that year's bottle, pretend to take a swig, and act drunk. At age eleven, she dropped it one day and noticed a hairline crack at the base. Petrified, she'd never touched Papa's "yuletide vice" again.

"Rumor has it that Prohibition isn't enforced on the island," Gabe said. "And you thought the beach was what attracted multitudes."

"Do you think we could order pink champagne?" Huck leaned in conspiratorially. "I've read about people having champagne brunch. It sounds so daring."

"It's too late for brunch," Gabe said, then laughed. "And since this meal falls between lunch and supper, we'd have to call it 'lupper.'"

"Champagne lupper," Huck replied.

"Doesn't have quite the same romantic ring, at least the lupper part. But the pink part sounds interesting, don't you think?"

When the waiter returned, Gabe ordered two shrimp cocktails, two cups of crab gumbo with extra rice, and a bottle of pink champagne. Since they weren't on any kind of schedule, they ate and drank leisurely, talking about favorite foods, books, and movies, while ocean clouds wisped high overhead and waves white-capped beneath their feet.

"I think my numb is getting nose," Huck said finally, then giggled.

"I think the lady's had a bit too much bubbly." Gabe reached for a cigarette. "Mind if I smoke?"

"Not in the least." Since childhood, the aromatic quality of tobacco was an odor Huck found comforting. She'd first smelled it on Gabe while riding the interurban, then at the beauty pageant when he whispered close. She laughed softly, reminded of a story.

"What's so funny?"

"Papa used to smoke," Huck recalled, "until Mother finally insisted his suit be sent to the dry cleaners for a proper going-over. The next Sunday, he wore the suit less than five minutes, saying it reeked of kerosene,

so he dunked it in her washtub. Said he 'baptized' it, the humorous analogy completely missed by Mother. And then . . ." Huck paused, the remainder of her story floating adrift her brain in the champagne's smoothness.

"And then your mother murdered him?" Gabe scooted an ashtray to his side of the table and thumbed open a book of matches.

"No, silly." She giggled a third time. "Slow torture is Mother's way." Huck peered into her empty champagne glass. "Where was I?"

"Your Papa dunked his suit in the washtub."

"Oh, yes. And then he never smoked again. Began chewing tobacco because he swore the kerosene odor wouldn't come out. Papa worried about fire and was afraid the flammable fumes had infiltrated his shirts and overalls as well."

Gabe laughed. "Why not just buy some new clothes?"

"What? And waste perfectly good garments?" Huck replied facetiously. "Threadbare/comfortable is Papa's way, and after almost fifty years of marriage, Mother still can't persuade him differently."

"Sounds like how my folks were." Gabe lit his cigarette, exhaling the smoke away from

Huck. "So what did your father wear to church the day he baptized his suit?"

"Oh, Papa never goes. Never has. Says he holds nothing against God's flock but doesn't need to visit the Lord's house because he hears enough preaching at home. So when Mother and the rest of the family attend Sunday service, he puts on his suit and quietly reads the Bible. Then he lays the Good Book aside and 'ponders,' while chewing tobacco and spitting off the gallery."

"I think I like your father." Gabe appeared lost in thought for a moment. "I'd bet he loves reading the Psalms."

"Why, it's his favorite book."

"And he enjoys discussing his ponderings? Especially with you?"

She raised an eyebrow. "How did you know?"

"The poetry in your voice."

Huck felt herself blush. "Mother's favorite book is Proverbs. I've memorized more than a few."

"My next guess."

"Because I'm so wise?"

"My next answer."

They laughed.

"A wise woman who speaks her mind is greatly respected," Gabe said.

"Is that a proverb?"

He shrugged. "I was thinking about your mother. I'd like her too."

Huck smiled. Contentment colored the afternoon.

Gabe signaled the waiter. "Two coffees please."

"How did you know I love coffee?" Huck asked, wondering if Papa felt this light-headed when he drank whiskey.

"I took a guess." He grinned. "Besides, doesn't the lady always get what she wants?"

Huck smiled back. Even if the champagne had clouded her mind, it was clear her heart wanted Gabe Alexander. And any unpleasant thoughts about ending things with Clark had evaporated, including how and when she'd tell her mother.

Several hours later, after poking through a variety of souvenir shops and applauding a troupe of sidewalk acrobats, they watched the sun set, munching salted peanuts and caramel corn on a deserted stretch of beach. At one point Huck commandeered Gabe's hat, which resulted in a merry chase, until both she and Gabe were hysterically out of breath. They kicked off their shoes and stockings beside a lonely log of driftwood, then wandered along aimlessly, the surf

slapping their bare ankles under the dusky soar of seagulls.

"I'm thirsty," Gabe said, then pointed to a rustic beach house built above the sand on stilts. "Bet there's a cistern. And that looks like a mighty comfortable porch swing hanging underneath."

"It would be nice to have some water and sit for a few minutes," Huck said. "No one appears to be home. Do you think they'd mind?"

"Honored." Gabe grinned. "It's the rule of the West to accommodate weary travelers or, in this case, beachcombers. Which means it would be okay to borrow the privy too."

"I was hoping you'd say that," Huck replied, scampering toward the privy. Lupper's pink champagne and coffee were begging for departure, and she'd about decided to tour the tallest sand dune.

"Be careful," Gabe called. "Bang on the door first, in case it's occupied."

She knew he meant occupied by varmints, recalling her childhood days before indoor plumbing and her mother's stern warning about scaring away any "uninvited visitors." The term always made her smile because it automatically inferred the opposite: guests receiving an invitation would be welcome. And who in their right mind would entertain

in an outhouse?

Five minutes later, they quenched their thirst from the same tin dipper, then lounged in the weathered swing as a brilliant moon rose, sparkling its path across the placid Gulf of Mexico. "Not exactly spring water, but a good clean cistern gets the job done," Gabe remarked, offering Huck his handkerchief. "You must have a hole in your chin. Your dress is wet."

"I beg your pardon?" Huck daubed the damp spots and returned the handkerchief. "You bumped the dipper."

"At least it's water rather than chocolate smears." His face crinkled into a grin.

"Was that today?" Huck thought back to the toddler on the streetcar. Morning in downtown Houston seemed a lifetime ago, but she was glad the boys had finger-painted her future.

"If it wasn't today, I've slept in this suit," Gabe said, then winked.

Huck laughed. "I've been up since dawn and should be exhausted, but . . ." She stood, twirling around on bare tiptoes, her shadow spinning happy girlish shapes against the white moonlight. "It will be May Day until midnight. Dance with me." She stuck out her hand and pulled Gabe to his feet.

They barefooted back and forth across the blanched sand to the soft rhythm of night waves, holding each other close while millions of stars popped to life. After dancing a hundred carefree dances to a timeless clock, they shared another dipper of water, then returned to the swing, Gabe speaking quietly in the pre-lovers' language of "what if."

*What if* this date led to another?

*What if* they began a serious courtship?

Into their mostly one-sided conversation, Huck inserted an occasional "I would like that" or "Sounds wonderful." But when Gabe paused to light a cigarette, her brain ricocheted thoughts like an answering line of melodic counterpoint. She knew that her roller-coaster romance with Clark was over, whether or not Gabe ever asked her out on another date. And when he'd mentioned the possibility of — how had he put it? — "future encounters," she was thrilled for them to spend more time together. She definitely longed to be with Gabe and was in the process of picturing them married when 'he uttered the words "our serious courtship." Even though Huck's mind had already considered a step even further than courtship, Gabe's words caught her off guard, catapulting her heart into a state of thrill. She had no choice but to laugh.

"Telling yourself jokes?" The ash end of Gabe's cigarette glowed orange in the night.

"Just happy." She rested her head on his shoulder, his clean smell now augmented with the pleasant leftover traces of sun and surf. Her mind whirled, wondering over and over when she'd fallen in love with him. Was it this morning, when she'd stumbled into his lap on the floor of the streetcar? Or was it that blustery March day they'd met . . . the corny oyster comment . . . the sea-sky eyes?

Huck listened to the distant surf and measured the pulse of her feelings. But more than mere feeling, her in-love-ness was a knowing, a severely protected knowing undergirded by the gentleness shared between soul mates. It felt safe, and it provided the freedom to communicate hidden fears and innermost desires without mock or rejection. She snuggled closer, and a joyful tear rolled down her cheek as she began to tell Gabe her story, her secrets. As she spoke, Gabe stroked her hair. She explained in detail about Mister Jack and the unusual Anacacho orchids. Finally, she revealed her mistaken engagement to Clark Richards and her decision to end it.

"I'm not surprised about the other guy," Gabe said tenderly, "not really. What man

wouldn't want to be engaged to you?"

She didn't answer but snuggled even closer as Gabe continued stroking her hair. Neither of them spoke for a moment. Then, after taking a few deep breaths, she told him about the foolish accident that had left her unable to bear children. "That's why I teach school," Huck finished. "It's my life's grand calling."

Gabe stopped stroking her hair. "I need to tell you something."

Huck said nothing, feeling his chest muscles tighten as a sudden tremor of doubt jarred her insides. Had she been wrong about her inner knowing, or had the lingering effects of alcohol made her bold? She wanted to look at him but was terrified she'd revealed too much. Not the Mister Jack or Clark Richards part. Angels were biblical, and engagement to another man could be remedied. However, being unable to bear children was another matter. Mocked by hard hindsight she closed her eyes, ready for the worst.

"Remember this afternoon when you said that we were so much alike, it was scary?"

"Yes?"

"Well . . ." Gabe briefly paused, then continued. "I decided years ago that married couples shouldn't base their happiness

solely on the children God chooses to give them . . . or not give them. It has to do with a concept I call 'The Long Division.' "

"Sounds like an arithmetic problem."

"It's more of a marriage dilemma," he replied, then explained his idea about how the pressures of career, multiplied with life's never-ending responsibilities, constantly divided and redivided a couples' time together, finally producing comfortable strangers rather than passionate lovers. "Unless I inherit a gold mine, working for a living is not a choice." Gabe cleared his throat, then chuckled lightly. "Do you think it's unrealistic to want lasting romance?"

"Of course not." Huck wanted to leap out of the porch swing for a hundred more moonlit dances. Besides calming her worst fear, Gabe was implying they might end up together. "Count me in on the concept."

"Since we're telling secrets," he continued, "there's more I need to say." He told about his near engagement to an old girlfriend, Amelia Addison, then recalled the terrifying duty of serving his country overseas during the Great War. Huck felt him tremble as he remembered the untimely deaths of his parents.

She sat up and faced him. His eyes were wet with tears.

"I love you, Gabe Alexander." Huck knew it was early in their relationship to say such a thing, but her words were spurred by the honest tenderness between them and the strong conviction that he was the soul mate she'd been searching for since age ten. She placed her arms around his neck, her child-bearing worries now weightless. "Want to know *why* I love you?"

"Tell me." Gabe wiped his eyes with the back of his hand.

"Because we've just bared our souls into the wee hours for the first time. And you weren't afraid to show your emotions."

Gabe grinned. "All cowboys cry, the real ones anyway. Bayou captains too." He paused for a moment, as if contemplating the silence. "Know why I love you?"

"You do?"

He smiled. "Want to know why?"

She nodded.

"Because you said 'first' time we'd bare our souls into the wee hours. That means many more wonderful nights together."

"How can you be so sure?"

With both his arms, Gabe drew Huck in, pressing his lips against hers with confident strength. "Marry me, Huck." He reached into his shirt pocket and produced a simple gold band. "This ring was my mother's. She

advised me to carry it always, so I could give it to the girl of my dreams."

"Oh, dearest Gabe."

He slid the ring on Huck's finger and they kissed deeply. This time, the tears belonged to Huck.

They remained in the swing awhile longer, holding each other until the hesitancy of new love evolved into deep, contented kisses. Then after a final visit to the privy, they located their shoes and stockings, retraced their steps along the beach, and climbed up the seawall to the boulevard. Gabe hailed a passing party trolley still loaded with drunken Splash Day revelers, the intoxicated driver singing about love, thrilled to deliver a pair of starry-eyed lovers to the interurban station. Then at two a.m., Huck and Gabe boarded the last scheduled coach and sped back to the mainland.

"Do we really look like starry-eyed lovers?" Huck clung to Gabe's arm, her head comfortably upon his shoulder.

"According to the singing trolley driver. I guess that makes you my dazed darling," Gabe replied, his answer trailing into a yawn.

"Me too," Huck agreed, then followed suit. "I mean, 'me too' about your yawn.

But you're also *my* dazed darling." She laughed softly, thinking how she'd awakened early that May Day morning with wild imaginings, never dreaming that almost twenty-four hours later, she'd be engaged to another man. A man who was undoubtedly her soul mate.

"Aren't we a pair?" Gabe's eyes rolled above a smile. "Staying out most of the night on our first date. Your father would have me executed."

"He'd never get the chance. Remember, Mother would torture you to death first."

Their lighthearted banter continued in spurts, with Gabe stealing a kiss every few miles in the dimly lit rail car. Huck knew they could have become much more *involved*. They were destined to be lovers, and lovers longed to be as intimate as humanly possible. But before the heat of her desire burned out of control, Gabe backed off.

Once, when she and Clark were in college, he wanted more physical passion than she was willing to give. So he forced his touch, until she finally convinced him to stop. The next day he was standoffish and pious, blaming her for enticing him during a weakened state. She refused to see him after that for weeks, until he showed up one day with a silver bracelet. As with the hair-

cutting incident and countless others, the man thought expensive gifts righted any wrong. Huck sighed, finally admitting to herself that her problems with Clark weren't entirely his fault. She'd accepted the gifts every single time.

"The Houston station's up ahead," Gabe said, gently interrupting Huck's thoughts. He checked his pocket watch. "It's almost three. We'll have to hire a jitney bus since streetcars don't run past midnight."

"I thought jitneys were outlawed two years ago."

"If they don't take business away from streetcars, the law looks the other way. Most of the drivers are former doughboys and friends of the cops anyway." He laughed. "Thought about going into the jitney business myself. After the war, several of my army buddies transformed their old jalopies to carry passengers."

"I'd ride with you," Huck said, noticing how handsome Gabe looked in the middle of the night.

At the station, they shuffled off the interurban to a waiting jitney bus. Even though it had room for eight, Huck and Gabe were the only passengers. Huck shouted her address over the engine's rattle while Gabe paid the driver.

"I live only a few blocks from your board-inghouse," Gabe said as they sputtered nois-ily along. "So I'll just walk home from there. I think this heap's on its last leg."

"Don't you mean 'last wheel'?" Huck laughed. "My older brother Andrew used to sing a popular song about a jitney." The cool night air was invigorating, awakening her weary senses. "Something about a jitney driver named Gasoline Gus who steals Satan's wife."

"Pardon my speech, but she must have been one *hell* of a woman." Gabe's face pos-sessed the same lively intensity as the stars that sparkled low overhead. "I remember the tune but not the words. Why don't you sing it?"

"Here?"

"Bet you're better than the drunken trol-ley driver."

"Okay," Huck agreed. "At least I'm sober, but I only know the chorus."

Gabe chuckled. "What a proper way to end the day . . . with a song."

By the time they reached Mrs. Thomp-son's boardinghouse, they were laughing hysterically, making up comical verses, then shushing each other, with Gabe singing harmony to Huck's melody.

"Good thing no one's home." Gabe

stepped off the jitney, then offered Huck his hand. "I hope we didn't wake the neighbors."

"They're all elderly and couldn't hear a locomotive steam through their yard." Huck hopped down and released Gabe's hand as the jitney motored away. She spun in a circle. "Dance me to the door," she said merrily, "to the tune of Gasoline Gus."

So with more laughter than song, they swayed across a dance floor of dew-covered grass, then scuttled up hollow wooden steps onto the front porch of the boardinghouse.

"It has been an enchanting day," Huck said, placing her arms around Gabe's neck, the warmth of his sea-sky gaze blazing through the predawn shadows.

"Our days have only started, my darling." He bent to kiss her, when the porch swing creaked in the darkness.

"Who's he?" demanded a surly voice.

Huck shuddered.

The voice in the darkness belonged to Clark Richards.

# NINE

We danced from moonlit laughter
Into a shadow cold as steel;
Sharp truth honed by jealous
    rage,
A fight for life, until
Love's desperate cry made
    madness flee. . . .
A miracle!
And our finality.

                Forever, Gabe

*May 1926*
*Houston, Texas*
In less than an instant, Huck felt the vise of
Clark's athletic grip, his rough thumb and
fingers twisting her forearm, jerking her out
of Gabe's protective embrace.

"I said, who's he?" Clark repeated, then
cursed. Bright moonlight reflected the shiny
six-inch blade of the hunting knife he
clenched in his right hand. "Answer me,

Huck. Who's the laughing moron?"

"Clark! No!" Huck struggled to break free. "You don't understand."

"I understand plenty." Clark's eyes bulged, revealing dark windows of jealous rage. He raised the knife.

"I'm Gabe Alexander," Gabe said coolly, edging distance between himself and Clark's weapon. "Let her go. Your argument is with me."

"Shut up!" Clark spun Huck around, encircling her with his left arm like an iron band.

"Clark, please." Huck's voice trembled, as hot tears streamed down her cheeks. She knew Clark was possessive and impatient but never in her wildest imagination had she thought he'd pull a crazy stunt like this. "Are you insane?"

"Insane?" Clark forced a laugh. "I ended a hunting trip early to surprise my fiancée. Rushed straight here to inform her of my promotion to a large bank in Chicago." His ranting grew louder. "Insane? I've waited for hours, sharpening my knife to pass the time. I'm glad my effort wasn't wasted."

Huck felt his grip tighten even more. "If you'll just let me explain."

"You don't deserve the privilege," Clark sneered.

Gabe spoke softly. "There's just been a simple misunderstanding, that's all."

"Simple? My fiancée's apparently been cavorting all night with another man, shouting senseless songs from the back of a low-class jitney, and dancing like a drunken fool."

"Just let her go before someone gets hurt."

"I'll decide who gets hurt!" Clark released Huck and lunged toward Gabe, the knife slicing through layers of moonlight and shadows.

Gabe ducked, the steel blade missing him. He motioned for Huck to stay clear, focusing on Clark and remembering that it had been seven years since he'd fought in the gas-filled trenches. Seven years since he'd last experienced the exhilarating, heart-pumping horror of kill or be killed. He'd learned the technique well, saving his own life more than once. "Drop the knife," Gabe said, his tone firm but calm. "Don't do anything foolish."

"You're the fool, Alexander." Clark faced Gabe in street-fighting fashion as both men began moving in a circle.

"Stop it, Clark." Huck's voice escalated into tearful hysteria. "You've gone mad."

"It's okay," Gabe said, keeping both eyes glued to Clark while trying to comfort

Huck. "Trust me. Everything will be all right." Even though he'd been up almost twenty-four hours, his newly awakened warrior senses were keen, evaluating every possible defensive measure. Clark was physically strong but obviously lacked the skill of hand-to-hand combat. If they tangled again, Gabe would end it. There would be no contest. "Just drop the knife and we'll talk."

"Talk is for cowards. No man touches my fiancée." Clark lunged a second time, slashing at Gabe's face with all his strength. Gabe dodged sideways into a low spin, then quick-punched underneath his attacker's rib cage. Gasping for air, Clark doubled over, dropping the knife. In a final swift movement, Gabe kicked the knife off the boardinghouse porch while twisting Clark's arm, forcing him facedown onto the wooden decking.

"I'm not . . . your fiancée . . . Clark," Huck managed between sobs. "Not now . . . not ever."

Clark's muscled rampage deflated then into limp silence, followed by a series of low whimpers. Gabe released his hold and backed a few steps away. Keeping his eyes on Clark, Gabe removed his suit coat, then laid it over the porch swing. He swallowed hard, having witnessed this very same

behavior on the battlefield when a defeated enemy thought his life was over. In a strange way, he felt sorry for Clark. Losing Huck would be difficult for any man to bear, if not impossible.

Clark sat up and scowled, rubbing his arm. "I love you, Huck," he whispered, his voice quivering. "Adored you since we were children. Remember?" He glanced at Gabe, then leaned back against the leg of a glass-topped table.

Huck sniffed and wiped her eyes. She wanted to leap across the porch into the safety of Gabe's arms, but knew she must come to terms with Clark herself. "You may have adored me, Clark, but . . ." She paused, allowing her voice to grow stronger. "But you've never *loved* me. And now you only wish to control me. I've tried to be frank, but you've refused to listen."

"That's not true. I've always loved you . . . and . . ." Using the table as support, Clark stood. "And I know you still love me." He glanced at Gabe again. "He's made you confused, hasn't he? Come with me to Chicago and everything will be clear. My new car is parked in the next block. I'll buy you one just like it the day we marry."

"No!" Huck stepped toward Clark, unwilling to carry the charade any further. The

salty burn of tears flowed again, but she didn't care. "I am getting married, but not to you." She held up her left hand, the gleaming gold band all too visible. "I've given my heart to Gabe."

"Never!" Clark shouted. "I won't allow it." In a renewed fit of rage, he slung the table in Huck's direction, smashing the glass. Before she could scream, Huck saw Gabe vault through midair, his lightning quick tackle forcing her legs out from under her. They landed with a *thud,* rolling clear of a thousand razor shards, the impact forcing all breath from Huck's lungs. She gasped for air, then glimpsed the punishing blur of Clark's hunting boot as he kicked Gabe in the head. Stunned, Gabe tried to stand as Clark delivered another powerful blow, its force almost knocking Gabe off the porch. Gabe moaned, then lay motionless.

Huck screamed. Clark towered above her. Just as in the hair-cutting incident, his eyes were glazed with darkness. But unlike the simple meat knife Huck had used to prove a point, what Clark now clutched was a long dagger-shaped shard, the finality of its horrible truth aimed directly at her heart.

Huck opened her mouth, producing nothing but a terrified silence. Then she heard a severe cry — unlike any human wail she'd

ever experienced — pierce the night. The sound was terrifying and completely foreign, yet at the same time caring and familiar. And desperately soulful.

The next thing she knew, Gabe was lying across her, his body protecting hers. Somehow, he'd rallied enough strength to cry out, leaping between Huck and danger, forsaking his own life to protect her from the madman's fury. There was a smaller smash of breaking glass, followed by Clark's panicked rush of footsteps, a car door's distant slam, a sudden squeal of tires. Why he'd dropped his weapon and run, Huck didn't know.

Gabe let out a guttural groan and rolled over onto the floor. "He's gone," he said softly. "Are you all right?"

"Yes, I'm fine." Fighting back more tears, Huck sat up, focusing her gaze upon the man who'd just saved her life. She began to ask about his unbelievable cry when she noticed the blood. "Oh, Gabe, your face is bleeding." She leaned forward and daubed his forehead with the hem of her dress.

Gabe raised himself into a sitting position. "Chocolate on one dress and blood on another. I wonder what time Foley Brothers opens."

"Stop cracking jokes. You could be seri-

ously hurt."

"Believe me. It's nothing but a scratch." He touched the wound. "See. The bleeding's stopped. Good thing I'm hardheaded."

"I think we should get you to a hospital." Huck stood. "Don't move. I'll go inside and call an ambulance."

"No, Huck . . . please." Gabe managed to stand with a wobble, then plopped into the swing. "I'm just a little dizzy. Been hurt much worse than this. All I need is a smoke." He located his coat pocket and pulled out a cigarette.

"But you may have a concussion." Huck sat beside Gabe. "Papa got kicked in the head by a mule and suffered double vision for days."

Gabe grinned. "I couldn't think of anything more wonderful than seeing two of you." He struck a match, holding it up to reveal a long but nonserious gash.

"Light your cigarette and hush," Huck ordered. "I'll run get some rubbing alcohol and . . ." She paused, almost cringing at how the alcohol would sting, then continued. "And a bandage."

Huck scampered inside, switching on lights as she searched for Mrs. Thompson's first-aid supplies. She vaguely remembered her landlady mentioning they were not

stored in the bathroom, but inside a cabinet somewhere toward the rear of the house, perhaps off the back hallway.

Huck's brain wanted to dwell on the horrible events of the past few minutes, but her heart resisted. Clark Richards was now in her past. He would move to Chicago, and she'd never have to see him again. Of course her mother, as well as the rest of the family, would hear about their breakup soon. It would be all over Huntsville, nothing even close to the truth. Clark would never be foolish enough to reveal what actually happened. Never admit he'd gone mad. She should probably call the police and press charges, but unless Gabe insisted differently, she'd just rather forget the whole ugly mess.

Huck located the cabinet and gathered gauze, a bottle of rubbing alcohol, and some hospital tape. She smiled. The man she'd been searching for her entire life was outside on another porch swing. And now she knew that his feelings for her were more than simple adoration. He loved her. He had shown sacrificial love by placing his life on the line without hesitation. That's what Gabe's caring cry of desperation had been about. It had to have been him, although it wasn't the same timbre of his gentle voice.

It was much deeper. She'd read stories where lovers in peril could suddenly perform miraculous feats of courage and strength, then have no recollection of what they'd done.

Huck shivered.

The cry in the night and Clark's sudden, inexplicable departure had certainly mirrored the miraculous. She wondered if Gabe may not have remembered doing it . . . unless . . . ?

Overcome with emotion, Huck began to tremble, dropping the first-aid supplies. She fell to her knees and wept. But this time her tears flowed because of a sudden realization. A knowing joy. An epiphany.

The cry in the night was what had made Clark run, saving her life and Gabe's. She had assumed it was Gabe's voice, a desperate groan as he leapt to save her. She had assumed the cry was abnormally human.

But it wasn't.

It was angelic.

The voice that had pierced the night was Mister Jack's.

# TEN

*Summer 2006*
*Adam Colby*

I'd waited exactly seventeen minutes when I received the disappointing text message from Yevette. She was my best hope toward filling in the many gaps of the Alexanders' story not included in the postcards. It was her third time to cancel our meeting. So I trudged to the counter and ordered a double espresso, my favorite pity-party beverage to symbolize life's bitterness.

"Strike three," I muttered, then returned to my corner table at the crowded Town Square Starbucks. One of the postcard albums lay open because I'd just read Gabe's poem about "love's desperate cry." I slammed it closed and uttered my own: "I give up."

For at least a nanosecond, everyone in the room looked my way. Beads of sweaty embarrassment dotted my forehead. I

swiped them with a napkin as an early-thirty-something woman with auburn hair approached me from across the room. She stopped beside my table and glanced down at the album. "You must be Adam Colby."

Before I could reply, the woman introduced herself as Yevette Galloway, then stepped over to the counter and ordered a sugar-free Italian soda. Except for a black opal pendant, she wore no jewelry. She was reed slender, dressed in handstitched western boots, designer jeans, and one of those fitted denim tops with fancy needlework. Even in boots, she moved with the delicate grace of a ballet dancer. For the first time in two years, I caught myself wanting to stare. Beautiful women were everywhere and most men noticed, some more discreetly than others. It was part of the male job description. It was how the game was played. But when Haley and I split, my girl-watching mechanism malfunctioned. I didn't care to ever watch or play the game again . . .

Until now.

It made me uncomfortable, so I shifted my gaze to the dark depths of my espresso and downed a big gulp, burning my tongue. Back when Haley and I were together, I felt free to admire other women — from a

distance — because it didn't mean anything. Now, I wondered if my past appreciation of the opposite sex had contained a hidden meaning, something threatening lurking about on a subconscious level. Had my eye antics produced negative vibes that over time ran Haley off? I glanced toward Yevette, then into my cup, crossing and re-crossing my legs as harsh reality stirred the brew in my stomach.

Yevette returned, placed her soda on the table, and sat across from me. "The post-cards," she said matter-of-factly, like an attorney submitting exhibit A. "I suppose I should've just taken them anyway."

"Anyway? Are they yours?"

Yevette shook her head. "Huck wanted them destroyed upon her death."

"Why?"

Reaching across the table, Yevette stroked the album with a finger. "During the last year of Huck's life, she wasn't in her right mind about half the time. I don't think she really wanted them destroyed. Anyway, I couldn't do it."

"So you hid them on the same shelf with the photo albums?" I asked, studying her heart-shaped face.

"I assumed they'd be overlooked and dis-carded."

"Your assumption almost proved . . ." I swallowed. "It was only a one-day estate sale, so in between my dealings with customers, I began gathering what we in the business call *dumpster collectibles.*"

"Trash," she said matter-of-factly.

I thought she'd tag her response with a slight smile, or even a chuckle. She didn't.

I cleared my throat and continued. "Sometimes people have their pictures taken with movie stars, sports figures, even U.S. presidents. Before I pitched the albums, I thumbed through a couple."

"That's what I get for not following Huck's wishes." Yevette sighed. "It's not your fault."

My hands trembled slightly as I clutched my espresso. "So . . . even though the postcards aren't yours, you didn't want anyone else to find them. Is that why you canceled our meeting three times?"

She nodded slowly, as if lost in thought behind her large hazel eyes.

"But today, you came anyway."

"Yes," she answered, then said nothing.

In the background, the hiss of steamed milk emphasized the thickening silence. My brain was pondering another question when Yevette spoke.

"I finally stopped resisting the inevitable,"

she said bluntly, "and decided that it was okay for someone else to know everything. But first, I had to see you for myself, without your knowing. Examine you up close. Then I'd determine if you were real."

I chuckled, probably for the first time in weeks. "So how long have you been in here watching me?"

"Long enough to text you a message and then change my mind."

"Am I real?"

"As best I can tell." Yevette leaned forward, her eyes changing from hazel to green. She curled a finger over her lips, then settled back in her chair.

"Good," I answered, wanting to laugh at the paradox. It was *this woman* who seemed to teeter upon the edge of reality. I was also a little unnerved about the eye-color thing — probably just the light — and wanted to get down to business before she changed her mind again. "Like I mentioned over the phone, there are some details about Mr. and Mrs. Alexander I need to know."

"Need or want?"

"Need," I said quietly, deciding she was intuitive enough to communicate on a deeper level than simple conversation. "My wife and I divorced a couple of years ago. I *need* to know where we went wrong."

"O-kay," Yevette said slowly.

"Look," I continued, "when I read Gabe's poems, I know it sounds really crazy, but I . . . it seemed like they'd uncovered some kind of secret."

"A secret?"

"Yeah . . . of lasting love.

"Like what?"

I stared at the postcard album, wondering if I should mention The Long Division. "They sacrificed for each other and had eyes only for the other. Reading the poems made me realize all the ways my marriage went wrong." I felt self-conscious opening up so quickly with Yevette, but I *did* need her to fill in the many gaps in the Alexanders' story.

"Look," I said, making eye contact. "Understanding exactly what made their marriage work makes me feel like I could . . ." I paused and cleared my throat a second time.

"Try again someday?" she finished.

"Maybe. If it's not too late."

"Your motives do seem genuine." Yevette smiled.

"Are you an attorney?" I asked wryly.

She shook her head. "Before Huck died, she told me everything."

"I thought she wasn't in her right mind," I said, then wished I'd kept silent as Ye-

vette's smile vanished.

"She became confused in her late nineties," Yevette replied, her tone slightly defensive.

"Alzheimer's?"

"Not exactly. A form of dementia caused by depression. On some days, Fridays especially, Huck thought Gabe was still alive. She even hallucinated about him coming to see her. On other days she was lucid."

"May I ask you about your mother?" I said, changing the subject.

"Okay."

"How long did Priscilla work for the Alexanders?"

"Twenty-six years."

"Did she know about the postcards?"

"Not to my knowledge. They were kept under lock and key." Yevette paused, her tone softening. "I didn't know about them until a few months before Huck died, when she was living at Bayshore Extended Care."

"She showed them to you?"

"I helped her put them into albums. It was her idea; said she'd meant to for years. We finished a couple of weeks before she called 911."

"You mean Mrs. Alexander called 911 from her room at Bayshore?"

"Twice in the same week."

"Why?"

"The first time she was determined to go to her own beauty shop."

I laughed out loud. "And the second?"

"Concluded her mail was being stolen." Yevette paused, her face thoughtful. "It's okay if you call her Huck. Most people did."

"And so EMS came?" I continued.

"Both times. With lights flashing and sirens blaring."

"Was Mrs. Alexander's . . . I mean . . . Huck's mail really being stolen?"

"In her mind, it was the logical conclusion. Since it was Friday, she thought someone had taken Gabe's weekly postcard. In truth, she'd not received one since his death eighteen years before."

"So prior to placing them into albums, where did she and Gabe store them?"

"The postcards were locked in a hidden compartment in a marble-top dresser. They'd bought it on one of their vacations because it was handcrafted by slaves in the 1850s. I remember my mother saying how valuable it was. The hidden compartment was used to hide letters passed along the Underground Railroad."

I smiled. A great-nephew of the Alexanders had been willed that beautiful historic piece of furniture. Little did he know

that the dresser that protected letters symbolizing human freedom had also protected the symbols of Huck and Gabe's love.

"I kept the skeleton key to the secret compartment," Yevette said. "You probably think it's odd, but it's one of the few things of theirs I wanted."

Not knowing how to reply, our conversation halted. My mind had a theory as to why she'd kept the key, but my heart pled the fifth. It was as if we stood in the wilderness before an uncharted crossroad. I desperately wanted to ask why Huck was finally willing to divulge what had been kept private for seventy-some-odd years, then remembered Yevette's resistance when I'd inquired earlier.

"Huck had her reasons for telling me about each card," Yevette said, then smiled. "Your face looks like a giant flesh-colored question mark." She sipped her soda, then leaned across the table and whispered beneath her green eyes. "Eventually, you'll know what I know. But the postcards will make little sense until I tell you about Mister Jack."

Then, as if creating a colorful quilt stitched with the careful tenderness of loving fingers, Yevette pieced together each event that molded Huck's childhood: her

family, the secret glen, the Anacacho orchids, the mysterious Mister Jack. She told me how Mister Jack had revealed things about Huck no one else knew, causing Huck to decide that he was her guardian angel.

Pausing for breath, Yevette curled her finger over her lips once again, then spoke. "I can see from your expression that you don't believe in angels. Is there a reason?"

"Because they turn into devils and leave their faithful husbands," I answered coldly, then smirked. "Nowadays, I'm not so sure I believe in anything."

"Angels included." Yevette blinked twice, her eyes still green.

"It was a joke." I gave a lighthearted chuckle to prove my point. "Don't you believe in humor?"

"Only when it's humorous." She smiled. "That was a joke too."

I couldn't help but grin. There was something mysterious about this woman. Something intriguing. Something satisfying. It made me wonder about her. What she was interested in, how she spent her time. Did she work? Or was she independently wealthy? My curiosity was sparked.

Yevette stirred her soda and continued her story, explaining Huck's fascination with the term "soul mate" and her youthful

desire to never bear children. How a freak car accident at age sixteen fulfilled that desire, aiding in her decision to teach, but instilling fear about ever finding a husband.

"Do you believe in soul mates, Mr. Colby?"

"Call me Adam. And why do you ask such deep questions?"

"Because, Adam . . . without deep questions, there are only shallow answers."

I shrugged, realizing the futility of reasoning with this woman. And yes, I did need answers. As far as I knew, Yevette was the only person who could provide them. "I believe the Alexanders were soul mates."

Nodding her approval, she proceeded, explaining how Huck was first engaged to her childhood sweetheart, Clark Richards. Then for the next thirty minutes Yevette talked nonstop. She told every romantic detail from Gabe's oyster comment, to Splash Day, to Mister Jack's wild cry in the night.

Yevette stopped talking and looked at her watch, then took a final sip of her Italian soda, which was mostly melted ice. I sat in stunned silence. Suddenly, Gabe's poems took on new meaning. Huge gaps in the Alexanders' story had been filled. With a little more work, I could begin to connect the

dots. But the cry in the night? Was Yevette being serious or making that part up?

"I've got to go race — literally — and you've got a lot to think about." Yevette stood.

"Race?"

"I race horses. Mostly Quarter Horses, but some Thoroughbreds." She smiled. "You've never met a female jockey?"

"Not to my knowledge. And speaking of never, you never said why you . . . uh . . . changed your mind and decided to stay," I managed, "except that I seemed real and my motives seemed genuine."

"I stayed and told you about the Alexanders because I sensed you believed in hope."

"And were you right?"

"Absolutely. Anyway, everything I've said is outlined in the postcards. But you already know that."

"But what about the rest? There's so many more blanks for you to fill."

Yevette's eyes had switched back to hazel. "Just call me."

Before I could gather enough wit for an intelligent reply, she walked out the front door and disappeared into the parking lot.

I ordered a latte and returned to my corner table, noticing an entirely different

group of patrons than when I'd first entered. How many times had the tables and over-stuffed chairs changed their humans in the last couple of hours? How many times would I meet with this unusual woman before I got answers to all my questions?

It was hard to believe two weeks had passed since I'd met with Yevette at Starbucks. Since then, I'd written the first part of Huck and Gabe's story. Read and reread the applicable postcards, filling in the blanks as best I could remember.

I still hadn't decided if Mister Jack was an actual person, a character in Huck's wild imaginings, or a mixture of both. There was a slim chance he could have been an escaped convict, since the state penitentiary was located near the Huckabee home. But it seemed, at least in the movies, that escapees hightail it as far away as possible. More likely, Mister Jack was a simple drifter and Huck's secret glen was his campsite, complete with rare Anacacho orchids. However, children do create imaginary friends. And logic told me that Huck wouldn't want or need an additional playmate with a house full of siblings. What really mattered was that Mister Jack had a profound impact on Huck's self-worth, which played directly

172

into her hope of finding a soul mate.

When Yevette assured me that I believed in hope, I thought I knew what she meant. Up until our meeting, I thought hope was more of an experience than a belief. I still *hoped* to love again, though I wondered if it had become more of a desperate desire. According to Yevette, Mister Jack instructed Huck to "grasp hope and never let go." I knew Huck was concerned with finding her soul mate, but after an intense amount of thought, Mister Jack's definition of hope seemed to include more depth, perhaps even a different meaning altogether.

I had to admit, before I discovered the postcards, I thought soul mates existed only in fairy tales. And couples lucky enough to stay together might live "ever after," but lied about the "happily" part. So the questions arose: Did soul mates evolve into lovers? Or did lovers evolve into soul mates? More plainly, were Huck and Gabe destined to be together forever, or did they make it happen?

The wisdom and insight of Gabe's Long Division concept had much to do with the success of the Alexanders' relationship. I was convinced that some males were born-romantics, where others broke out of the womb as athletes or musicians. What woman

wouldn't sell her soul for a man thoughtful enough to mail her an original love poem each week for sixty years? Even men who lacked Gabe's creativity should adopt that idea and apply it to their own marriages in some form or fashion.

I'd not yet written about, nor discussed with Yevette, the postcard Gabe penned for their wedding night. The poem for that significant event highlighted this phrase: *two hearts commanding devotion.* When I considered how they practiced this idea early in their courtship — each putting the other's needs first — I decided it most likely set up a lifelong pattern of selflessness. Haley and I had selfishly *demanded* each other's devotion, even while dating. As a result, we were never in *command* of our relationship. So was their altruism fundamental to avoiding The Long Division? I expected I already knew the answer, but there was still so much to consider.

Yevette and I had made plans to meet the next afternoon at a steakhouse in one of the older parts of Houston. She wanted to show me something. Our plan was to discuss more of the postcards, which for me would probably result in as many new questions as answers. In some ways, I felt that she was hiding something. Something significant.

I was better, but most days I operated like a confused snail running the hundred-yard dash. At least I'd started, and at that point I just wanted to go the distance. My hope was that I had the guts to keep moving forward. Then perhaps . . . just perhaps . . . I'd find the secret to a lasting marriage.

# Eleven

*Bayshore Extended Care Facility, 2004*
*Mrs. Alexander*

"Oh, Gabe, must you go? Can't we read the postcard today?" Huck whispered.

She knew it was morning but refused to open her eyes. Refused to wipe away the tears, some falling onto the silver strands of hair that covered her pillow. Tears of sadness turned to joy. Tears of long-awaited anticipation. For the third Friday in a row, Gabe had appeared just before daylight. Walked right into her room and sat on the edge of her bed, then drew her into the comfort of his sea-sky gaze.

She smiled.

On Gabe's first visit, he'd apologized for not arriving sooner. Gently teased her about calling 911. Before she could explain, his lopsided grin burst into a laugh. "I'll bet the expressions on those nurses' faces were well worth it," he repeated over and over,

until his words and laughter no longer lingered with the dawn.

Then he was gone.

Raising one eyelid, Huck glimpsed the present day's growing brightness and sighed. Wasn't that just like Gabe? Not bothered in the least about their precious postcards being stolen. She toyed with the silly idea of becoming upset with his nonchalance, but that had never worked. Instead, she decided to remember his return on the previous Friday. How wonderful it had been to feel the familiar warmth of his breath brush across her lips, awakening her from a dreamless sleep. She meant to ask if he'd brought her a card, but their brief conversation centered upon Yevette. Gabe was delighted about the albums and the fact that Huck had shared every detail of . . . how had he worded it? Oh yes. "Shared every detail of our love's radiant hope."

Opening her other eye, Huck smiled again at the now week-old memory of his second visit. Her caring man sure had a way with words. He knew Yevette was struggling with the nightmarish ghosts of two past relationships and needed expert guidance. And even though the albums were complete, he'd asked Huck to continue telling Yevette everything she could remember.

After blinking several times, Huck focused upon her drab surroundings: antiseptic walls, viewless window, plain curtains. Except for a fresh bouquet of yellow daises from Yevette, the only flowers in her room were artificial. Huck would've thrown the plastic eyesores away — along with an appalling imitation of Van Gogh's *Starry Night* — if those items hadn't belonged to Bayshore.

Pushing a button, Huck raised her bed into a sitting position. She touched her face, feeling a leftover happy tear slide down her wrinkled cheek. This morning, Gabe had arrived on the leading edge of sunrise. As before, he was young and healthy, and dressed in the same gray linen suit he'd worn on their first date. But unlike his two previous visits, he'd held a colorful postcard.

"Oh, dearest Gabe, you remembered."

"I've wanted you to see this card for the longest time," Gabe said softly. "But may I show you something else first?" Even though Huck was in her bed, she suddenly envisioned Gabe standing in the center of her secret childhood glen. The same circle of soft Bermuda grass. The same crisp blue sunlight. It was the place where she'd met Mister Jack.

Gabe grinned. He was no longer in the

glen but back sitting on her bed. "Next Friday, let's meet at the glen. I know it was one of your favorite places."

"But, Gabe. They won't let me leave this room. And I can't get out of this bed without . . ." Huck began to cry.

"I know, darling." Gabe leaned close, the light from his smile illuminating Huck's soul. "So when they're not looking, I'll come back to read the postcard." Gabe stood, his handsome form fading into a shimmering glimmer. "And then I'll carry you to the glen . . . in my arms."

---

## TWELVE

Tonight,
Sweet mystery we explore. . . .
A timeless understanding
Of how The Long Division's
  foiled by more
Than tender touch along love's
  way,
But two hearts commanding
Devotion. . . .
On our first
Forever Friday.

                    Forever, Gabe

*May 1926*
*Houston, Texas*
Huck and Gabe secretly wed the Friday evening after Mister Jack's wild cry in the night. Their week-long engagement had been fun but hectic: securing a marriage license, buying rings, packing Huck's belongings, transporting them to Gabe's

garage apartment. They'd even purchased a shiny new Oldsmobile they immediately dubbed Blue Norther, due to its azure color and whirlwind speed.

On "Elopement Friday," Huck taught school at Sidney Lanier in her colorful pastel shift, while Gabe worked the books at Cecil's in his gray linen suit. At five o'clock sharp, he selected a dozen perfect pink roses from a nearby florist, then drove across town to pick up his bride. An hour later, they knelt in the stained-glass glow of Christ Church, where a portly rector announced them man and wife, his emotional spouse insisting they come to the parsonage for a celebratory supper of chicken-fried steak and banana pudding.

"I shouldn't have had that second helping of pudding," Gabe said as they motored away from the parsonage in the humid Houston twilight. "I don't want to be a fat married man." He laughed.

"Let's promise to keep an eye on our waistlines," Huck replied, thinking how many couples she'd known had gained weight shortly after they married.

"It'll be a pleasure watching yours, Mrs. Alexander."

"I love my new name." Huck slid over to Gabe and planted a kiss on his cheek. Blue

Norther swerved.

"So Mrs. Alexander likes to sit close and live dangerously." Gabe grinned.

"She does. From now on, next to you is my assigned seat. Yours is behind the wheel."

"Yes, teacher. But what if I become distracted and we crash?"

Huck scooted closer and clung to Gabe's arm. "Mrs. Alexander won't allow that to happen . . . I mean the crashing part." She leaned her head back and laughed, her mind repeating her new name in various ways, mimicking the scribbles of a lovesick school girl:

Mrs. Alexander.

Mrs. Gabe Alexander.

Huck Alexander.

She'd wondered if the transition from "Miss" to "Mrs." would make her feel old. It didn't. It just made her feel warm. Warm and wonderful.

Peering through the top of the windshield, she could see a speckle of stars peeking out from underneath the vast blanket of heaven. Just like on their first date, the stars seemed to shimmer with excitement. "I love you . . . Mr. Alexander."

"Kiss me again and prove it." With a squeal of tires, Gabe braked the car to a sudden stop. They kissed deeply, until

someone honked. Waving an apology, Gabe let out the clutch and moved on.

"I wonder why at a wedding the preacher always says, 'You may now kiss the bride'?" Huck let go of Gabe's arm long enough for him to shift gears.

"Didn't you want to be kissed?" Gabe turned his head to meet Huck's gaze, this time almost swerving into a pair of oncoming headlights.

"You watch the road and I'll watch you," Huck replied. "And to answer your question . . . of course I wanted to be kissed. But ever since I was a little girl, I've wondered why the preacher doesn't say, 'You may now kiss the groom.' "

"I don't want to kiss the groom."

"That's not what I mean and you know it."

At the corner of Louisiana Street and Texas Avenue, Gabe pulled up to the newly constructed Lancaster Hotel. They'd toured, then chosen the Lancaster because it was small, only twelve stories and a mezzanine, but the most luxurious and romantic hotel in the city. After checking in, they followed the bellman up to the entrance of the honeymoon suite on the top floor. He gently set down their bags. Instead of opening the door after inserting the key into the lock, he

merely grinned. "Sir. Everything is exactly as you've requested. Happy honeymoon." Before Gabe could offer a tip, the bellman spun on his heel and was gone.

"What exactly have you requested, Mr. Alexander?" Huck reached up and placed her arms around Gabe's neck. His eyes twinkled like an entire galaxy.

"Why don't we open the door, Mrs. Alexander? Then you'll know." Gabe turned the key and the door swung open.

"Oh, Gabe . . . When did you . . . ? How did you . . . ?"

"I had some connections," Gabe answered, his voice mirroring the excitement in his eyes. "The owner of this hotel is now one of Cecil's most satisfied customers."

Huck wanted to laugh and cry at the same time. The entire sitting room was aglow with hundreds of candles attached to tiny blocks of balsa floating in leaded crystal punch bowls, their rainbows of brilliant light flickering over walls and ceiling. The floor, removed of its Persian rugs and elegant furniture, had been covered with a large tarp upon which pure white sand had been sprinkled. In the room's center, a weathered porch swing swung from a wooden frame, with "his and hers" emerald silk robes hanging from one end. The swing was identical

to the one in which they'd snuggled the night their love was born. A large covered picnic basket and modern Victrola completed the room's furnishings.

Huck kicked off her shoes and twirled around in a circle. "Oh, Gabe. You've re-created our own private beach. Come dance with me. Come dance with the happiest girl in the world."

Gabe removed his shoes and socks and wound the Victrola. Strains of the waltz "Waves of the Danube" filled the room, its gypsy-like melody lovely, haunting. He stepped toward Huck, placing his arms around her.

"I can't believe you remembered." Huck melted into his embrace as they moved with the passion of the music. "But you did."

"It's only been a week, my darling."

"Not the beach. You remembered that 'Waves of the Danube' is my favorite waltz."

"That's what porch swings and secrets are for," Gabe said softly. "Things about you I didn't know, I get to remember."

"And what will you remember about . . . tonight?"

Gabe stopped dancing. Pulling Huck into the depth of his firm embrace, he lowered his head, brushing his lips against hers as he spoke: "Tonight, we are the music.

185

Tonight, we are the rhythm. Tonight, we are the mystery."

A little while later, they put on the emerald robes and returned to the swing, sitting side by side. Huck cuddled next to Gabe and shivered with delight. Wearing only a robe beside a man who was dressed the same way was daring, even if he was her husband. She laughed.

"What's so amusing?"

"My parents."

"Your parents?" Gabe lit a cigarette. "Why would a girl think about parents during her honeymoon?"

Huck stroked the delicate silk, feeling the softness of her body underneath. "Mama would die before she'd let Papa see her dressed like this . . . and vice versa."

Gabe chuckled. "I'll admit, that's not quite how I pictured your folks." He inhaled slowly and released the smoke. "So when do we tell them?"

"About these beautiful robes? Never!"

"About us," Gabe replied softly, meeting Huck's gaze. "I can't wait to see the two people responsible for making you."

"I'm starved," Huck said, wiggling forward in an attempt to stand. "What delicious snack is in the basket?"

"Why are you so worried?" Gabe gently placed his hand upon her leg. "I'm a lovable man."

"Extremely." Huck sighed and scooted back into the swing. Her stomach tightened. "You're my lovable man and that's all that matters." She paused, struggling with her hidden fears. "We'll tell Mother when the time is right."

"Because of the church thing?"

"Please, Gabe. Let's not discuss that now." A single tear rolled down Huck's cheek. She swallowed hard, refusing to cry about her mother's stubborn religiosity, even though the entire evening had brimmed her heart with emotion. "There's no telling what Mother's heard about you already."

"Because of Clark?"

"Oh, Gabe, this is our wedding night. Let's not ruin it."

"I agree." Gabe snuffed his cigarette, then held Huck close, wiping the tear trail with the hem of his robe. "I guess your lovable guy needs to learn when to ask his wife questions."

Huck buried her cheek against Gabe's chest and sniffed. "You've already asked the most important question . . . and I said yes."

Their lips met once again, this time with

the unquenchable fire of rekindled under-standing. As the blaze burned hotter, their lovers' symphony flamed into a tone and rhythm more impassioned than before. Then gradually, their music slowed, fading into the softness of satisfied slumber.

A few minutes before midnight, there was a knock at the door. "Telegram!" It was the voice of the same bellman who'd carried their bags.

Gabe leaped up.

"Dearest. Don't forget your robe." Huck giggled, then covered herself. "Who would send a telegram at this hour?"

"Who even knows we're here?" Gabe grabbed his robe and strode to the door.

"Mr. Alexander! Telegram!"

A dozen reasons, all of them tragic, sud-denly ricocheted inside Huck's head. Only bad news would be delivered at midnight.

After opening the door, Gabe thanked the bellman and faced Huck as the latch clicked behind him. His eyes were full of tears.

"Gabe? What is it?"

"It's not a telegram. It's a postcard."

"A postcard? Who's it from?" Huck felt her voice tremble. "Aren't you going to read it?"

Gabe stood still. "I already know what it says."

"You do? How could you —"

"I wrote it," Gabe interrupted, his face bursting into a grin. "Happy first Forever Friday."

"I should chop off your head for scaring me like that." Huck threw on her robe and scampered toward Gabe. "What have you done, sending me a postcard when it's almost midnight?"

"Something I plan to do each Friday for the rest of our lives, that is, if I get to keep my head." He handed her the postcard. "And the United States Post Office will take care of all future deliveries during normal business hours."

Huck read silently.

"Oh, my genius man of endless surprises," she whispered before flinging her arms around his neck. "I didn't know you were a poet."

"Guess I inherited the gift from my father." He paused. "Do you really think I'm a genius?"

"Of course, silly. I love the line 'two hearts commanding devotion.' And your Long Division concept should win a Nobel Prize."

Gabe laughed. "A Nobel Prize for love. Now that's a pretty genius idea too. Perhaps you should win a Nobel for creating a new Nobel category." He kissed her tenderly.

189

"Look at the lovers on the front of the card."

Withdrawing one arm, Huck held the card in the candlelight and studied the striking couple. "They're perfect. Young. Beautiful. Happy. He's gazing into her eyes as she gazes into his. They could be us."

"Exactly what I thought the day I bought it."

"Oh, Gabe! Postcard poems on our Forever Fridays. They'll be our most cherished secret, held by *our* hands only."

"Then stored safely in our hearts." Gabe pulled Huck close for another kiss when her stomach growled.

"Oops." Huck laughed. "That wasn't my heart, nor was it ladylike. Guess I'm definitely hungry . . . and thirsty." She eyed the picnic basket, remembering their May Day lunch at Mermaids on Galveston Beach. "I don't suppose there's shrimp cocktail?"

"Lounging on ice for your midnight eating pleasure," Gabe replied, then raised his eyebrows. "It took some doing, but I managed to barter for something else that's in that basket. Something one keeps secret *and* on ice."

"Would that have to do with my midnight drinking pleasure?"

"More like your pleasurable bubbly personality."

Huck smiled, recalling the giddiness she'd felt that first day while drinking pink champagne. But more than that, remembering her childhood vow of only sharing deepest secrets with her soul mate.

Suddenly Huck couldn't stop laughing.

Their clandestine Forever Friday postcards were pure glee.

# THIRTEEN

Morning's coolness bright and
  fair
Reminds me of my girl so dear;
To share with her this early
  hour
And hold her close is my
  desire. . . .
The morning of our love.
Forever, Gabe

*June 1926*
*Houston, Texas*
Huck stood behind her teacher's desk and watched twenty-four students crowd out of her classroom as the final bell rang, ending another school year at Sidney Lanier.

Summer at last, she thought . . . well, almost.

Even though Huck was an adult, the season still evoked the carefree gladness of uninhibited freedom. Freedom from stale

studies and chalk dust. Freedom to run barefoot down a warm sandy lane. Freedom to spend time loving the soul mate of her girlhood dreams.

She glanced at the clock as anticipation pulsed through her veins. Three thirty. Only ninety minutes before Gabe would pick her up and their weekend would officially begin. Huck smiled. It was Friday and she couldn't wait to get home and check the mail.

Kicking off her shoes, she plopped down in her chair, mentally organizing tasks for the following Monday. It would be the final workday for teachers. An entire day to turn in grades and ready classrooms for the next school year. The coolness of the polished oak floor soothed her tired feet. Pushing aside a stack of graded essay tests, she let her mind wander again to thoughts of Gabe.

It had been almost a month since their porch swing honeymoon. And marriage to him was every bit as wonderful as she'd imagined. On weekdays, he'd hop out of their bed the minute the alarm sounded and put on the kettle, allowing her time to snooze awhile longer. The next thing she knew, he'd be under the covers again, gently rubbing her back while two cups of Admiration Coffee steamed on the nightstand. She'd prop feather pillows against the

headboard, and they'd sit, sip, and snuggle while the sun lit the eastern sky. After a few coffee kisses, Gabe would shave and dress while Huck cooked a breakfast he said was "fit for a Texas cattle baron." He'd tie on one of her aprons and wash dishes while she got ready. Then they'd scuttle down the apartment stairs and zoom away in Blue Norther.

Huck smiled. Her cowboy-captain looked so silly wearing a frilly apron. In a way, it reminded her of the day they'd met at Cecil's — Gabe covering his suit with an apron — except her aprons were starched and not spattered with fish scales.

On Sundays, they'd attend the eleven o'clock service at Christ Church. Since the weather was sunny and warm, they'd pack a picnic lunch and head over to Hermann Park. Before munching fried chicken and an assortment of fresh fruit, they'd thank God for His bountiful goodness. Then while eating, discuss the day's sermon. Afterward they'd stow their picnic basket back in Blue Norther and stroll through the zoo. Their favorite animals were a pair of Asian elephants: Nellie and Hans. "Now there's a couple who lives *large,*" Gabe said.

Opening her grade book, she wondered if every week of their marriage would receive

an A+. There had been a few "together tweaks," a phrase coined after their first disagreement. She now realized how juvenile she'd been, and Gabe too. Neither of them had argued like adults. And even though Cutter — her twin — was a paltry six minutes older, she'd been branded the youngest Huckabee, accused by her family of expecting to get her way. And Gabe had been an only child.

"Well, maybe just an A for that particular week," she whispered. They'd been married only ten days when she'd mentioned wanting to sleep on the right side of their bed, the side she'd always favored. She'd just come out of the bathroom from brushing her teeth when Gabe turned back the covers.

"I didn't know there was a *wrong* side." He chuckled and leaped into bed.

"Gabe . . . I wanted that side."

"What difference does it make?" He pulled the top sheet up over his head.

"Evidently, lots." Huck tried to uncover him but couldn't, so she hit him with a pillow. "You're not being fair."

"But I've always slept on this side," Gabe said, peeking out at her.

"So have I." Huck dropped the pillow and folded her arms, surprised at his selfishness.

She realized they were both on the verge of hurt feelings but wanted to prove a point. Her cheeks grew hot. "Before we married there was only one of you living here. That means you always slept in the middle."

"Great idea." Gabe rolled to the center.

"I can't believe you," she said.

Neither spoke for a moment.

"I can't believe *you* clogged the bathtub drain with your long hair." He frowned.

"That's a ridiculous male observation that has nothing do with one's favorite side of the bed."

"Are you implying I'm being unfair?"

"If the toenail fits, wear it."

"The toenail?"

"More precisely, toenails. Yours. It's not just my hair clogging the drain." Huck stomped back into the bathroom and locked the door. She'd not really discovered his toenails in the bathtub, but he must cut them somewhere. Several minutes passed in silence. She'd started to open the door, but changed her mind and sat on the toilet lid instead, crossing and recrossing her arms. Surely Gabe knew they weren't seriously fighting . . . were they?

Standing slowly, she tiptoed to the door and listened. Nothing. Had he gone? Suddenly, a car engine roared to life on the

street below. Huck reached for the doorknob as mental images of her new husband disappeared in a dark cloud of automobile exhaust. "Oh, Gabe!" She flung open the door.

"I'm a selfish ignoramus." Gabe stood only inches away. "It's all my fault."

"No. It's mine. My feelings were hurt and I made up the toenail story." She melted into his arms. "I don't care what side of the bed I'm on, as long as I'm next to you."

"And if I'm ever tempted to do something as disgusting as clip my toenails while bathing," Gabe whispered, "I won't. I'll just buy larger shoes."

They laughed and held each other close, then kissed like long-lost lovers.

"So what were you doing out here all this time?" Huck asked.

"I'll never tell." Gabe grinned. "What were you doing in there?"

"I'll never tell either." She laughed.

"You don't have to. I was watching through the keyhole."

"Gabriel Robert Alexander! You should be horsewhipped."

"How 'bout you scratch my back instead?"

The memory of their first "together tweak" made Huck laugh out loud, jiggling her thoughts back into her classroom. She'd

been mad enough to claw Gabe's eyes and ended up scratching his back. And just today, one of the other teachers had told her that men who have their heads scratched every day never go bald. Gabe would love that.

Huck studied her grade book, then closed it, debating what to do next. She'd much rather think about Gabe than record essay scores. Besides, she'd worked ahead and had little to do on Monday. Opening a desk drawer, she then pulled out a hand-held mirror and a small brush. Gabe might arrive early, and it wouldn't do for her hair to be mussed. He'd done that last Friday . . . arrived early.

Satisfied with her hair, Huck put away the mirror and brush. She walked over to a window and peered outside. Blue Norther was nowhere in sight.

"At least we have tonight," Huck said aloud. They'd made no definite plans, a late movie date perhaps, but it didn't matter. Spending a Friday evening together was enough. Once again, she pictured what would be waiting in the mailbox, and her insides tingled.

"I wish tonight would never end and we could cancel tomorrow," Huck muttered. The next day was Saturday, so they'd

decided to drive to Huntsville because Gabe had not met "the folks." The plan was to arrive after lunch, then spend the night and attend church there if all went well. If it didn't, she'd make a job-related excuse and they'd drive back to Houston.

Huck had written her mother a long letter, not referencing marriage specifically, but hinting how she'd met Gabe and it had changed her life. Annise had mailed back a quick reply. Not a word about Gabe. But since none of her children lived in Huntsville, it would be wonderful visiting with her youngest daughter face to face.

*Face to face* meant a private talk, which Huck wanted to avoid. However, her mother's letter could've been worse. Clark wasn't mentioned, so perhaps he'd not spread rumors about his and Huck's violent breakup, at least none vicious enough to cause a hometown stir. And there was a bit of good news: Cutter would be home. Huck believed without reservation that he'd adore her new husband. Well, maybe not *adore,* but be so relieved she'd not married Clark, would probably award Gabe season tickets. Two years ago, Cutter had signed with the Beaumont Exporters, a top-rated minor league baseball team. He wasn't usually free

on summer weekends but had a rare open date.

A car resembling Blue Norther pulled up outside Huck's classroom window and honked. She knew it wasn't Gabe — he considered honking for ladies as rude — but checked the clock anyway. Only ten minutes had passed. So the start to their wonderful evening would have to wait awhile longer.

She returned to her desk. As good as it would be to see family, she dreaded the possible outcome. The whole thing made her stomach hurt.

When Gabe arrived at Sidney Lanier ten minutes early, Huck was waiting out front. He offered a brief kiss and opened the passenger's side door.

"I missed you today," Gabe said as he steered Blue Norther out of the parking lot.

"Not as much as I missed you." Huck leaned over and pecked him on the cheek. "Can you believe school's out for the summer?"

"It's predicted to be a scorcher," Gabe said. "So I think we should install a swimming pool."

"That sounds refreshing, darling, but with whose money?"

"Well . . ." He rubbed his chin. "We do okay. And we did sell my parents' ranch."

"Gabe dear, we agreed to spend some of that money on a house, save some, and invest the rest."

"So, not a good plan?"

"I'd rather have a house." She studied his face. "What are you up to? You know as well as I that we can't install a swimming pool on rental property. Our landlord would . . ." She paused. "Why are we driving north?"

He shrugged again. "Just gave Blue Norther her head, and this is the direction she chose."

"Gabe Alexander. Where are we going?"

"You have been kidnapped." He chuckled. "Thought we'd head on up toward Huntsville tonight. I've already been home and packed everything we'll need."

"Oh, Gabe, no." Huck's bottom lip quivered. "I'm prepared to deal with Mother for an afternoon and perhaps one night, but not two. Anyway, it's *our* Friday."

"I said we'd head *toward* Huntsville, not that we'd actually get there. Not tonight anyway." He grinned, his mouth lopsided with mischief.

Huck sighed, relieved that the confrontation with her mother was still a day away. "Since I've allowed you to kidnap me, I

insist on knowing everything." After the stunning romance of the honeymoon, she didn't know what to expect.

"Okay. About halfway to your folks' place is an elegant country inn that's just been refurbished, complete with a French chef. I read about it in the *Chronicle.* Thought we'd have a nice dinner there and stay the night . . . to celebrate."

"Celebrate?" Huck took a deep breath. "Dearest. I know I said that Mother could be handled, and she can, but when she discovers her youngest daughter has married . . ." She stopped, realizing he wasn't paying attention.

"Gulf Oil Corporation offered me a job," Gabe interjected. "Starts July 18."

"Gabe!" Huck threw her arms around his neck. "I can't believe it!"

"Careful. Last time you attacked me like this we almost crashed."

"I'm not worried." Huck kissed his cheek. "Introducing you as an oil executive is exactly how we'll handle Mother."

"Accountant," Gabe corrected. "Lowly accountant."

"Doesn't matter. Mother knows nothing about the oil business. The second I introduce you, I'll mention Gulf Oil. Papa will be impressed."

"Sounds a little slick to me."

"Very funny."

"What about that private talk your mother wrote about?"

"I've been intensely praying for wisdom."

Gabe wrinkled his forehead. "Hmm. I'll bet your mother has offered a few intense prayers as well. I wonder whose side God will take?"

"We're both on *His* side," Huck said.

"Well stated, my wise wife."

Huck smiled. Hopefully their private talk wouldn't even happen.

"Any further advice on meeting your father?" Gabe asked.

Huck kissed his cheek again and snuggled close. "Are you skilled at dominoes?"

"Not if you don't want me to be."

"Then you'll do fine. Papa would love it if you challenged him to a game."

"What about Cutter? Is he any good?"

"Against Papa?"

Gabe nodded.

"Hasn't been for years."

At the inn, Huck discovered Gabe had stuffed Blue Norther's trunk with her entire wardrobe, along with all her makeup, jewelry, shoes, and anything else she could possibly need. It was a ridiculous amount for one weekend, but he wanted her to have the

proper choices, and she was touched by his thoughtfulness. He even brought their Friday postcard and had the waiter deliver it to their secluded little booth, along with flaming cherries jubilee.

Huck read the card before the flame died. "The morning of our love," she repeated softly.

"May its fire continue well into the evening," Gabe added.

"A double-meaning metaphor," Huck replied.

He took her hand and kissed her. "I love being married to an English teacher."

The next morning they ordered coffee and hot cinnamon rolls for breakfast, then walked and window-shopped. After browsing for over an hour through a used bookstore, they enjoyed a bite of lunch at a local soda fountain.

"I'm titling this weekend *Kidnap Surprise*," Huck said as they strolled hand in hand back to the inn.

"I like that," Gabe replied. "Is the surprise what happens later in Huntsville?"

She made a sour face. "It's too fine a day for anything to go wrong. You stick to your domino challenge, and I'll handle Mother. Trust me."

"Always," he said.

When they arrived at the Huckabees' in the middle of the afternoon, Huck immediately introduced Gabe as her husband, explaining that he worked for Gulf Oil.

"Well I'll be," said Ethan. "An oil man in the family."

Gabe shook Ethan's hand and grinned. "Sir, it's a pleasure to know you."

"Likewise," Ethan said.

"You too, ma'am." Gabe smiled at Annise. "I've so looked forward to meeting my fine new kinfolk."

Annise stared blankly at Huck. "I had a feeling you'd married."

Huck's mouth dropped.

"You've had a mind of your own since birth. But that's no excuse for not letting your mother know beforehand."

For the next few seconds, the raspy buzz of cicadas intensified an awkward silence.

Huck felt beads of perspiration pop across her forehead. Her plan of introducing Gabe as an oilman had failed. "I'm sorry, Mother," Huck said finally.

"We wanted to surprise you," Gabe added.

"Reckon it worked," said Ethan.

Annise stepped toward Huck and hugged her. "After thirteen children, I've learned to expect the unexpected, especially from my

most headstrong child."

"Are you sure you know what you're getting into?" Cutter asked Gabe.

Huck shot her brother a playful sneer.

"Positive." Gabe shook Cutter's hand. "But what I'd really like to get into is a lively domino game. Huck assures me I've come to the right place."

"Set up the table, son," Ethan said. "Let's welcome this boy into the family."

Huck embraced her mother as the men headed toward the veranda.

"Why don't we serve cobbler and lemonade?" Annise suggested awhile later. "The peaches this year have never been sweeter."

It was a warm afternoon, so Huck sat beside her mother on the wide front porch, each in a comfortable rocker. On the opposite end, Cutter had set up a card table, and the game was in full swing. The rattle and shake of the *bones* was a comforting sound, as well as Ethan's triumphant "Skunked ya."

"I'm sure they wouldn't turn it down," Huck said. It meant being alone with her mother in the kitchen, the prime location for their private talk. But so far, their conversation had been nothing more than catching up on various neighbors and fam-

ily members.

"Would you men like some refreshment?" Huck called as she followed her mother inside.

"That and several pairs of socks," Gabe answered. "Mine keep getting beat off me."

"And I might as well be shirtless." Cutter laughed. "Good thing Papa wears a different size."

Ethan slapped a domino on the table. "Fifteen," he said.

The women donned aprons, then washed their hands in a basin of water atop a dry sink. Huck glanced out the kitchen window. "Looks like you've had some decent rain." Her mother's garden was as beautiful as ever.

"We've been blessed," Annise said, digging lemons out of the icebox. "These were on sale at the market and need to be used." She placed them on an enamel-top worktable.

"I miss a garden," Huck said. "One day, Gabe and I will have one just as grand."

"You didn't miss it when I made you pick green beans."

"And my back still hurts," Huck said. She grabbed a knife and began cutting lemons. "How did you ever put up with me?"

"By the time you came along, Papa and I

207

were worn out. That's why you're spoiled." She raised her eyebrows.

"And not Cutter?"

"Remember, he's six minutes older, so we had more energy."

They laughed. Annise removed five bowls from the cupboard and set them on the long kitchen table.

"Gabe was an only child. I think I said that in my letter."

Annise opened a pie safe and retrieved the cobbler.

Silence.

Huck cut a lemon. "Mother? Did you hear me?"

"I did."

"So . . . ?"

"It was a long letter." She set the cobbler next to the bowls and began filling them.

"I had much to say." Huck paused. "I thought you liked a good newsy letter."

Annise cleared her throat twice.

Huck felt her stomach drop. It was a clear signal of what was coming next.

"Speaking of news, I ran into Florence Richards a few Sundays ago," Annise said.

"That's a coincidence. You've only attended the same church for over forty years."

"Don't get sassy, Huck." Annise cleared

her throat again.

"If you're wanting to discuss Gabe's and my Christian denomination," Huck said calmly, "we're Episcopalian."

"Do you think that's why I wanted to speak face to face?"

"Isn't it?" Huck felt lightheaded.

"I've made my wishes very plain on that subject, have I not?"

"Yes ma'am."

"And my grown children have the right to agree or disagree, as well as their spouses, do they not?"

Huck nodded.

"And even if we're members of different denominations, we're all believers in Christ?"

"Of course." Huck's knees weakened, so she sat on a nearby stool.

"Then that's all settled. Now, back to what I was saying."

Trying to regain her composure, Huck stood. What *had* they been talking about?

"Florence Richards is as shocked as I about you and Clark. Whatever happened?"

"I outgrew him I guess."

"That's not what I'm referring to."

"Then what, Mother?"

"The altercation between Clark and Mr. Alexander at the boardinghouse."

"Please call him Gabe." Huck cut another lemon. "Why ask me to explain what you obviously already know?"

"I want to hear your side of it."

"Does it matter?"

"Of course, child." Annise motioned to a nearby chair. "Come sit."

"No, thank you. I'd rather stand."

"Then I'll sit. Have you married a violent man?"

"What?" Huck nearly sliced off her finger.

"Is that a yes?"

"No!"

"Of course Clark asked Florence not to tell anyone but me because he didn't want to ruin your reputation."

"My reputation?" Huck realized she'd raised her voice but didn't care. "Clark's the one who should worry about a soiled reputation."

"And since when does one of *my* daughters, engaged no less, think it proper to stay out all night with another man?"

"The other man is my husband!" Huck yelled. "And Florence, of all people, shouldn't spread false rumors."

"Lower your voice," Annise said sternly. "We don't talk that way in this house. You may be an adult, but I'll not have you speak in such a disrespectful tone."

Huck walked to the dry sink and stared out the window.

"Come sit," Annise said. "Please."

Huck wiped her hands and sat across from Annise. "Clark started it." A tear seeped out of one eye. "If you must know, he practically tried to kill Gabe."

"Don't be maudlin, dear. Clark would never behave in such a manner. Perhaps you don't remember."

"Not remember?" Huck felt her voice tremble. "I think I'd *remember* when a man I've known my entire life, and thought I trusted, pulled a knife."

"You were drunk," Annise said.

"What?" Standing, Huck removed her apron.

"Calm yourself, daughter."

"No, Mother. And I wasn't *drunk*. And here's the sober truth whether you want to hear it or not: Clark intended to hurt me as well. If not for Gabe, he would have."

Annise stood. "Perhaps I've misjudged. I only wanted the best for you."

"And you think the best is Clark Richards? Mother, he would've been the *worst*. I never want to see him again."

Huck walked back outside. The game had stopped and the younger men sat smoking,

while Ethan enjoyed a plug of chewing to-bacco.

"I was expecting peach cobbler," Cutter said.

"Or at least some socks," Gabe added. He looked at Huck. "What's the matter?"

"We're leaving," Huck said.

"Where's Mother?" Cutter asked.

"Spooning up cobbler, I guess." Huck placed her hand on Gabe's shoulder. "You know I have those teaching duties to complete before Monday. Remember?"

Gabe nodded dumbly.

"But y'all just got here." Cutter scratched his head. "Did you and Mother have an argument?"

"Stay clear," said Ethan. "A man who tries to stop a wildcat fight will get clawed for his noble intentions."

"I love you, Papa, but I resent the negative gender implication," Huck said.

Ethan grinned. "You boys see what I mean?"

As Gabe started the car, Huck watched her mother step out onto the veranda. She offered a small wave and Huck returned in kind.

"I don't get it," Gabe said after they'd been driving several miles. "You two obviously had words, and —"

"And we still love each other," Huck said. "Very much."

They motored along in silence. "Do you want to talk about it, my wise wife?"

Huck scowled. "Are you making fun of me?"

"Of course not. Was it the church?"

"No, not really."

"Then what?"

Huck didn't answer.

"Was it . . . Clark?"

"Oh, Gabe, let's not discuss it."

She reached for his arm, feeling it stiffen. "What did she say?" he asked.

"Mother heard some false rumors, that's all. But I set her straight."

"She still looked crooked to me."

Huck let go of his arm. "Is everything a joke to you?"

"I'm sorry," Gabe said. "Please." He took her hand in his.

She continued. "I assured her — quite dramatically — that you were the man for me."

"I appreciate that."

Gabe released her hand, then reached his arm around her and she snuggled close.

"Here's what I think," he said.

"Tell me."

"I can't remember meeting two men I'm

213

prouder to know than your father and twin brother."

"I knew you'd get along. It's obvious they like you too."

"So what about your mother?" Gabe asked.

"She tried to apologize, but I was too angry to let her. Now I feel horrible." Huck thought a moment. "I think I'll write her another letter. It's the right thing to do. And I'm off after Monday."

"I agree," Gabe said. "So . . . you think she'll ever accept me into the Huckabee clan?"

"I suspect that the next time we visit she'll be your most ardent admirer."

"Good." Gabe released a long breath. "Wait a minute. I thought you were my —"

Huck reached up and pinched his lips. "Ardent *lover,* dear. And since we're concerned about proper word usage, *passionate* is the best adjective for us."

"I agree, Mrs. English Teacher," Gabe said. "You are a wise wife."

# Fourteen

A house of wood and stone
Will never be a proper home
Till faith
Fills every room
With love.
For more than hearth and kettle
  warm
Our grateful hearts;
An orchid blooms!
This gift
Comes from above.

*June 1926*
*Houston, Texas*
An entire week had passed since the trip to Huntsville, and Huck sat at the garage apartment's little kitchen table, brooding. School was out until September, Gabe had left for work an hour ago, and she'd finished the morning chores.

Standing, Huck stretched her arms. They

were sore from carrying boxes home from her classroom, even though Gabe had toted the heaviest ones. Sidney Lanier was getting a summer facelift, so she'd had to remove all her teaching materials.

After pouring herself more coffee, Huck grabbed a pencil and a box of stationery, then plopped back into her chair. The plan of introducing Gabe as an oil man had not veered Annise away from her uncomfortable "face-to-face." And now, she must write her mother an apology. It couldn't be put off any longer.

Huck sipped her coffee and sighed. Procrastination had put her in a frightful mood, which wasn't fair to Gabe. Honestly though, there hadn't been time to write. Monday she was still at school. On Tuesday and Wednesday she'd organized, then filed everything she'd brought home. And yesterday she'd washed clothes and shopped for groceries. Her man deserved clean shirts and a hot supper, didn't he?

She sharpened her pencil, then scolded herself for her listlessness. Gabe had tried to be encouraging, and she'd snapped at him more than once. And today was Friday, which meant another postcard would arrive with the mail. On top of that, after Gabe got off work, they had plans to go house

hunting. She should be ecstatic.

"Perhaps I'll address the envelope first," Huck said aloud. After picking up an envelope, she wrote the ever familiar address, then licked and applied a stamp. *I'd better sharpen my pencil again,* Huck thought. She started to stand but, instead, lifted the topmost stationery piece and began.

Mother,
Please forgive my disrespectful attitude last Saturday afternoon. I was wrong, and I'm sorry. You wanted to make amends, and I refused to listen. It's clear you only want the best for your children, and I know that. But please understand: Clark is not "best" anymore. At one time I thought he was God's choice and we were meant to be together. But as you say, "People change; Truth remains." Gabe Alexander is a man of God, and truth. And, Mama, he's my soul mate. Once you get to know him, you won't be disappointed.

Dearest love,
Huck

The Market Square clock chimed two o'clock. Just as Gabe was leaving Cecil's,

Charlie drove up in his delivery truck.

"How about a smoke?" Charlie hollered.

"Can't," Gabe yelled back. "Got plans."

"With the missus, I'll bet." Charlie shook his head. "It's always with the missus."

Gabe grinned and climbed into Blue Norther. He had plans, all right.

Waving at Charlie, he cranked the engine and sped onto Main. It was already a fine Friday. He'd ordered a word rhyming book, which had arrived at his office earlier in the week. It made writing poems so much easier. If he'd known how challenging it would be to compose an original verse each week, he might have come up with an alternate plan. But now that he had his *rhymer . . .* why that flung open the poetic door of endless possibilities.

He felt like E. E. Cummings.

The traffic up ahead slowed, so Gabe turned and motored down a side street, then pressed on the gas. He'd planned to take Huck house hunting, but he'd spied a chic women's apparel shop not far from the Rice Institute. In the window was a pair of those new duck pants he'd seen advertised in the newspaper. He'd always dreamed of buying his wife stylish outfits, and today seemed as good a day as any, especially after Huck's talk with Annise. Few men he knew

had any interest in their wives' wardrobes, and no clue about size and style. They just weren't using their brains. All a man had to do was study the ads. In Gabe's opinion, it would be another connecting thread to deterring The Long Division. And there was nothing more satisfying than seeing Huck's pleased expression.

When Gabe arrived at the garage apartment a little after two, Huck was sitting on the steps, humming.

"Well, well," he said, still seated behind the wheel. "I see a letter clipped to the mailbox for the postman to pick up. Is that why you're so happy?"

"I feel much better." She stood and twirled, causing her dress to slightly billow.

"Would you do that again?"

She smiled. "Absolutely not."

Before he could think about opening her door, she was already seated next to him. "Writing Mother an apology wasn't hard once I started."

Gabe backed out of the driveway and grinned.

"Looks like you've had a good day too," she said.

"Yep." He sped toward the Rice Institute.

"I thought we were going house hunting."

"Thought we'd start over by Rice. There's

a classy new housing addition out that way called Boulevard Oaks."

"Fine by me," Huck replied. "Isn't that where they've planted trees along the roadway?"

"One day the branches will canopy the streets," Gabe said.

They traveled along a wide boulevard until Gabe slowed and stopped in front of a series of shops. "I think my leg hurts," he said.

"Which one?"

"I'm not sure. Maybe both."

Huck looked around, knowing Gabe was up to something. "What have you done, Mr. Alexander?"

"Guess I pulled a muscle at work this morning."

"Keeping the books? Smells fishy to me," Huck said.

"Mind if we walk a minute?"

They stepped onto the sidewalk and passed a few storefronts. Suddenly, Huck stopped walking and pointed to a headless female mannequin. "Gabe, look."

"What happened to her head?"

"Not that, silly. She's dressed in trousers."

"Why I've never . . ." He bugged out both eyes. "And without a head, she won't have to worry about a matching hat."

Huck laughed. "Trousers for women are the daring new rage."

"Maybe for city gals. Ranch wives have been wearing their husbands' britches for years. Can you imagine riding horseback and working cattle all day in a dress?"

"True. But these trousers are designed to fit. Some of the teachers at school were whispering about them. They're called 'duck pants.' "

"Do they make women waddle?"

"Cute. The material is called white duck. Mother would have a conniption."

"Why don't you try on a pair?"

Huck smiled, remembering their first date and how he'd so easily convinced her to buy a new dress at Foley Brothers. Then moments later while she was in the dressing room, Gabe selected a pink sailor blouse that fit her perfectly.

"I've seen a few husbands come in with their wives," the young female clerk said as they stood at the cash register, "but they couldn't wait to leave."

"I tried to," Gabe whispered. "But I'm being held against my will under the spell of her beauty. Can you help me?"

The salesclerk laughed and handed Huck her packages. "I don't think she'd want me to."

Huck felt herself blush. "If you're single, be careful. You never know *who* will try to win you over with clothes."

After leaving the clothing store, they bought double-dip chocolate cones in an adjacent ice-cream shop and climbed back into Blue Norther. They passed many beautiful homes for sale, but none seemed like what they wanted.

"Perhaps we don't know what we want," Gabe said while motoring sluggishly through a sleepy neighborhood.

"We'll know it when it's right," Huck replied.

"You think living near a university might make us smarter?" He licked his cone.

"Of course," Huck answered, wishing she'd been wise enough to have eaten hers more slowly. "Look where I grew up." She laughed.

"I'd rather just look at you." Gabe faced Huck, bulging out his eyes again.

"Stop that. We're supposed to be finding For Sale signs. And anyway, you have a chocolate chin." She leaned over and kissed his chin clean. "Watch the road, Mister."

"Oops!" Gabe smeared ice cream on his cheek. "Now I have a chocolate cheek."

"Too bad because I'm full and my head hurts. You'll have to kiss yourself."

"A man can't be expected to find a house with ice cream smeared on his —"

"Gabe! Look!" Her eyes were focused on a brown Tudor-style brick home. "Stop the car."

With a screech of tires, Gabe brought Blue Norther to a stop. Huck hopped out and headed toward the house. It was well landscaped, with a steep green-tile roof and a series of slightly rounded arches that framed the front porch and each window, then fanned out to form the entrance to a flower garden on one side. In the center of the garden was an Anacacho orchid bush in glorious bloom.

"Oh, Gabe, look." Huck ran to the garden. "Anacacho orchids. This must be our home."

"But . . . honey . . . ?" Gabe said, catching up. "We're standing in somebody's yard. There's no For Sale sign."

"That's because no one else was meant to find it." Huck scampered to a window as a pang of fear jolted her insides. What if Gabe was right? But he couldn't be. The orchids were a sign of her destiny. She cupped her hands and peered inside.

"You're going to get us shot."

"No I'm not. It's vacant. Come look."

They spent the next few minutes peeping

into each window on the property. Huck couldn't see everything, but the fine craftsmanship of rich wood paneling and deep molding was obvious. The garage was enormous, with room for Blue Norther, a workbench, and tools. There was even a sailboat with a small cabin stored on top of some wooden supports.

"Look at that," Gabe said. "It's like the boat I sailed as a kid, just larger."

A car honked, then pulled up the drive.

"It must be the owner." Huck straightened her dress. "Let's buy the house today."

"In all the excitement, I left our car in the middle of the street." Gabe grinned. "Hope it's not the *new* owner."

"Go move Blue Norther," Huck ordered sweetly. "Then come back and negotiate me a home."

It wasn't the owner after all, but a Realtor who'd driven out to plant a sign in the yard. He gladly showed the house, explaining that the middle-aged couple who owned it had moved unexpectedly and were eager to sell at a fair price. They had no more use for the sailboat, so it was part of the deal.

As warm summer dusk settled on the city, they returned to the garage apartment. They'd had nothing to eat since the double-

dip cones, now hours earlier; however, neither Huck nor Gabe could stop smiling.

"I'm starved," he said as they exited Blue Norther. "How about we celebrate with supper at Benny's?"

"Oh, Gabe, I feel so grimy. I'd need to bathe first."

"Yeah, I'm a little sweaty." He wiped his face with a handkerchief. "So how about a sandwich and onion rings at The Pig Stand? That way, we don't even have to leave our car."

"A yummy idea." Huck headed toward the mailbox. "I'm too excited to cook."

"I'm going to run tell our soon-to-be-disappointed landlord the news," Gabe said, then winked. "I'll bet there's mail."

"Whatever could it be?" Huck replied as he scampered toward Mr. Blane's back door.

The mailbox was out at the curb, so she removed her shoes to feel the cool grass beneath her feet. What a day it had been. First she'd finally written her mother — a major relief — and then the unexpected shopping adventure. She laughed. It was a bit paradoxical that she'd apologized to Annise and then bought *pants* of all things. But to find the perfect home complete with Anacacho orchids? Her new address would

be 3315 Glen View Lane. Because of the orchids, it might as well have been 3315 *Secret Glen* View Lane.

Thoughts of Mister Jack had flooded Huck's mind ever since she saw the bush. Had he somehow been involved? She'd mentioned it to Gabe, who said he wouldn't discount the idea completely, but it had probably just been a coincidence. Oh well, he was *her* guardian angel, not *his*. It would be nice, but they couldn't share everything.

She reached the mailbox and removed the contents. It was almost dark, but she could see the anticipated postcard, which she'd wait to read inside with the proper light. There were also a couple of bills and a letter. She wondered who the letter was from. Mother might have written, but it wasn't her typical envelope. And her siblings mainly corresponded around the Christmas holidays. Of course it could be a letter for Gabe, but —

And then she recognized the handwriting, transforming her former joy into a cold shiver.

The letter was from Clark.

# FIFTEEN

As the fingers
Of souls
Who are one
Intertwine
To form complete and perfect
  trust,
Our todays and yesterdays
Eternally refine
Tomorrow's most precious
  gift . . . not just
That we are lovers . . .
But each other's "bestest"
  friend.

                    Forever, Gabe

*July 1926*
*Houston, Texas*
A polished brass teakettle steamed a happy
song as Huck dried and put away the
breakfast dishes. The modern three-
bedroom design of her new home was

exactly what she and Gabe had wanted, complete with a fireplace, formal sitting and dining rooms, large kitchen, and cozy breakfast nook. They slept in a four-poster bed in the largest bedroom and transformed the two smaller ones into a study and their own private parlor . . . a candlelit room containing fresh-cut flowers, favorite books, a rose-colored love seat, and, of course, the postcards.

Huck smiled.

The parlor idea had entered her brain when she was sixteen, the same afternoon her secret glen had been bulldozed. Undaunted by the din of the powerful dozer, she vowed to one day create a special place for herself and her future husband. It would be a beautiful room, secluded, off-limits to most visitors. And she'd die before seeing *it* destroyed.

Remembering the glen made her think of Huntsville and the apology letter she'd written to her mother, who'd responded in kind. They'd both corresponded a couple of times since, finally fine-tuning their differences into a bona fide truce.

Clark's letter was another matter. Huck's smile vanished because she'd not yet told Gabe. When they'd bared their souls on the night of their first date, they'd vowed to

never keep secrets. But with the excitement and bustle of moving, she'd kept putting it off. Clark was a sore subject, one that Gabe would rather not discuss. Was he jealous of her former beau? Yes. He'd be livid if he knew there was a letter she'd not told him about.

Huck thoroughly dried the silverware, then inspected it for water spots. After reading the letter carefully, she realized that Clark had apologized and even asked for her forgiveness in his own proud way. He told her he'd married a girl in Chicago whom he swore was "his unexpected pot of gold at the end of fate's rainbow." She thought it an odd statement, if not a little spiteful, but was relieved Clark had finally shifted his romantic focus.

Last weekend, she'd intended on casually mentioning the letter after breakfast. But her intentions were thwarted when the beautiful love seat they'd ordered for the parlor was delivered. So they'd brewed more coffee and spent the rest of the morning lounging on it. She hadn't wanted to ruin the fun.

"This parlor thing is downright antisocial genius," Gabe had joked. "No guest room, no weekend guests."

"I'll take that as a compliment, I think."

Huck pinched his cheek. "Weekends are our time. And besides, I don't see you offering up your study to the visiting relative pool."

Gabe laughed. "Touché! And that *is* a compliment."

Returning to the task at hand, Huck dried a delicate cup and saucer. Two weeks of serving meals on the fine china she'd stored in her hope chest was so . . . satisfying. Even more was the way Gabe looked at her when he sat at their maple breakfast set each morning, his smooth face bright with appreciation. But most satisfying of all were his lingering good-bye kisses, communicating she was the one person in his world who mattered most. Their kisses were a kind of "lip linguistics": a romantic language without words.

Warm anticipation transformed Huck's mouth back into a smile. This was Gabe's last day of work at Cecil's. Beginning tomorrow, they'd share fifteen summer days of total freedom before he started his job with Gulf. To celebrate, she'd planned two surprises.

The first had occurred last evening, a casual supper at Benny's Diner with Gabe's closest friends. She'd wanted to hostess the event in their new home, but the breakfast set, bed, and love seat were their only

furniture. Except for two sentimental lamp tables and some bookshelves, they'd sold everything from the garage apartment to a secondhand dealer, deciding to invest in higher quality. "Better craftsmanship means we can only buy a piece of furniture every few months," Gabe had emphasized more than once, "but it will outlast us both. Besides, it would be embarrassing if our bed collapsed under the strain of heavy passion."

Huck dried a silver serving spoon, inspecting it for tarnish. *Heated* defined their bedroom activities much better than *heavy.* After rubbing a water spot, she studied the spoon again. Her reflection was upside down. She laughed. Gabe had certainly turned her world topsy-turvy.

Putting away the last bit of china and silverware, Huck pitched the dishcloth into a pile of soiled table linens, then spooned ground coffee into a small drip-style pot before adding boiling water. While the coffee brewed, she retrieved a large mixing bowl and wooden spoon. Gathering eggs, flour, and baking soda, she recalled the fun she'd had last night eating supper with Gabe's friends.

Benny, who reminded her of a grizzled chuck-wagon cook, had called her "a pretty little heifer — pretty ornery." Cecil exuded

the pleasant kindness of a southern gentleman, but with sad eyes. His wife, Norma, was "under the weather" and sent her apologies. And Charlie? Funny, opinionated, spinning one joke after another. Some were slightly off-color. Wife Chloe would roar with laughter, then suddenly gasp, slapping her hand over Charlie's mouth.

Huck shook her head at the memory of Gabe's diverse friends, then lit the gas range. Part of her second surprise was baking Café Chocolate Cake, Gabe's favorite. The recipe had been handed down through his south Texas roots, and to her husband's delight, she'd made it the first week they were married. Cocoa was a prime ingredient, but this cake also called for one cup of strong coffee, cinnamon, and brown sugar. The icing boasted the same rich flavors and was decorated with toasted pecan halves.

With a wooden spoon, Huck creamed butter and brown sugar, stirred in the dry ingredients, then added coffee and eggs. As a child, she'd learned the secret to a moist cake was beating each egg into the batter separately. It took a lot more work, but the final result was worth the extra effort.

As the cake baked, Huck grabbed a pencil and a secret to-do list hidden in her recipe box. Sitting at the table, she checked off

final preparations for her second surprise:

Cake: Check.

Food and water: Check.

Bedding: Check.

Swimsuit: Check.

Ever since their interurban journey to Splash Day, when they'd discussed a real sailing adventure, she'd dreamed of exploring the jetties and coves around Galveston Bay with her soul mate. And when they'd bought a house with a sailboat, it was serendipity, something one must never ignore. So she'd planned their trip to last an entire week. Daylight hours would be spent gliding silently across the calm waters. At night, they'd build a fire on the beach and hold each other under the clear Texas stars.

Huck smiled and returned to her list:

Sailboat: Check.

Without Gabe's knowledge, she'd hired a boatman to inspect the hull, rudder, lines, and sail. The little sloop passed with ease. And as part of the deal, he'd promised to trailer it to the bayside town of Seabrook. The only things not already stowed in the boat were the cake and a few personal items.

Releasing a satisfied sigh, Huck checked "Sailboat to Seabrook." As planned, the boatman had arrived that morning only mo-

ments after Gabe sped away in Blue Norther. All she had left to do was pack the rest of their clothes.

"Running away to join the navy?" Gabe joked later that afternoon. He'd raced home after his final day at Cecil's to find Huck sitting atop the front porch steps, smiling and holding a cake tin.

He whistled.

The girl of his dreams was dressed in the white duck pants and pink sailor blouse. She had never looked more appealing. "Perhaps you're posing for a fashion magazine?"

"With a cake in my lap?"

"Guess not." Gabe removed his hat, sat next to Huck, and lit a Lucky.

"Aren't you going to ask what kind of cake I baked?"

"Don't have to. Here, hold my cigarette." He handed it to Huck and grabbed the tin.

"Give that back. It has to do with a surprise."

"Another one . . . for me?"

"You don't change jobs every day. And this surprise, you'll *really* like."

"It'll be hard to beat the dinner at Benny's last night." He grinned and studied the

cake tin. "Can I at least smell what's inside?"

"One brief smell. But barely open it."

Prying the lid up a crack, Gabe sniffed. "Mmm. Just what I hoped . . . Café Chocolate. So when do I get to know the rest of your plans?"

"Right now." She handed back the cigarette. "You and I are going on an adventure." Huck giggled.

"Big game hunting?"

"In this outfit?"

"How about deep sea diving?"

"Gabe. Be serious."

Leaning close, he kissed the top of her head. Something about being outdoors, the way she was dressed, the fresh scent of her hair . . . made him crazy. "A man can't think properly in the presence of a beautiful woman wearing duck pants," he whispered, "especially during his first hour of jobless freedom when all he wants to do is celebrate."

"Oh, Gabe darling," Huck snuggled close. "It is your first hour of freedom. And since you picked out this blouse and said I'm beautiful . . ." She paused, planting a breathy kiss at the base of his neck. "I suppose we could go inside and celebrate by having a little, you know . . ." She paused

again, nibbling his ear lobe.

"I think we both know," Gabe whispered.

"Then you're sure?"

"Absolutely." He snuffed out his smoke.

"Good." She giggled. "We'll have a little cake. Open the tin."

Pooching out his bottom lip, Gabe sat up straight and lifted the lid. A paper sailboat sailed atop an ocean of chocolate icing and toasted pecans. Lettered across the stern was the name *Cleopatra*.

"Now would you look at that." Gabe chuckled. "I'd completely forgotten. On our first date, we talked of a swashbuckling adventure someday on a boat named *Cleopatra*."

"Someday." Huck smiled and nodded.

Gabe paused, studied the cake, then stood and pointed toward their garage. "You mean, today? In our new boat?"

"In *Cleopatra*. But she's not here."

"What?"

"She's moored over at the dock in Seabrook. Shipshape and loaded with a week's worth of supplies." Huck laughed. "I had to do something exciting while you worked. Now, as Mister Jack told me when I was ten, close your mouth before Mister and Mizz housefly change address."

236

■ ■ ■

It didn't take Huck long to become an "old salt" like Gabe. She quickly learned the difference between fore and aft, port and starboard. In less than two days, she could raise and lower *Cleopatra*'s sails, command the helm, and tack into the wind. They didn't need to worry about complicated navigation because they never left sight of land, dropping anchor close to shore each evening.

Breakfast and lunch were prepared in *Cleopatra*'s small galley, while suppers were cooked on the beach over a driftwood fire, the orange and blue flames disappearing into glowing embers. On some nights, the cool Gulf breeze would gust, scattering redhot coals like hundreds of fiery cat eyes across the dark, deserted sand. Not bothering with suits, they'd swim in the warm shallows, then wrap in a blanket and hold each other close. After sharing deepest secrets with the moon and stars, their spoken words transformed into soft murmurs of lovemaking, lasting well into the wee hours. Then with heavy eyelids, they'd return to *Cleopatra,* falling asleep to the gentle lap of waves against her bow.

Days were spent exploring and relaxing. There was always coffee to drink and subjects to discuss. The Long Division was a favored topic, and how they'd defeat it best.

First was their strong faith — which was a given — along with mutual respect. And when it came to household chores, they'd decided that gender didn't matter. All work outside their day jobs, whether washing dishes or weeding flower beds, would be shared. Each would have a preference, but if they pulled together, there would be more time to spend doing the activities they enjoyed most.

Saturday mornings would be a period of reconnecting. A time to lounge in their cozy parlor and talk without the demands of schedule. If the weather was dreary, they'd just snuggle on the love seat, while a slow rain pattered against the panes. Some Saturdays they'd plan projects, then spring into action. Others would be spent rereading the postcards. Touching. Dreaming

Above all, they vowed to protect their privacy and never take part in matri-"moan"-y, that all-too-common practice of constantly griping about one's spouse. If there was a problem, they'd face it head-on, allowing each other the freedom to air any grievance. Hopefully, arguments would be

rare but, when they did occur, would be mutually solved under the unified stance of their marriage vows.

At midafternoon on their last full day, Gabe sailed *Cleopatra* into a small clear-water cove off Atkinson Island and dropped anchor. Huck climbed up from the galley carrying an apple and paring knife. "Want half?"

"Are you going to peel it?" Gabe licked his lips.

"Don't I always?" Huck sat on the edge of the cockpit, hanging her legs off the starboard side, feeling free. She'd still not told him about Clark's letter, and tomorrow they'd be back to their normal routines. The entire trip had been ideal, and she didn't want to ruin a moment of it. So last night at supper's campfire, she'd decided *not* to show him the letter, burning Clark's final words while Gabe gathered driftwood. Clark was happy and out of her life, so what good would producing the letter do? And the fact she'd saved it this long might be cause for even more hurt. She and Gabe had promised to share their deepest secrets, but this one had become shallow at best.

Huck watched the apple peel drop into the water. She'd still tell him Clark had married. That would be a good thing. But it

might require a tiny fib.

Several small fish bolted for the peel, catching her eye. And then she spied something shiny on the sandy bottom.

"Gabe! Come quick. We've found money."

"Where?"

She pointed the knife toward half a dozen small round objects. "Coins. Think they're Spanish doubloons?"

"It's possible." Gabe rubbed his chin. "Legend says that Jean Lafitte buried treasure around here. Treasure that's never been found." He studied the coins. "Water looks to be about fifteen feet deep. The sun must be at exactly the right position for us to see them."

"Maybe it's a pirate treasure," Huck said conspiratorially.

"Maybe. Unless it's man-eating sharks fishing for greedy humans. I've heard they use coins for bait."

Huck ignored the comment. "Well, we must take a closer look. It could be a significant historical find."

"Or some local fisherman had a hole in his pocket."

After an apple break, they agreed Gabe should dive to the bottom and retrieve the coins. "If I get eaten by a shark, take good care of Blue Norther," he said, then grinned.

"Don't you even suggest it."

"Okay. Don't take care of our car. I won't be around to know." He dove into the water.

"Gabe Alexander!" Huck scolded. A dangerous shark in this part of the bay was unheard of, but still, one never knew when tragedy might strike. An icy shiver inched up her spine as she watched Gabe descend into the depths. "Mother said to never borrow trouble," she said aloud. "So I won't." Still, an ominous feeling surrounded her.

Fifteen seconds later, Gabe had retrieved the coins and signaled he was on his way to the surface. Huck breathed a sigh of relief.

But after five more seconds passed, he was still at the bottom. Then five more. What was he doing? "This is no time to show off how long you can hold your breath," Huck shouted as the coins fell from Gabe's hand. Why did he drop . . . ? No! He was struggling. Caught in something. Trying to free himself!

Grabbing the paring knife, Huck leaped off the boat. For a split second, she lost her bearings, almost swallowed some water, then saw Gabe. As a child, she'd been a good swimmer, but East Texas creeks were narrow, shallow.

*Swim faster,* her brain and heart screamed in unison.

241

*Not like that. Use both hands. Grip the knife between your teeth like you did when playing pirates with Cutter. Swim deeper.*

Eyes stung.

Ears popped.

Deeper!

Lungs begged to explode.

Fingers too weak now to hold the knife.

And then Gabe's strong hand grabbed hers, hacking the blade through a giant ball of tangled fishing line.

Everything went black.

The next thing Huck saw was the shape of his face, silhouetted against bright sunlight. "I thought . . . I'd lost you," he said, barely above a whisper.

She tried to talk but coughed, shooting raw burning pain from lungs into sinuses.

"Just lie still. We're back on *Cleopatra.* You're going to be fine."

Huck coughed again, motioning to sit upright.

Gabe cradled her in his arms. "You're going to be fine," he repeated.

Within thirty minutes, she was wrapped in a blanket, sitting in the cockpit, nursing hot tea sweetened with honey. The weakness in her muscles made her arms tremble. Her sinuses were still sore, but she was on the mend.

"You saved my life . . . our life together." Gabe stroked her cheek with the back of his hand. "How you freed me from that web of fishing line with a little paring knife I'll never . . ." A tear slid down his cheek.

"But I blacked out. You saved me."

"You saved me first," Gabe countered.

They laughed.

"It's a good thing you could hold your breath like that." Huck sipped her tea.

"I learned how during the war. Our gas masks didn't always work properly." He smiled and lit a cigarette. "By the time you showed up with the knife, I could only have lasted . . . say . . . another hour or two."

"If I wasn't so exhausted I'd hit you."

"Oh. I almost forgot." Gabe held up a shiny silver coin. "Found it in my trunks. It's Spanish all right."

"A doubloon?"

"I'm afraid not." He handed it to Huck. "Date's 1891. Has a picture of King Alfonso the Thirteenth minted on the front. And he's *still* king. I've been reading about him in the newspaper."

Huck rubbed her thumb across King Alfonso. "Isn't he the king who saved himself and his bride from an assassination attempt on their wedding day?"

Gabe nodded as he inhaled smoke,

thought for a moment, then exhaled. "Probably from a jealous fiancé."

"Probably." Huck smiled. "Did I tell you that in Mother's last letter, she mentioned Clark was married and living in Chicago?"

"Good. I hope he stays that way."

"Married or in Chicago?"

"Both." Gabe frowned, then tossed the rest of his cigarette into the water and stood. "How 'bout I head down to the galley and rustle up some supper? I'm too tired to build a fire on the beach." Without waiting for her answer, he disappeared below.

After taking her last sip of tea, Huck set the cup aside. She'd already asked God to forgive her for the fib and would never tell a lie to Gabe again, even a white one. Gazing at King Alfonso, she considered how close she'd come to losing Gabe. The first time was when he'd fought with Clark and she'd heard Mister Jack's wild cry in the night. Until this moment, she was certain Gabe had guided the knife in her hand, even though he didn't seem to remember. Huck shivered.

Now she wasn't so sure.

# SIXTEEN

*Summer 2006*
*Adam Colby*

Smatterings of windblown rain pelted against my darkened study window like handfuls of pea gravel flung by small children. I sat up in my makeshift bed and checked the time. Twenty minutes after midnight. It had been raining off and on for four days. Four gray, colorless days that matched the cloud of gloom surrounding my heart.

Lightning flashed. I counted the seconds. One-thousand-one, one-thousand-two, one-thousand-three. A distant rumble. Cursing the uncomfortable couch, I tossed my pillow to the floor, stood, and grabbed my robe.

Another flash. Another three seconds. Another rumble.

My computer hummed and the screen crackled to life with a message from the

National Weather Service. *A low pressure system remains stalled over Harris and Chambers Counties,* the message read. *Flooding possible. Avoid driving in low-lying areas.*

"Tell me something new," I mumbled, plopping into my computer chair. I switched on a small lamp, then picked up the silver coin I'd left atop my mouse pad for the past week.

King Alfonso.

Yevette had handed it to me during our second meeting. The now troublesome king had been the catalyst for our continued discussion about Huck and Gabe. A conversation resulting in more questions . . . some of them hard to stomach.

We'd met at The Braided Rein, a smoky steakhouse that boasted the tenderest cuts of beef south of the North Pole. Cute cowgirls with braided ponytails poured beer from frosty ceramic jugs into thick-handled mugs. Rumor was if a patron complained about the food, he'd be served an actual braided rein — or some other piece of horse tack — grilled to perfection. A live band encouraged patrons to dance, and ladies were welcome to do a little "boot scootin' " on top of a century-old bar.

"I'm surprised this is where you wanted

to meet," I'd said to Yevette amid the driving pulse of drums and bass guitar.

"Why? I love a good steak."

I sipped my beer. The dance floor was empty, but five p.m. was probably a little premature for the two-step bunch. "So . . . would you like to order?"

"Too early. But you can."

"Not hungry." I took another sip while the band segued into "Cotton-Eyed Joe."

"I like the energy in here," she said finally, then furrowed her brow. "We don't have to stay if you're uncomfortable."

"Uh . . . no. This is great. It's just not Haley's kind of place." I shrugged. "We never came. No offense."

"None taken." She smiled. "Huck and Gabe loved coming here."

"Here?"

"This building's one of Houston's oldest and has been several establishments over the decades. During Prohibition it was a speakeasy." She paused. "Know what attracted Huck?"

"Pink champagne?"

"That and the fact it's haunted."

"You're kidding?"

"A wealthy cattleman originally built this as a saloon in the late 1800s. Called it 'Bull on the Bayou,' or something similar."

"How about 'Cow on the Canal'?" I interjected, then chuckled.

Yevette's lips turned up, but she continued without comment. "According to legend, a saloon girl entertained the cattleman upstairs in her room on a regular basis. His jealous wife walked in one night and blasted him with a buffalo rifle."

"He didn't survive?" I chugged what was left in my mug.

"Not physically."

At that moment, fingernails slid across my back. I jumped.

Yevette laughed.

"Sorry, sir." A blond cowgirl heaved a large jug onto the table. "There's a slick spot on the floor and I almost lost my balance. We don't make it a habit of scratching customers' backs unless they're big tippers." She giggled and refilled our mugs. "Let me know when y'all are ready for another round."

"Serves you right." Yevette's eyes changed from hazel to green.

"Are you saying that Huck believed in ghosts?"

"Mostly in the 'spirit' of fun." Now Yevette chuckled. "But I think Huck was disappointed she never saw one here."

"What about Gabe?"

"Huck never said. I do know he believed in her wild imagination."

"And Mister Jack? Did Gabe think he was imaginary?"

Yevette dug a shiny coin out of her purse. "We'll talk more about Mister Jack in a minute. First I want you to see this." She slid it across the table.

"Looks foreign." I read the date. "1891. Old and foreign."

"Read the name."

"Alfonso the Thirteenth. Wasn't he King of Spain?"

"How did you know that?"

I smiled. "Estate-sale professionals naturally become history buffs. We have no choice."

"Makes sense. Now read the inscription."

"*Por La G. De Dios.* For The Glory Of God?"

"Exactly." Yevette's eyes grew round with excitement.

"Why did Spain abbreviate the word *glory*?"

"Not enough room for the entire phrase I guess, but that's not important. What matters is what happened when Huck found it."

"Tell me," I said, feeling better than I'd felt since Haley left. Yevette was really open-

ing up. If we talked long enough, I might even get brave and ask her to dance.

After draining her mug, Yevette folded her hands and leaned across the table in my direction. "The day Huck found this coin, she and Gabe almost died."

"Really? How?"

"They nearly drowned." Yevette paused, as if pondering what to say next.

"And? Don't leave me hanging."

"I'll get to that part of their story because it deals with Mister Jack, but you should know what happened that next month in 2004 after Huck called 911."

"Okay. But don't forget the drowning story."

"I said they *nearly* drowned." Yevette sighed, sat back, and continued. "As you remember, Huck was almost bedfast in her room at Bayshore Extended Care and . . ."

I raised my eyebrows.

Yevette took a deep breath. "She told me that Gabe came to see her on three separate occasions."

"You can't be serious. He'd been dead for what . . . eighteen years?"

"She swears he was there."

I scratched my head, incredulous. "Huck was obviously hallucinating."

"Perhaps. Unless like the Alexanders,

you're a person who believes that the power of love is not limited to time and space."

"No disrespect, but I stopped believing in Santa Claus when I was ten . . . if you catch my meaning."

"Caught."

"So then what happened? I'm anxious to hear the near-drowning part."

Over the next hour, Yevette revealed everything Huck had remembered about Gabe's visits to Bayshore, their wedding day, porch swing honeymoon, first home, *Cleopatra,* and finally . . . narrow escape from death.

I stared into my empty mug. The tale had been so intriguing, I'd forgotten about asking her to dance. And just as she did in our previous meeting at Starbucks, Yevette ended the story once again with Mister Jack. Last time it was his life-saving howl. This time, his underwater heroics.

"Common sense tells me that Gabe grabbed the knife and freed them from the tangled fishing line," I said, "especially since he'd mastered holding his breath. The stress of being so close to death caused him not to remember."

"That's exactly what Huck thought, until she read the coin's inscription. To her, the phrase *For The Glory Of God* was a divine

message, proving Mister Jack had inter-
vened."

"Did Gabe agree?"

"In a way. His thoughts about death are
included in the final postcard."

"They are? I don't remember reading —"

"You don't have it." Yevette stood. "It was
never part of the collection."

"Why not?"

She smiled. "That postcard belongs to me.
I'll tell you all about it at our next meeting."

"Okay," I managed, suddenly growing
weary of her cat and mouse routine.
"Where? When?"

Yevette tossed a twenty on the table. "I'll
let you know."

A lightning flash returned my thoughts to
the dreary study. I'd had a sneaking suspi-
cion Yevette was hiding something significant.

Now I knew. Gabe's final card.

At times, I felt as though we were playing
a form of Texas hold'em: all my money on
the table and Yevette with the winning ace.
Unless she was bluffing, why make me wait
to see her hand? Furthermore, I didn't
understand why she considered the last
postcard hers when she didn't the others.

Since our meeting at The Braided Rein, I'd written every detail Yevette recounted. Haley and I were amiable but never friends, much less "best" friends. And facing problems head-on just wasn't our way, not that we ever discussed "our way" about anything. Politely ignoring the uncomfortable was . . . comfortable. Now I realized our marriage was like an unopened bottle of soda pop, shaken periodically, ready to explode. If only we'd been wise enough to release the pressure a little at a time.

On the one hand, it had been depressing to write about the Alexanders' relationship, a connection uncommon in today's cynical age. On the other — and I hated to even use this word — the "magic" they shared was what I so desperately desired. Angels aside, the disturbing thing was this: their happiness seemed to have been linked by body *and* soul, a depth of spirituality most couples never even consider, much less understand. Huck and Gabe recognized a higher power greater than themselves, and this belief system anchored them.

Most painful was King Alfonso. For Huck, the coin was a sign of divine protection. But for me, it signified the threefold wealth of their union: Total trust. An unbreakable bond. Completeness. It hurt, but I was

beginning to contrast the strengths of their marriage against the weaknesses of my own.

Haley and I never took the time nor trouble to find a "coin." Consequently, what trust we had soon evaporated, leaving completeness wounded at the matrimonial starting gate. For the most part, neither of us was unfaithful as such, but as I'd already reasoned, we each had a scandalous love affair with our own selfishness. And under the twelve-year strain of making "me" happy, our link weakened until it finally broke.

Not long ago, I'd asked myself whether soul mates evolved into lovers or lovers evolved into soul mates. An answer I considered was that the trail we took to reach the top of the mountain mattered not, as long as we arrived. But now I'm thinking that the *journey* itself was key. Romance wasn't what saved Huck and Gabe from The Long Division. In fact, romance was simply an external result of the willingness each of them had to continually choose each other over their own selfishness.

*Two hearts commanding devotion.*

So my new question was this: Since I'd lost my way on the first journey, was it still possible for me to travel to the summit with someone new? Or was I destined to travel the lowland's lonely path, haunted by a

single set of footprints . . .
   My own.

# Seventeen

After the market crashed in
   twenty-nine
Our hearts were tested for a
   time,
And in the gloom
Of parted days did usher
Fate's way of turning 'round
That rumbling, roaring, rushing
   sound. . . .
Boom!
Our love's a gusher!
               Forever, Gabe

*August 1931*
*Houston, Texas*
Saturday morning dawned bright and full of promise. Huck sat on the love seat sipping her second cup of Admiration. The phone in Gabe's study had rung, so he'd gone to answer it. They'd planned a delightful day of selecting bulbs at the nursery for

their fall flowers. She'd joined Houston's elite garden club and was thrilled at what she'd learned.

Gabe returned to the love seat and lit a cigarette.

"Who's brave enough to disturb our morning?" Huck said, then laughed.

"Chuck Browning."

"Your boss?"

"Honey. I hate to ruin our day, but I've got to travel to Kilgore this afternoon."

"Kilgore? Why?"

"Our accountant there was involved in some kind of trouble, so they had to pull him."

"Trouble? What exactly?"

"Chuck didn't say. He told me to tell you he's sorry for the short notice."

"He needn't be. It's your duty to go."

"Well, I'll . . . You're a wife who never ceases to amaze. Most might balk because of all the rough and seedy characters. Money really is the root of all evil, especially in a boom town."

"Oh, but Gabe, Kilgore was the hot topic in the teachers' lounge all of last year. It's so scandalous. So daring." Huck smiled. "Kilgore. For how long?"

"Five days, maybe longer. Gulf has purchased a few independent wells and needs

me to finish the books. I don't want to scare you, but Chuck suggested I carry a gun."

"To fight off prostitutes?" Huck laughed.

Gabe frowned. "Last night's *Chronicle* said the Texas Rangers have sent in El Lobo Solo."

"Who?"

"The Lone Wolf. His real name is Manuel Gonzaullas, a Ranger every outlaw better think twice about messing with. He's vowed to shut down the gambling houses, dope rings, and bootleggers."

"Can he do it?" Huck snuggled close.

"Of course. He's enacted martial law. Lone Wolf also believes that God has called him into crime fighting and will protect him." Gabe stared at his cigarette's growing ash. "He takes Bibles, underlines the passages about sinning and forgiveness, then hands them out to criminals."

"Sounds like something Mother would do."

"Except your mother hasn't mounted a machine gun on the passenger side of her car."

"Only because she doesn't own a car." Huck laughed, then stood. "I'd better start packing."

"Packing?"

"Unless you want Lone Wolf arresting us

for indecent exposure."

Gabe ground his cigarette in a glass ashtray. "Honey. You're not going. It's much too dangerous."

"Don't be silly. I still have a month of summer vacation. Any woman who can handle junior high students nine months a year can certainly deal with roughnecks and drillers for a few days."

"I'm not talking about the law-abiding work force. There've been gunfights in the streets. And besides outlaws, there are hundreds of greedy, no-good drifters who'd love to steal the company of a beautiful woman. When a town's population explodes overnight from a few residents to over ten thousand, it's not filled with Sunday school teachers."

"You will protect me."

"Always." His face remained stern. "But I said *no.*"

Not believing what she was hearing, Huck felt her cheeks grow hot. She fought back tears. "We've never been apart for one day, much less five. And more than that will be an eternity."

"I thought you said it was my duty."

"If it's that dangerous, then it's *my* duty to go with you. We've always faced life together." Huck knew she was being selfish.

But so was Gabe.

"Honey, I have no choice," Gabe said softly.

"No choice? You're a top accountant, and Gulf wouldn't dare fire you if you refused. They'd just send someone else."

"Until the economy rebounds," he continued, "we should be thankful to even have jobs." He lit another cigarette. "The boys downtown say this depression is gonna get worse before it gets better." He shook his head. "Never know what might happen, especially in a lawless place like Kilgore."

For the next few minutes, neither spoke. Turning her back, Huck ignored his negative silence, even though her initial excitement waned. She hadn't really considered the danger and knew Gabe was right about their jobs. After the stock market crashed two years ago on Black Tuesday, thousands of people across America had been sleeping in rail cars and standing in soup lines. Houston had taken a glancing blow. Most Texans were lucky.

"I agree about our jobs," Huck said finally. "And you're right, we don't know what will happen next." She faced him, then spoke, her voice trembling. "That's why I need to go with you. What if something . . . happens?"

"It won't." Gabe stiffened. "You're not going and that's the end of it."

"Don't you even care about my feelings?"

"Not as much as I care about you."

"My feelings are me!" Huck shouted as fear transformed into anger. "What about our agreement?"

"What agreement?"

"That we'd always discuss our problems and come to a mutual solution."

"We have. The answer is no."

"But it's not mutual!"

"Yes it is. I've decided for us both. Now go cool down before saying something you might regret."

It was Gabe's constant level of controlled calm that made her the angriest. The heartbeat of hot blood pounded inside her ears. It made her want to curse.

"And think pleasant thoughts," he added. "You'll feel better."

"Pleasant thoughts?" Huck muttered. "Think pleasant thoughts?" She marched down the hallway. "That's what an adult would tell a child. Well . . . If Gabe wants a child, I'll show him one."

She stomped into the kitchen and faced the cabinets.

Open. Open. Open. Open.

Slam! Slam! Slam! Slam!

Huck flung open four more kitchen cabinets, reared back, and slammed them shut like rapid machine-gun fire. Dishes rattled. If some of their precious china shattered, then so be it. How dare Gabe refuse to let her witness the largest oil boom in the history of the country. Thrill to the sight of a mighty wooden derrick on every street corner. Step into the instant wealth and excitement of a town boasting the world's richest acre.

Huck reopened the first four cabinets, paused, and listened. She heard no reaction from Gabe. He was still sitting on the love seat, she thought. Still frowning. Still smoking. After five years of marriage, the man could be so . . . so frustrating!

Huck's third round of cabinet slamming channeled her anger into an idea. Actually, it was a *pleasant thought.* On Monday she'd take her own daring excursion. Not to a place as wild as Kilgore, but one rich in resources.

First National Bank.

She'd visit their joint savings account and then enjoy a little wardrobe shopping spree. As in solving relationship problems, they'd agreed that withdrawing from savings would be a *mutual* decision. A decision *she* would gladly make for them both.

262

Huck laughed. Gabe was right again. She did feel better. And later, when he left for Kilgore, she'd even consider kissing him good-bye.

By eleven a.m. Monday, the mercury in downtown Houston already hovered near ninety degrees. Huck exited the stuffy streetcar, thankful that First National Bank was on the shaded side of Main. Pausing in front of a glass storefront, she checked her reflection.

Good.

She didn't look too exhausted. Two sleepless nights worrying about Gabe's safety had tired her body but reawakened a simmering indignation. How dare he ignore their rule about shared decisions and refuse to take her to Kilgore.

Refuse!

Weren't shared experiences and decisions fundamental in avoiding The Long Division, or had Gabe abandoned the concept and not told her? It seemed her opinion no longer mattered.

At first, shopping seemed fair retribution. But after stewing over the entire affair for forty-eight hours, she decided money drawn from their savings account would only be a small down payment toward what she'd

later refuse him.

She checked her appearance one last time, then strode the half block to the bank's entrance. Being properly dressed was important, especially for a woman doing business. Everyone knew that a disheveled dress meant a distorted mind.

"Mornin', ma'am." A doorman tipped his hat. "Gonna be another hot day."

"Scorching." Huck forced a weak smile, passing through double brass doors to a row of mahogany cashier cages.

"May I help you?" A bald teller sporting a thin mustache snapped to attention.

"Good morning. I'm Mrs. Gabe Alexander."

"Of course. And Mr. Alexander?" The teller peered in both directions.

"He's doing well." Huck managed another smile. "I'd like to withdraw twenty-five dollars from our savings."

"Absolutely. I'll just need to look up your account." He stepped over to an enormous ledger.

After opening her purse, Huck retrieved the list of stores she planned to visit. Twenty-five dollars was much more than she'd spend, but it never hurt to be prepared. And with the entire day at her disposal, there was no telling what might

catch her fancy.

"Um . . . Mrs. Alexander?" The teller returned. "Mr. Alexander will be joining you, I assume?"

"No. He's away on business."

"I see." The teller paused, then spoke in a low tone. "Are you aware that withdrawing funds from this account requires his signature?"

"But it's in both our names."

"Your checking account is in both names, not savings."

"I'm positive you're incorrect." Other customers were now in line. Huck felt herself begin to perspire. "Please double-check your records."

"Right away, ma'am."

She cleared her throat. The week after they married, all of their personal accounts had been switched to joint ownership.

The teller reappeared. "I'm sorry, Mrs. Alexander," he whispered. "The account *is* in Mr. Alexander's name, thus his signature must accompany the transaction. It's bank policy."

"But I'm his wife. There must be some mistake."

"Obviously."

Chuckles erupted from the growing line.

"I . . . I didn't mean it's a mistake you're

his wife," he stammered. "I'm sure Mr. Alexander is a very lucky man." He rubbed his bare head. "However, the proper signature is bank policy."

"Then I insist on speaking with your supervisor," Huck commanded, her strict tone reminiscent of dealing with an unruly student.

"But ma'am, my supervisor is —"

"In a meeting," interrupted a smooth voice from her past. "Now isn't this a lovely surprise."

Huck's heart froze. She recognized the scent of familiar aftershave before she met his gaze. But it was the timbre of his voice that had first punched her in the stomach. "Why . . . Clark Richards?" She swallowed hard, as panic invaded the corners of her mind. "You said in your letter that you'd relocated to Chicago."

"That's where my wife and son live." He chuckled. "The financial industry requires that the road be my home, at least for now. Last week, I examined banks here in Houston. This afternoon, I move on."

"I see." He was thinner than she remembered. And even though he was smiling, his eyes mirrored a hint of sadness. She quieted her voice so the people in line wouldn't hear her. "Perhaps you should just *move on,* as

you say. Our business finished long ago."

"It was extremely long ago, and I apologized and even begged your forgiveness . . . in my letter." Clark seemed sincere but hurt. "A letter you never answered."

Huck felt her knees weaken. "You attend to your day and I'll attend to mine."

"The joy of my day is serving the public." Clark smiled.

The teller craned his neck forward. "I don't mean to intrude, but —"

Clark frowned. "Mrs. Alexander may withdraw whatever amount she wishes and I'll sign for it. Understood?"

"That's generous, Clark, but please don't go to any trouble."

"It's no trouble at all. Just doing my job."

"But sir? First National Bank's policy states —"

Clark cut him off. "My signature overrides unforgiving policy." He grinned broadly at the teller. "A bank's business is to serve the public, even if it means bending the rules. I suggest you do *your* job and remember that."

"Yes sir."

"Very well then," Clark said. "I believe enough of Mrs. Alexander's valuable time has been wasted. To avoid her further delay, place the cash in an envelope with her name

on it to be picked up later. She'll be joining me at Club Prosperity for lunch."

"I most certainly will not," Huck said, quiet but firm, feeling a surge of strength in her knees.

"Nonsense. It's the least one friend can do for another." He smiled. "We are still friends, correct?"

Huck could feel the people in line staring. "May we please not discuss this here?"

"My thoughts exactly." He turned to the teller. "She'll take her withdrawal without delay."

"Thank you," Huck replied, when the teller handed her an envelope. She stepped away from the teller's cage and faced Clark. "I'll be on my way. My streetcar will be arriving soon. Take care of yourself."

"It may be decades before I see you again, if ever. So may I escort you to the proper corner? It's the least I can do."

Huck thought for a moment. It would be rare for their paths to cross, especially if Gabe had a say in it. She was still furious with him.

"Only to the corner," she said.

On the way to the stop, Clark spoke tenderly about his wife and child and asked so sweetly about her parents. He even inquired about Gabe. So instead of lunch,

she agreed on something cool to drink.

Huck had heard tales of the lavish Club Prosperity, with its 360-degree view of the city, but had never been invited to partake. And even though Prohibition still reigned, the alcohol flowed freely among petroleum financiers, stockbrokers, ranchers, and bankers. Before Huck knew it, she was sipping rum punch, and Clark had ordered lunch.

"Tell me about your wife and son," Huck said. She felt a little guilty enjoying lobster bisque without Gabe, but leaving her at home had been his decision. And the punch was delicious.

"Haroldson Lafayette Richards." Clark sipped scotch and smiled. "Named my boy after H. L. Hunt."

"The Texas oil tycoon?"

"The one and only. Before long, Hunt will be the richest man in the United States. He just opened his own pipeline. This time next year, most of the black gold wealth in East Texas will ride in his back pocket. I'm headed that direction this afternoon."

"East Texas?"

Clark laughed. "There's a bank in Kilgore that wants to drill an oil well right through the expensive terrazzo floor in their lobby.

It's my job to make sure no funny business is involved."

"Kilgore?" Huck couldn't believe what she was hearing. "Isn't it dangerous?"

"Oh, you know how the papers blow everything out of proportion. I'm sure there's been some petty thievery, but most of it's rumors."

Huck smiled. "You're not going to believe this . . . Gabe is in Kilgore."

"I heard you say he was away on business, but I had no idea. What oil outfit is he with?"

"Gulf. He landed an executive position."

"That's strange. Most corporations don't send their top dogs out into the field."

"Then I suppose the same would hold true for your company?" She laughed. "Of course, one would assume that there would be exceptions."

"Naturally." Clark chuckled and raised his glass. "Here's to all of us who are 'executive exceptions.' "

Huck laughed again and met his toast. Now that Clark was a father, not to mention being married, he'd developed a mature charm. It was obvious that some of her good feeling was the luxurious lunch, but couldn't a former beau grow up and be forgiven? Within a few more years, they might even

270

be friends. After all, she had loved him once. But it had been a shallow, self-centered love, the kind that only made her feel good about herself.

After the bisque followed shrimp cocktail, an entire platter of delectable seafood choices, crème brûlée, coffee, flavored brandy. As they ate and drank, conversation centered around their growing-up years and juicy tidbits of hometown gossip. Before the brandy was gone, Clark had apologized again for his past dishonorable actions, thanked Huck for not reporting him to the police, and said he was ashamed for the false rumors he'd spread.

"You'd best stop while you're ahead," Huck said. "Mother still thinks I was drunk that night."

Clark laughed gratefully. "Your kindness allowed me to meet and marry my perfect girl," he whispered. "Thank you."

"I'm so glad this day happened." Huck wiped a tear from her eye.

"Me too." Clark finished his brandy. "So when does Gabe get back?"

"Tomorrow. I hope one day you two can spend time together. You'd like him."

"I know I would, but business is business." Clark paused. "Wait a minute. Why don't you drive up to Kilgore with me this after-

noon? We could find Gabe and have a nice dinner."

"Oh, Clark. No. I've forgiven you, but Gabe —"

"Listen." He leaned toward Huck, placing his hand atop hers. "Like I said back at the bank, it may be years before I get down this way again, and I sure would like to right things. If your husband is the man I believe him to be, he'll forgive me." Clark squeezed her hand gently. "Besides, you could witness the excitement of a real oil boom, then travel back to Houston with Gabe in the morning. What do you say?" Clark removed his hand and sat back.

The scene of Gabe's refusal flashed across Huck's memory. But more important than a shopping spree to pacify her own hurt feelings was Clark's need for forgiveness. She *had* known his family her entire life. And what had happened on the front porch of Mrs. Thompson's boardinghouse was history. Maybe taking Clark to see Gabe was the honorable thing to do. Gabe would be mad at first. In fact, he'd be furious. But she'd been married to the man for over five years now and knew his heart. Gabe would quickly see the merit in her actions. "I'll need to go home and pack a few things."

"How 'bout I pick you up in an hour?"

"Fine. Here's our address."

The trip north was delightful, and since the summer had been dry, they didn't have to contend with muddy or washboard rutted roads. It was hot, so Huck had worn a lightweight sleeveless dress hemmed just below the knee.

"I love this part of the state," she said as they motored atop a ribbon of reddish sand beneath the towering sway of emerald pines. They'd just stopped to fill up at a rural gas station. She sipped a grape soda pop, allowing the sweet fizz to cool her dusty throat. The owner lived in the back, his wife selling soft drinks out of their kitchen icebox. "Think you'll ever move your family to East Texas?"

"Too hot and humid." Clark tossed his empty bottle out the window.

"Clark Richards. A car could crush that bottle and blow a tire."

"Nah. Some country bumpkin will find it first and redeem it for a penny. Think of it as helping the ignorant poor."

Huck ignored the comment. "What I miss most is dogwoods blooming in the spring."

"What I miss most . . . is you." He reached across to the passenger side and rubbed up her bare knee.

273

Stunned, Huck pushed him away. "Stop that."

"Just an innocent little pat between friends." He placed his hand back on the wheel. "I guess old habits die hard."

"Make sure that one's dead." Until now, Clark had been a perfect gentleman. He'd even sat in his luxurious automobile while she finished packing, after mentioning how his joining her inside the house might give neighbors the wrong idea. She scooted closer to the door. If he touched her like that again, she'd demand he stop and let her out.

Clark smiled. "While you were getting our drinks, the kid pumping gas told me that we're about twenty miles from Kilgore. Said when the wind is right, they can smell the oil field."

"Lovely." Huck stared straight ahead. Why would a family man try to place his hand where it didn't belong? What had been intimate when they courted was now repulsive. She glanced his way. Hopefully, that would be the end of his shenanigans.

"I think the oil field smells like money. Can't think of a more pleasing scent." He breathed deeply. "Except for the scent of . . . you."

"You'd best keep your nose on the driver's

side." She folded her arms.

"I was joking." He raised his hands in a show of innocence. "Did marriage destroy your sense of humor?"

"I don't think your wife would consider it funny." She faced him. "Come to think of it, you've never mentioned her name."

"Maiden name was Michaels. Eleanor Katrina Michaels. Family calls her Elli for short. Met her on a train from Dallas to Chicago. She was born and raised in the Windy City to a family rolling in old money. Her father is a major stockbroker."

"What about her mother?" Huck asked, trying to keep Clark's thoughts aimed in a suitable direction.

"Glad you asked. Elli's mother is crazy for baskets."

"Baskets?"

"Collects them from around the world. She read about some backwoods woman living near Kilgore who weaves baskets out of thousands of pine needles. Wants me to locate the woman and buy one."

"Mother has a small pine needle basket, but I think it was woven by the Alabama-Coushatta Indians." Huck relaxed. It would be easy to keep Clark talking about his wealthy in-laws for the next twenty miles. "Does your father-in-law collect anything?"

275

"Piles of silver dollars." He chuckled. "But get this. The kid back at the gas station says 'basket woman' lives nearby. How's that for a piece of luck? We should be nearing her road any minute."

"Her road? We're out in the middle of nowhere."

Clark nodded. "I guess she's one of those reclusive types who prefers living off the beaten path." He slowed the car. "See that creek up ahead?"

Huck nodded.

"Just this side of the bridge is a culvert. That's our turn."

They entered what looked like an overgrown logging road, the entrance partially hidden by a thick stand of wild dewberry bushes. After a few hundred yards, the road narrowed to a sandy trail, then all but disappeared, the forest floor covered in an expanse of pine cones, dead branches, and jungly undergrowth.

"I think we made a wrong turn." Huck peered out her open window into the dim, breezeless shade. If Clark didn't stop the car, they'd run over a stump or get stuck between the impenetrable trees. "Turn back. We've gone too far."

"My thinking exactly." Clark braked hard, skidding to a stop beside a giant pine inches

from Huck's door. He switched off the engine.

"What are you doing?" Huck said. She tried to open her door. "I can't get out." The dark forest felt suddenly as if it were closing in on her. "Put it in reverse. Start the motor and back up!"

"Can't go back. Like you said, we've gone too far. Much too far." He faced her, his eyes now wild with a demented glow.

"Clark, please. I don't like it here." Gabe was only thirty minutes away, and she'd never needed him so desperately.

"Don't feel safe being away from civilization?" He began unbuttoning his shirt. "Why don't you call for help? Scream the way you did that night you dumped me out of your life." He flung his shirt into the backseat. "Dumped me like a piece of useless garbage."

"No. Please no!"

"Oh, come now. Your voice is much stronger than that." He cupped a hand behind his ear. "Release that ungodly scream, not that anyone will hear it."

"You're a madman." Huck grabbed the doorframe, pushing her upper body out the open passenger window. Clark lunged across the seat, his big hands digging into her ribs like meat hooks, cutting off her air.

She screamed.

"I'm disappointed. Not as good a scream as last time." He squeezed tighter.

"Someone help me! Gabe!"

"That's right. Try yelling for that pitiful excuse of a man you married. Couldn't save you then. Can't save you now."

"You're hurting me. Let go."

"Not until I get what's been rightfully mine."

"You're insane." Huck twisted onto her back, braced herself against the door, and kicked her feet, pummeling his face.

Catching her legs, Clark spread them apart like scissors. He spoke in broken sentences, his breathing heavy. "All our lives. You've . . . denied . . . me." He crawled forward, pressing her down into the seat with his full weight. "Now . . . denial ends." With one hand, he grabbed both her wrists. With the other, he ripped her dress and slip, exposing her bare skin.

"No." Huck sobbed. "Oh God. Help me!"

Clark smashed his mouth against hers.

Huck bit down hard, finding a piece of his lower lip. She tasted blood.

*Whack!*

The sound of his slap echoed in her ears before she felt the dizzying sting. For a split second, she saw a knife. A blade exactly like

the one he'd pulled on Gabe. Then darkness.

"Oh no you don't." She regained semiconsciousness amid another series of slaps. She could hear Clark's voice, but his face was a blur. "Not like this!" he yelled. Huck felt him release her wrists. "Wake up. I want you to remember this." Clark gripped her shoulder, shaking her entire body.

As her right hand dropped to the floorboard, she felt something smooth. Something heavy. Clutching the neck of her empty pop bottle, she swung it toward Clark's head with all her strength.

An explosion of glass rained onto the car seat as Clark's body fell limp.

Trapped underneath him, Huck tried to move but had no strength. Tried calling for help but had no air.

Lungs too empty to scream.

Body too weak to cry.

Something wet and warm pooled at the base of her neck, then trickled down her chest and shoulders.

Lightheaded. Sleepy. If only she could doze for a moment. If only . . .

Images of Gabe flooded her groggy thoughts. His sea-sky eyes. His crooked grin.

The grin widened, transforming into a booming laugh. A laugh that wasn't Gabe's

at all, yet somehow familiar. A powerful vibration that traveled into the secret places occupied by her dreams. Suddenly she was free, weightless, floating upward, longing to soar into the cool blue dampness.

And then she heard a voice.

Felt moisture on her brow.

Opened her eyes. Tried to focus.

"Ma'am? Are you all right?" A tall man wearing a Stetson hat mopped her face with a wet handkerchief.

"What? Where's Gabe?" She needed his arms. His comfort. Not a stranger's.

"I'm Ranger Gonzaullas. You passed out. I've pulled you from the car and everything's okay."

"Who?"

"Don't try to talk. Just lie here under this tree. The man who attacked you is dead."

"Attacked? Me?" And then as suddenly as Huck had lost consciousness, her mind cleared. She'd been traveling to Kilgore with Clark. They'd turned off the main road and he'd gone mad. There was a knife. An empty bottle. Warm blood.

"No! Clark! Why would he . . . ?" Tears streamed down her face. She'd killed him with an empty grape soda pop.

"Clark Richards is dead," Gonzaullas repeated. "Shot through the head."

■ ■ ■ ■

Several hours later, Huck and Gabe entered the café connected to his hotel.

"Please sit anywhere," said a waitress.

"We're meeting Ranger Gonzaullas," Gabe said. "He'll be here shortly. He said to ask for his table."

She nodded and seated them near a window away from the other customers. "Would you like to see a menu?"

"Just coffee," Gabe said flatly.

After the waitress delivered two cups, they sat in silence. Gabe lit a cigarette and Huck peered outside. The sun would be down soon, but the street was crowded with people.

"You want to talk?" Huck asked.

"We have. There's nothing else to say."

"Then let's go back to the room."

Gabe shook his head. "We have to meet with the Ranger."

"Was he the one who killed Clark?"

"I don't know." Gabe blew out a cloud of smoke. "He's dead and you're alive. That's what matters."

She couldn't believe Clark was dead, the shock of his actions numbing the grief over his death, at least for now. Everything

seemed like a horrible nightmare, none of it real. A Texas Ranger had killed Clark, then removed her from the car while she was still unconscious. When she regained consciousness, another Ranger sped her to a kindly doctor who'd declared her to be "one bruised but lucky young lady." Then Gabe had arrived at the doctor's office.

"And the doctor is sure Clark didn't . . ." She looked across the table at Gabe. A tear slipped down his cheek.

"I'm positive. We can thank the Rangers for that."

"How did they know I belonged to you?"

"There was an envelope in your purse with cash and a withdrawal slip with both our names on it. The law knew I was here working for Gulf, so it wasn't hard to figure out."

She stared out of the window. Did Clark think the police would never find out? Or that Gabe wouldn't hunt him down and make him pay? She did feel sorry for his family and wondered what would drive a man to such a bitter and tragic end.

And where was Mister Jack when she'd needed him most?

"Are you sure you're not hungry?" Gabe asked.

"Coffee's fine." They'd both been too

upset to eat. She reached across the table for his hand. He loosely held it a moment, then released it. Huck felt hot tears roll out of her eyes. Shameful tears. Was what happened her fault? If she could start the day over, she would. But what was done couldn't be undone. And because she'd been so childish, so impulsive, she was almost raped.

And Clark was dead.

Gabe held out his handkerchief, so she took it and buried her face in her hands. It was all she could do to look at him, never having seen such anger and hurt occupy one man's face at the same time.

At the doctor's office, Gabe had been visibly upset. But after hearing the story, he was overcome with emotion, saying at least a dozen times how blessed he felt that she was alive. So he took her back to his hotel room, where she bathed and changed clothes. Then they'd lain on the bed and he'd held her for over an hour. Feeling guilty, she'd confessed about Clark's letter, explaining between sobs how he'd not only apologized for his former actions but sought their forgiveness. That's why she'd traveled to Kilgore with him.

"I wanted to tell you about . . . the letter . . . when we sailed on . . . *Cleopatra*," Huck said finally, "but I burned it instead.

I'm . . . so . . . sorry."

"If I'd read the letter, none of this would have happened," Gabe snapped. "I would've known it wasn't a sincere apology." He stopped holding her and stood, then crossed to the window and peered outside. The next thing she knew, he was facing her.

"Tell me the truth," Gabe said, his voice an angry whisper. "Did you really expect me to forgive him? Do I need to forgive a dead man?"

Before Huck could reply, Gabe had walked out of the room.

The café door opened with a squeak. Huck looked up and wiped her eyes as Ranger Gonzaullas entered. He still wore the Stetson, and his uniform looked as clean and starched as if he'd just stepped out of the dry cleaners. The famous Lone Wolf Gonzaullas had saved her.

Gonzaullas approached their table and removed his hat. "I've done a little research, and there's something you folks need to know."

"Have a seat. Please." Gabe stood grimly and the two men shook hands, even though they'd already met. "Cigarette?"

"Just coffee, thanks." The Ranger signaled to a waitress, then sat. "Are you folks aware that Richards was connected to gangsters in

Chicago? Had planned to rob the Kilgore National Bank?"

"Heavens, no." Huck stared in disbelief. "I thought he was a bank examiner."

"He was." Lone Wolf paused as the waitress delivered his coffee, then leaned forward and lowered his voice. "Borrowed massive amounts of money from the mob. Missed a payment, so they threatened to put rocks in his pockets and give him an underwater tour of Lake Michigan. That's when he started stealing from the banks he examined."

Gabe lit another cigarette. "I guess he was privy to any account he chose."

"Right." Gonzaullas sipped his coffee. "Skimmed a little off the top from folks who'd never notice. Then he got greedy. Mob did too. So they made a deal to work together. That's how we found him."

"What about his wife?" Huck asked. "Did she know?"

"Left him three years ago. The reason he'd borrowed money in the first place was to fight one of the wealthiest families in Chicago for custody of his son. Six months ago, the boy died of pneumonia."

"Oh no!" Huck gasped. "We had no idea." At least what Clark had done was not just about her.

Gabe tapped his cigarette on the edge of an ashtray. "So how did you find him?"

"My partner and I arrested one of the two gangsters Richards planned to meet. Recognized him from a mug shot. After some thorough questioning, this lowlife copped a plea. The boys in Chicago had learned that when this bank job was over, Richards planned to relocate somewhere down on the Mexican Riviera with most of the cash. Mafia's not big on being double-crossed, so they ordered a bullet put through Richards's head."

"Then it wasn't . . . you?" Huck could barely speak.

"No ma'am. Best we can figure, these two goons had planned to meet Richards in town, but he didn't show. So one gangster hung around the bank, while the other patrolled the road from Houston. When Richards sped by with a passenger, he followed. Sneaked some distance on foot and shot Richards through the rear windshield. Luckily, my partner and I got there and apprehended the shooter before he was able to finish —" He stopped. "It's a miracle I noticed that old logging road. Thought I heard something in the distance, even though my partner didn't. Just before we crossed Sandy Creek, we saw fresh tire

tracks." He furrowed his brow. "I'm glad you're okay, ma'am."

"What did you hear?" Huck faced the Ranger. "Please tell me."

"Can't really say." He rubbed his chin and thought for a moment. "A low rumble. Almost like what you'd hear just before a gusher. But different. Closest rig I know about is fifteen miles away. Out west, I'd swear it was a quake. The odd thing was that I heard it until I saw Richards's car, and then the sound stopped. Guess this place is getting to me."

"We can't thank you enough," Gabe said.

"And by the way . . ." Lone Wolf stood and put on his Stetson. "Spoke on the phone awhile ago with our office in Houston. They questioned a teller at First National Bank who swears a beautiful woman distracted Richards this morning. We think it delayed his being able to be alone in the vault. Kept him from making off with thousands." The Ranger tipped his hat. "And folks think men make the best crime fighters."

As soon as Gonzaullas left, Gabe signaled the waitress and ordered two grilled cheese sandwiches to go.

"That's a good idea," Huck said. "You might be hungry later." She didn't know

how long the café stayed open, but they were the only customers left.

"It's not for me," Gabe replied.

"I can't eat —"

"I telephoned Cutter. Even though baseball season's in full swing, the Exporters have a few days off. He's driving up from Beaumont and will take you to your folks. Should be here in about twenty minutes."

"What?" Huck began to cry again. "We're not going home?"

"I've got to stay here awhile longer."

"How long?"

He ignored the question. "You'll be just fine. Cutter knows what happened. Your folks don't."

"But what should I tell them?"

"Don't tell them anything. You're good at that."

They were waiting in the hotel lobby when Cutter arrived. Gabe grabbed Huck's bag, and they headed outside to her twin's car. Gabe hugged her good-bye, then opened her door. Neither spoke.

"Thanks for the grub." Cutter started the engine. "I think I'll take her back to my place in Beaumont. The news about what's happened is liable to find its way over to Huntsville."

"Good idea," Gabe said. "Should I phone your folks?"

"I'll take care of that."

"Thanks."

"Any idea when you'll be coming to get her?" Cutter asked.

"Sometime later in the week. I've still got a few days here."

"On Thursday, I'm headed out of town with the team. Y'all stay on at my place as long as you need."

Gabe nodded. "There's a sandwich in the sack for Huck, but she probably won't eat it."

"I'll take care of that too." Cutter depressed the clutch and shifted into gear. "I passed a little soda fountain at the edge of town. We'll stop there for a couple of root beer floats. It's gonna be a hot night."

Gabe watched the car disappear into the still evening. When he'd hugged Huck goodbye, they'd tried to act as though nothing was wrong between them.

But for the first time in their marriage, things were very wrong.

And Cutter wasn't stupid.

For the next three days, Gabe worked in his temporary office at the bank in Kilgore from dawn until dusk. He only spoke when

necessary and ordered all his meals to go, eating them at his desk. Thoughts of Huck occupied his psyche during every waking moment and even dominated his dreams. In his mind, her perfume still lingered in his hotel room. He'd tried to change rooms, and even hotels, but everything was full. So he walked the uneven plank sidewalks until the nightfall curfew, blankly staring into the eyes of strangers. After that, he roamed the nearby wooded trails and darkened alleyways for hours. It wasn't safe, and he'd be arrested and thrown into jail if caught. He didn't much care and, in a way, hoped some lowlife would be itching for a fistfight. But all he ever saw were stray animals and a few sleepy drunkards.

On Thursday evening he finished the Kilgore job, but wasn't required to be back in his Houston office until the following Monday. He knew he should at least telephone Huck, and had started to several times after his initial anger subsided into numbness. But numbness soon morphed into guilt, which incurred another round of anger. And since she'd not tried to contact him, he wondered if things could ever be right between them again.

So he packed his briefcase and trudged back to the restaurant adjacent to his hotel

a little before dark. He wasn't hungry but remembered the grilled cheese sandwiches he'd ordered for Cutter. Everything he'd eaten during the past four days had tasted like fried sawdust. For some unexplained reason the grilled cheese sounded good, and he might want a bite of nourishment during the night. He wasn't sleeping much anyway and had to muster the strength to decide what he'd do next.

After paying for his order, Gabe clutched his bag of sandwiches and stepped outside, pausing in front of the hotel to smoke a cigarette. He peered down the dusty main road, now fading into the twilight. It was the last place he'd seen Huck. Recollections of her had been so painful, he'd forced most of them from his mind. He'd envision her face and then see Clark forcing himself on her. It made Gabe break into a cold sweat, made him want to vomit.

The cigarette had lost its taste, so he flicked it into a nearby spittoon. It was a good thing Richards was already dead because Gabe might've finished the job. The thought was both satisfying and terrifying. When he'd fought in the trenches during World War I, he swore he'd seen enough killing to last a lifetime. Apparently, a man's view of "enough" might change.

"You planning on eating them sand-wiches?" croaked a voice from the shadows.

Startled, Gabe turned. A whiskered old man with a wooden leg — probably a drunkard — sat on a bench in front of the hotel. "All yours," Gabe said, handing over the sack. The man obviously needed them worse than he.

"I appreciate it. Don't get grilled cheese too often."

"How did you know what — ?"

"The smell." The old man sniffed the sack and laughed. "I may hobble around on a pine peg, but my nose still works."

Gabe dug in his pocket for a few coins. "This will buy you some coffee."

The old man waved him away. "Son, don't waste my time, or yours. You've got more important things to think about."

It wasn't worth asking him what he meant, Gabe thought, then noticed the old man's eyes — probably the clearest he'd ever seen. Maybe he wasn't a drunkard.

The man sniffed the air. "Is that a pack of Luckys I smell?"

Gabe reached into his shirt pocket and produced the cigarettes.

"Throw in a book of matches, and I'll give you some advice for your trouble."

"Take my lighter," Gabe said. "Keep your advice."

The old man's smile glowed in the dusk. "A man can't see ahead till he's first looked back. Then he can look up."

"Need anything else?"

"I ain't the one who's needy. Now you'd best get out of here. Like I said, you got more important things to consider."

Gabe walked back inside the hotel. After almost a week in this town, he'd seen a wide cross-section of humanity; now, his first mental case. In an odd kind of way, the old man was right. But there was no way a total stranger would know or understand what Gabe was going through. The man's advice was nothing more than a coincidence. Suddenly Gabe felt fearful and realized he needed to be more careful. The man could've gone berserk and pulled a gun. So instead of heading for the alleys, he returned to his room.

The instant the door swung open, his eyes focused where Huck had lain on the bed and the pillow that had been stained with her tears. A lump rose in his throat. He'd never purposely avoided her before and wished he could take back the past four days. But that was impossible. And the more he contemplated the infamous Clark letter,

the more Gabe realized how unfair he'd been.

Would he have read it, even if she'd shown it to him?

Probably not.

And if he had, remained levelheaded enough to view it rationally?

He knew the answer.

Gabe's eyes grew moist. Not only had Huck almost been raped, a childhood friend she'd once loved had been killed.

Killed.

Whether a man deserved death or not, the outcome was the same for those close to him.

Gabe rubbed his eyes. Because of his stupid pride, he'd almost sent Huck where the tragic events would remain forefront. Thank goodness Cutter had taken her to Beaumont instead of Huntsville.

Gabe dropped to his knees and wept.

What had he done?

The woman he loved more than life itself needed his protection now more than ever.

"Oh God, please forgive me," Gabe said as tears streamed down his cheeks. "And please comfort Huck."

He stood and threw his things into his suitcase. Beaumont was a good four-hour drive south. Cutter wouldn't be there, and

Huck might be fearful of the dark. If he hurried, he could still right things with his Forever Girl before midnight.

Huck lay on the bed in Cutter's spare bedroom and stared out the open window into the night. She'd cried more the past three days than she thought humanly possible, but the tears still found ways to pour from beneath her swollen eyelids. That afternoon, her twin had left town with the Beaumont Exporters and wouldn't return for a week. He'd been sweet and had seen to her every need. But he wasn't her husband. So she'd pasted a smile across her face and told him she'd be fine until Gabe arrived.

Gabe.

Would he even come for her? She'd never been more scared.

Since he'd not called, she'd halfway expected a letter. When she'd walked out to Cutter's mailbox that evening, she prayed with every step, but her hopes had been dashed. Worse, it reminded her that tomorrow was Friday and there would be no postcard this week, if ever again. So a round of tears burned anew.

Huck glanced at the bedside clock. Eleven thirty. Three days and three nights without

Gabe seemed an eternity. And now she was well into night number four. Cutter had suggested she not contact Gabe but give him the freedom "to do what a man needs to do." Huck knew that meant Gabe needed time, but not phoning him was the hardest thing she'd ever done. Her thoughts flashed back to Mister Jack and how he'd taught her about hope. But since her guardian angel hadn't bothered with an appearance in Kilgore, the only hope she could manage was that her marriage wouldn't fall apart.

She sat up and took a sip of water from a glass on the bedside table. Cutter had called their folks, who were genuinely upset. He'd said nothing about the attempted rape, but only about how Huck had been traveling to Kilgore with Clark to see Gabe, who was there on an assignment for Gulf. Boom towns, as everyone knew, were dangerous, and Clark had been fatally shot. Cutter went on to explain that specific details were sketchy, but Huck was fine and would be in Beaumont with him until Gabe finished his assignment.

Huck shivered.

The Richards family would keep the sordid details of what had happened out of the newspaper, but versions of the truth would gradually seep into town, and the

gossips would have a heyday. Even though it still seemed surreal, Clark's death would eventually become a reality. So Huck prayed that when the numbness passed, she could cope not only with the tragic loss of a lifelong friend, but with the pain of his betrayal.

Suddenly, she heard a familiar car drive up.

Blue Norther.

Without taking the time to grab a robe, she ran out of the house in her nightgown and into Gabe's arms.

"I'm sorry," Gabe said, tears pooling in his eyes. "I should've never stayed."

"No. It's me. What happened was —"

Before she could finish, Gabe kissed her deeply. Huck didn't know how long they stood on Cutter's front lawn, but she could've remained in Gabe's arms forever.

"Salty kisses are the best kind," he said finally, wiping both their eyes with his handkerchief. "I don't suppose you've got a cup or two of coffee handy this time of night?"

"For you," Huck replied, "I'll drip an entire pot."

While the water boiled, Gabe showered, and then they sipped mugs laden with heavy cream, talking into the wee hours. Things

weren't perfect between the two of them, but they discussed the dangers in forgetting The Long Division and came to an understanding. Realizing they'd stepped apart through mainly selfish acts, they asked each other for forgiveness, then bowed their heads and thanked God for His ever-present goodness. And just before turning out the bedroom light, Huck recited Gabe's first postcard poem about "two hearts commanding devotion." From now on, the phrase would be their motto.

When dawn broke a few hours later, Huck lay wide-eyed, wrapped in Gabe's protective embrace. On her pillow was a new postcard. She didn't know how he'd managed it, but she read it over and over again, her back pressed against the comforting rhythm of his sleeping heart. She snuggled closer as a tear of eternal gratitude rolled down her cheek. It was Friday, her soul mate had returned, and she felt safe.

She'd not dreamed since the terrible incident, but sometime during the night an idea — dreamlike — danced along the fringes of her thoughts. The rumbling sound that guided Ranger Gonzaullas to Clark's car was no oil well or earthquake. It was the same vibration she'd felt during her state of semiconsciousness. Only, Gonzaullas had

heard it first.

Another tear joined the first one.

The mysterious sound was the powerful echo of a booming laugh she'd first heard at her secret glen when she was ten.

A powerful laugh meant to defy evil.

A laugh belonging to Mister Jack.

# EIGHTEEN

Love's laughter and tears
Are the colors we brush
On life's canvas.
And try as they might
The passing of years
Will never control or demand us
To paint . . .
What we ain't!

                    Forever, Gabe

*October 1940*
*Huntsville, Texas*
"The traffic this year's worse than ever,"
Huck said as they sped up Highway 75
toward Huntsville. "We'll spend the entire
afternoon trying to find a parking space."

"That's because the *Chronicle* has touted
this year's prison rodeo as the most un-
bridled show in captivity." Gabe glanced at
Huck. "Thanks for the surprise."

She smiled, remembering how much fun

it had been to surprise her husband of nearly fifteen years with a pair of the most sought-after rodeo tickets in the Lone Star State. Even though it was held each Sunday afternoon in October, more people wanted to attend than there was room. She and Gabe had even skipped worship services that day in order to drive up from Houston and make the two o'clock start time.

"I can't think of a finer way to spend our afternoon than watching man wrestle beast."

"If Papa were still alive, I'd have stayed home and graded papers."

"Did he miss a single rodeo?"

"Not to my knowledge."

"Think your dear mother — God bless her soul — knows we missed church?"

"My guess is that Mother is still much too busy gawking at folks in heaven she thought wouldn't be there." Huck smiled. "That or scolding Papa about how he should be spending eternity."

"Seems hard to believe your folks have been gone four years." Gabe patted her leg.

"I know." She sighed. "It's even harder to believe their old home place has been sold to the college. Molly Beninna says there are plans to tear it down and build a men's dormitory."

They drove along in silence as Huck

301

remembered the quiet deaths of her parents. It had been the summer of 1936. Cutter had moved up to the majors and was playing for the White Sox. She and Gabe had taken a two-week vacation, boarded a northbound train to Chicago, and spent three glorious days sightseeing and watching Cutter play at Comiskey Park. It unnerved her a little that Chicago was where Clark lived before his death, but she'd not dwelt upon it.

At the end of their vacation, they'd driven to Huntsville to help with her mother's annual pickling and preserving. Annise had grown to love Gabe as one of her own sons. In fact, the family joked he'd become the most beloved Huckabee child. By midafternoon of the first day, they'd peeled and cooked a bushel of tomatoes, had two bushels of sliced cucumbers soaking in lime water, and finished canning three dozen quarts of peaches. Annise announced she was "done in" and was going to lie down. She did and never got up again.

Two weeks later, Ethan passed. As was his habit, he'd retired to the veranda after Sunday's breakfast for a little Bible reading, to be followed by a fresh chaw of Brown's Mule tobacco. He'd accomplished the reading but expired in his favorite rocker, the

plug still in his shirt pocket, unopened.

Family consensus was that since both Mama and Papa were well into their eighties, they'd lived a good life. And after fifty-eight years of marriage, plus providing for a large family, their physical bodies had simply worn out. Moreover, without Annise around to tell Ethan what to do, he'd lost the direction to continue living.

Huck agreed with her siblings only to a point. In her mind, Ethan lived life on his own terms, complying with Annise's wishes because he loved her. In turn, she met his every need because she loved him. Whether the others realized it or not, her parents had been soul mates of a sort.

When they reached Huntsville, Gabe took a series of back roads to beat the traffic snarl. It wasn't long before they reached the rodeo arena and located a parking spot.

"Saved just for us," he said. They hopped out of Blue Norther and headed to the main gate. He took a deep breath. "It smells like our Splash Day first date."

"Except for the salty air."

"And roasted corn on the cob."

Gabe pointed to a long row of concession stands. "Tell you what . . . Next year we'll quit our jobs and open up a cob stand. We'd only have to work one month a year."

"Sounds appealing," Huck said as they passed through the gate. "But so does eating and paying our bills the other eleven months. And speaking of food, why don't you get us a snack while I claim our seats?"

"Okay. What sounds good?"

"Anything."

"I've been dreaming about hot roasted peanuts."

"Section R," she said as they parted. "Seats 1207 and 1208. I'll wave if you get lost."

Huck watched her husband walk toward the delicious smells. In a way, she enjoyed the rodeo because it reminded her of Papa. On rodeo day, Ethan had insisted on a quick lunch. So before attending worship, Annise would make roast beef sandwiches with all the trimmings, including onions. Keeping with tradition, Huck had made the same meal for her and Gabe to eat in the car. The rule was that if one of them ate onions, the other did too. It was no fun having onion breath alone.

Thoughts of Papa naturally brought to mind her mother, whom she missed dreadfully. They'd had their differences, but Annise understood her woman to woman. Her death had left an irreparable hole in Huck's heart.

As she passed a group of trustees picking up trash, she stopped cold. One of them looked exactly like Clark. She still sometimes had nightmares of Clark's attack in the car.

"May I help you, ma'am?" a guard asked.

"Excuse me?" she replied.

"You seem lost."

"No, um, thank you. I'm fine." She gazed at her ticket stub. "Section R."

The guard pointed. "You're right by the entrance. Climb up the ramp and someone will help you find your seat. Hope you enjoy the show."

Huck stood frozen until the guard and his inmate crew were out of sight. She knew without a doubt Clark was dead, and the inmate lookalike was the Clark of ten years past. Still, the likeness was unnerving. One of the reasons she'd wanted to come to Huntsville was to keep abreast of the town's recent changes, perhaps even drive by the site of the Huckabee home place. Not seeing the spacious old house would be difficult, but thoughts of her past had been haunting her dreams.

"Ladies and gentlemen! Welcome to the tenth annual Texas Prison Rodeo. The wildest, woolliest show behind bars!"

Composing herself, Huck climbed the

ramp as the announcer's voice echoed above the roaring crowd. After locating section R, she scrambled up the steps of the massive wooden bleachers to row 1200.

The announcer's booming voice continued. "Each convict competing today must have a year's clean record and a lifetime of guts."

Huck located seats 1207 and 1208, then gazed across the thousands of eager rodeo fans for Gabe. A few minutes later Gabe slid into the seat beside her.

"Did you have trouble finding me?"

"Nope. Want a fresh roasted peanut?"

"Only if you'll crack it open for me."

"Kind of like a safe?"

"Cute. You should be the announcer."

"Fellow at the concession said cattle for the show are gathered from wild herds that roam the bottomland along the Trinity River," Gabe shouted to Huck above the noise.

At that moment, a bull lunged into a tailspin and the convict lost his grip, almost falling underneath several thousand pounds of stomping hooves.

"Oh, Gabe, I can't look!" Huck covered her eyes.

The afternoon continued with the usual rodeo events, along with bareback basket-

ball, cow belling, wild mare milking, and the crowd favorite, hard money. Forty convicts wearing red shirts competed against the tick of the clock and each other to retrieve a money-filled Bull Durham tobacco sack from between the horns of a surly Brahman. The winning prisoner found over a hundred dollars stuffed in the sack, much of which had been contributed by the crowd.

"A dollar of that money was ours," Gabe said later as they climbed into Blue Norther. "Hope he sends it to his family."

"If he's lucky enough to have one," Huck added, glad that the rodeo had come to an end. She knew the inmates looked forward to it each year but felt strangely sorry for them. Even though some of the men had come from good families, they'd made poor choices and suffered for it.

Like Clark.

She pictured the inmate again and shivered.

Clark would have ended up serving time behind the high red brick walls if he'd lived. As far as she knew, the factual story about his death had never been widely circulated. Huntsville's local paper, *The Huntsville Item*, had mentioned a few sketchy details, stating he'd been killed in an incident near Kilgore.

"How about some ice cream?" Gabe suggested. "You seem a little sad. We haven't been to King's Drug Store since . . ." He paused.

"Since Papa passed?" Huck smiled, remembering how her father had loved for them to bring him a "cream cone." She faced Gabe. "I'm fine. But how about a root beer float? Then let's drive by the old home place site and go sit by the pond at Sam Houston Park."

It didn't take long to pull up in front of King's and honk for service. Within thirty minutes, they'd finished their floats and were relaxing on a grassy bank beside the Texas-shaped pond. Nearby stood the Sam Houston Museum and his historic homes.

"We haven't been inside the museum in years." Gabe stood and stretched. "It's open another thirty minutes. How 'bout we wander through? See what's new?"

"You go." Huck reached up and squeezed his hand. The rodeo, thoughts about her parents, their old home place, Clark. So much had changed. "I'd just like to sit here awhile longer."

"Thirty minutes, sweetheart. Then we'll head home. We both have to work tomorrow." Gabe grinned. "I'll come back soon."

After picking up a smooth flat rock, Huck

skimmed it across the placid water. It skipped several times, then sunk, sending tiny ripples back to shore. Just like life, she thought. We bounce from one phase to the next until we finally run out of energy. Our hearts stop, but the waves of our actions return to those who love us. Some waves roll in with a splash of gentle foam. Others crest and crash.

Huck lay back and peered heavenward. A handful of autumn stars poked through the dark blue canvas of early dusk, a sign the days were shortening.

She took a deep breath, then slowly emptied her lungs. Change was inevitable, she knew that.

So was death.

An image of Mister Jack flashed across her mind. What was it he'd said the day they met? Oh yes. "There ain't no guarantees about living long."

She knew that too.

Clark had died young. A violent death that had been harder for her to accept than she'd first thought. At the time, her sadness didn't make sense, not after the way he'd behaved. But it was the "good" Clark she'd sewn into the fabric of her memory.

The adventurous Clark.

The fun-loving Clark.

So she'd kept her grief buried, finally crying hysterically one Saturday afternoon three months later while Gabe was out getting his hair cut. It was one of the few secrets she'd ever kept from him.

"Oh, dearest Gabe," she whispered. "*My* soul mate."

She smiled. The term had been more of Mister Jack's mysterious wisdom. He'd also compared life to a poker game, admonishing her to look deep in order to find the best card.

She had.

Gazed into the depths of Gabe's being and discovered an ace.

The thought of ever losing him was . . . unthinkable. So she must be the one to die first . . . except . . . he probably felt the same about her. Perhaps if they were fortunate, they'd go together.

"It's been thirty minutes." Gabe's voice floated into the center of her thoughts. "Ready to go?"

Huck slowly stood, meeting his sea-sky gaze.

"Only with you, darling . . . I'll go only with you."

# NINETEEN

*Summer 2006*
*Adam Colby*
I'd just entered my study after an exhausting day when my phone rang. I glanced at the caller ID. "Hi, Yevette," I said, hoping she'd decided to meet again soon. Our last meeting at The Braided Rein had ended rather abruptly.

"Have you had supper?"

"Um . . . grabbed something at the drive-thru, but it's still in the sack."

"Save it for tomorrow," she replied. "Can you meet me at 3315 Backstretch Road? It's near Jensen Road and Highway 59."

"Backscratch?"

She laughed. "Back*stretch.* S-t-r-e—"

"Got it," I said, grabbing a pen. "Sounds like a racetrack."

"It was. Ever heard of Epsom Downs?"

"In England? Horses, right?"

"Good on the horses, but *this* track was in

311

Houston. It only lasted for a decade or so, but Huck and Gabe attended opening day back in 1933, on Thanksgiving no less."

I thought for a moment and couldn't remember seeing a postcard about a racetrack.

"Adam? Did I lose you?"

"Still here," I replied, wondering if her question had a double meaning. "You said 3315?"

"The same address the Alexanders had on Glen View Lane."

"That's odd. What's the house out there look like?"

"No house, just a dented rural mailbox with the address painted on the side."

"Is this about the final card?" I asked, feeling a nervous tingle.

"It's about Mister Jack. Look for an old '63 tan Chevy pickup."

"His or yours?" I muttered, wondering what was about to happen.

"Pardon? It's a little breezy and I couldn't hear you."

"Are you already there?"

"Yes. It's up on a little rise and is my favorite place in the city to watch the sun go down. There's not many streetlights, so hurry before it gets dark."

This time I hung up first. Yevette sounded

different than the other times we'd met. Perhaps I'd finally become completely real, like the stuffed animal in the children's classic.

Backstretch Road wasn't at all what I'd expected, especially 3315. The old pickup was there, but Yevette had neglected to inform me that it would be parked a good one hundred yards from the mailbox. The property would make a decent-sized football field, or even two.

"Did you have trouble finding me?" Yevette sat on the pickup's tailgate. Beside her was a cooler and a gallon of what looked like brewed tea.

"Guess I never pictured empty land inside a big city."

"It's not how Gabe pictured it either, at least not this long after he purchased it. He was hoping for more residential development."

"You mean a fancy subdivision."

"Exactly. But it never happened, so he never sold it. As you can see, there are many undeveloped lots."

I gazed west. The sun was almost gone. "I wonder why their estate lawyer never mentioned this property."

"Because before Gabe died, they willed it

to me." She stood. "Iced tea?"

I nodded, not really knowing what to say next. She wore the black opal pendant I'd noticed each time we met. And it was the first time I'd seen her dressed in shorts. I'd always heard that horsewomen had shapely legs, and it was no lie. But there was more to Yevette than looks; I was beginning to sense an inner beauty, both simple and complex.

Yevette grabbed two large plastic cups and filled them with ice from the cooler. "I'm not much on cooking," she said, "mainly because I'm on the road so much. But I've got a knack for brewing sun tea." She poured both cups.

"Delicious," I said, then sat on the tailgate.

She sat next to me.

"When I was a kid, I loved riding in the back of a pickup." I took another sip.

"Which is now against the law," she added.

"Guess we didn't realize how dangerous it was."

"Guess not."

We laughed.

I wanted to inquire about her childhood, but it didn't feel right. The light was almost gone, and the breeze had calmed. Hopefully, the mosquitoes wouldn't notice. "So . . . you have something to tell me about

Mister Jack?"

She nodded. "It's not connected to a postcard, not in an obvious way. So I thought you needed to know." Yevette looked at me. "Hungry?"

Before I could reply, she slid off the tailgate and opened the passenger side door. She returned with a grocery bag and the largest silver candelabra I'd ever seen outside of a 1930s movie.

"Where did you get that?"

"At the health food store. Hope you like fresh wholegrain bread, hummus, carrots, and fruit."

"Sure beats what I've been having. But that's not what I'm referring to."

She laughed. "Why don't you light the candles while I unpack supper. We can eat while I tell you about Mister Jack."

I lit the candelabra and gazed again at this unusual woman. A candlelit supper from the health food store, eaten in the back of an old pickup, in the middle of big-city-nowhere. It was exactly what Huck and Gabe would've done.

"Okay," she said. "How about we bless it first?"

"Do what? Oh, you mean say grace."

Yevette understood my apprehension and voiced a simple thank-you prayer. The only

time Haley and I ever prayed was when the Texas Lotto grew above thirteen million. And even then, we never actually *prayed,* only joked about it.

"This property is where Epsom Downs was located," Yevette said. "And we're parked on the backstretch." She dipped a carrot piece into the hummus. "After betting was outlawed and the track folded, they sold off the land at bargain prices."

"And Huck and Gabe purchased it as an investment."

"Gabe did. Huck wanted it because of what happened here."

I laughed. "And opening day was on Thanksgiving?"

"It was the largest pari-mutuel track in Texas, seating some ten thousand people. However, twenty-five thousand showed up for the first race." Yevette ate her carrot.

"Are you a historian?" I followed suit with the hummus, but with an apple slice.

"A *Huck* historian. Even with dementia, she rarely forgot an important detail. Huck said that outside the gates, vendors sold everything from hotdogs to furniture."

"So . . . they bought the candelabra at the racetrack?"

Yevette took a piece of bread. "Don't get ahead. You'll miss something."

"Yes ma'am. Now hand over the bread."

She continued. "Get this: a group of sailors calling themselves The Epsom Salts entertained the crowd with Texas swing music. Bob Wills's intricate fiddle arrangements."

"So famous Bob sold the candelabra to them?"

"Hardly, but an old cowboy did. While Huck sat and listened to the music, Gabe walked to a nearby booth. The proprietor was a saddle maker and a silversmith. I remember Gabe laughing and mimicking his western drawl. I was little and had no idea why. But I'd sit on his lap and beg him to talk that way."

"So, lil' lady," I said in my best John Wayne imitation, "how much did they give fer it?"

"That's the strange part. It was during the Great Depression, so Gabe was only willing to spend five dollars."

"Five dollars?" I almost choked on the bread. "Even back then, a sterling silver candelabra this size would be way more."

"The cowboy ordered Gabe to get *Mr. Abraham Lincoln* out of his pocket and bet him on Humdinger in the fourth race."

"And Gabe won?"

" 'Life's too short not to take a chance,'

the cowboy told him, *'specially when yore in love.'* Gabe's winnings were the cost of the candelabra, to the penny."

"And Huck thinks the old cowboy was Mister Jack?"

"She had her suspicions but didn't let on. Then, before they left the track, Huck saw an old cowboy in the distance who walked with a familiar limp."

"Lots of old men walk with a limp," I said.

"She just left Gabe standing there and ran after him, but lost the cowboy in the crowd. Remembering the booth where Gabe had gone, she ran back to it. The old cowboy wasn't there, but propped in the corner was a handmade yellow-pine cane." Yevette faced me. "Go ahead and say it."

"What?"

"That thousands of canes in this part of Texas were handmade, most out of yellow pine."

Yevette met my smile, then gazed at the burning candles. "This particular cane had playing card suits carved on the handle."

Again, I was at a loss for words.

Yevette reached into the sack and handed me an envelope.

"What's that?" I asked.

"Gabe's final postcard. But don't read it now."

"Why?" I stared at the envelope.

"Because you'll need awhile to think about it."

I got the feeling it was time for me to leave. "And after I think about it?"

She reached over and squeezed my hand, the one holding the envelope. "Call me. We'll meet again so I can finish telling you their story."

"How about here?"

Yevette smiled brighter than the candelabra. "If it's all right with you, I'd like to meet in Texas City."

# TWENTY

Twenty-one?
Lucky for some.
And the age in which a man is
   able
To play the odds at a blackjack
   table.
But for you and me
The number's more
Than law or magic spell;
It's passion's coveted "second
   score" . . .
'Cause we beat the fires of hell!
                    Forever, Gabe

*April 1947*
*Galveston, Texas*
Huck and Gabe stood under the marbled
portico of the swanky Hotel Galvez as a
valet delivered their third version of Blue
Norther, a new Oldsmobile 98 convertible.
Its gleaming white canvas top and sky-blue

320

exterior made it the most beautiful and luxurious automobile they had ever owned. Both previous cars, hard tops and darker in color, had been more than adequate, providing dependable transportation from the beginning of their marriage past the end of World War II. But Gabe had been promoted to a top-level accountant at Gulf, so they'd splurged.

After opening Huck's door, Gabe tipped the valet and walked around to the driver's side. He slid in behind the wheel, shifted gears, and sped down the palm-lined drive to Seawall Boulevard.

"You should have let the valet open my door," Huck said casually. "It's part of his job."

"I tipped the man." Gabe smiled. "Why give him the pleasure of opening your door too?"

Huck returned his smile and scooted closer. After twenty-one years of marriage, he still loved to surprise her. "So where are you taking me this evening? Dinner? Dancing?"

"Since we're in Galveston, I thought it might be fun to go somewhere from our first date."

"The International Pageant of Pulchritude?"

"Nope. Those gals are homely compared to you. Besides, the pageant folded during the Depression." He gazed toward the beach. "Let's see. Somewhere out over the water, there's a romantic little restaurant that serves pink champagne. We have reservations at seven."

"Mermaids?" Huck squeezed his leg. "Don't be silly. It was destroyed in a hurricane."

"Exactly why we've never been back." He glanced in her direction, raising his eyebrows. "But when I phoned the owners last month and explained that we'd be on the island for three nights, they rebuilt it just for us."

"Anything you say, darling." Huck kissed his cheek. There had been a piece in the newspaper about Galveston rebuilding some of its most popular beachfront businesses, but she hadn't paid much attention.

"What? Don't you believe my story?" Gabe grinned a crooked grin.

"Absolutely not. But I will say it's hard to doubt a face so insincere."

"My sentiments exactly . . . I think."

Huck laughed softly, thrilled to be away from Houston in the middle of the week. Sidney Lanier was on spring holiday, and she didn't have to teach. Since Gabe had

business the next two mornings across the bay in Texas City, she'd grade term papers while he worked, but afternoons would be spent relaxing together.

She studied her husband's strong profile, his hairline receding slightly more than it did when they'd met, beginning to gray at the temples. A year or so back, she'd noticed some gray in her own hair, so had it dyed once a month at The Lady Texan Beauty Salon, a ritzy downtown establishment whose sign boasted: "A Place Where Men Are Rare And Women Are Well-Done!"

A few minutes later, Gabe pulled into the newly paved parking lot of Mermaids. The restaurant was much larger than Huck remembered, most of the inside reconstructed into open-air seating. In the center, a beautiful blonde wearing a mermaid costume swam in a giant champagne glass. A group of sailors shared cocktails at a nearby table, vying for her attention.

"She's almost indecent," Huck whispered after the headwaiter had seated them. "Swimsuits have become risqué since the Pageant of Pulchritude."

"That's a mermaid suit," Gabe replied, then chuckled. "And it's why those navy boys are sitting there."

Huck wrinkled her nose with playful

indignation. "All men have disgusting minds, even you."

"We try not to disappoint."

After ordering a bottle of pink champagne, they decided on the house specialty: grilled red snapper, served with a tangy chili-lime sauce.

"Oh my," Huck said, reaching for her glass after the first bite. "I've never tasted fish so . . . grilled."

"A spicy innovation from our Mexican neighbors." Gabe chuckled. "It is much different than the fried fare we're accustomed to."

Huck could eat only half of her order and pushed the rest across the table for him to finish. She sipped her drink and peered out into the vast Gulf of Mexico. There was a certain majesty about ocean sunsets. The brilliant ball of light, transforming into every color of the rainbow before dipping into the darkening sea. On their first date, this was the time of day they'd stumbled upon the porch swing, which Gabe had later copied for their honeymoon.

"What lovely thoughts lie behind those coffee eyes?" he asked after lighting a cigarette.

"Oh, just remembering when we discovered that beach house."

"And you had to use the privy?" He laughed.

"You would recall that part." She reached across the table for his hand. "Remember the porch swing?"

"Vaguely."

"Gabe Alexander!"

He exhaled, the soft sea breeze pushing the smoke inland. "My guess is that unless a storm reclaimed that section of beach, our special swing is still there."

"Let's go and see."

"Tonight? But I have to work in the morning."

Huck leaned across the table and whispered. "Remember how we cuddled close in the swing?"

"I'll never forget."

"And you behaved like the perfect gentleman?"

Gabe nodded.

Turning her head, Huck stared at the mermaid, then returned her attention. "There's no need to be a gentleman tonight . . . sailor boy."

Gabe snuffed out his smoke. "Waiter," he called. "Check please!"


"I think I ate too much," Gabe said as they drove west along the island. "Either that, or

my trousers have shrunk."

"The day we married we promised we were going to watch our waistlines," Huck said, then laughed.

"My stomach must have been sleeping during *that* conversation."

As predicted, the swing was still there, hanging underneath the crude bungalow built on stilts. And even though a row of modern weekend houses had been constructed just up the beach, they had no trouble locating the secluded spot where they'd first bared their souls.

"Isn't trespassing exciting?" Not waiting for Gabe's answer, Huck hopped out of the car and kicked off her shoes before twirling around in a circle. "I don't think this place is ever used."

"We have the world to ourselves." Gabe climbed out of the driver's side and walked over to the swing. "This is it all right. A good bit more weathered than I remember and full of sand."

"Let's write down the address and send the owner an anonymous thank-you," Huck said, scampering back to the car. She put the top down and turned on the radio, keeping the volume low so they could still hear the gentle splash of surf along the beach.

Gabe emptied the sand, then laughed. "To

whom it may concern: Thank you for the use of your gritty swing and old-fashioned restroom facilities." He paused. "Now would you look at that. Privy's gone. What's my dear wife going to do after all that champagne?"

"Hush and take off your shoes so we can dance," she ordered. "The DJ just announced he'd play 'Moonlight Serenade.'"

"Okay, but first let me loosen my belt. You don't want to dance with a man who's miserable."

As stars began to glitter the sky, they barefooted to a romantic selection of big-band ballads. And just like so many years before, Huck felt herself drift helplessly under the enchanted spell of soul mates. But this time it didn't matter how deeply she showed her affection.

This time she wasn't engaged to another man.

This time she was with her husband.

Gazing into his sea-sky eyes, she kissed him. Throughout their marriage, she felt it proper for him to make the first move, but not now.

Not tonight. Where other couples their age had selfishly drifted apart, they'd grown closer over the years, working hard to avoid the effects of The Long Division. Thanks to

forgiveness and their continued desire for romance, they still treasured the time they spent alone together. "Two hearts commanding devotion," she whispered, then kissed him again.

"Wow," Gabe said. "I never knew you could be this . . ."

"Brave?" Huck laughed. "Want to see how brave?"

The DJ's melodic voice carried softly into the night. "And now for all you married couples out there, here's a number that will strum the heartstrings. New on this week's hit parade by Mr. Al Jolson: 'The Anniversary Song.' "

"It's 'Waves of the Danube,' " Huck cried. "From our wedding night. Only now there's words."

"Darn that Jolson." Gabe sat up. "This had better be good."

"Shh! I can't hear." She ran to Blue Norther and upped the volume as Al Jolson crooned. When the song ended, Huck switched off the radio and returned to the swing. "I can't believe our music has words." She kissed him a third time, more deeply than ever.

"My own beautiful moonlight serenade," Gabe whispered as she dove into his arms.

With a loud snap, the swing fell to the ground.

They burst out laughing.

A light upstairs switched on.

"Oh no!" Huck screamed. "We're not alone."

"Who's down there?" A gruff voice sounded as if it was directly above them, followed by a clomp of loud footsteps.

"Quick, I'll grab my coat and shoes. You run for the car!" The instant Gabe stood, the button on his trousers popped and they slid down around his ankles.

"My shoe! Gabe, I've lost my other shoe!"

"This is no time to play Cinderella. Leave it for Prince Charming up there!"

Huck reached the safety of the car first as a flashlight beam shot through the darkness. She glanced back at Gabe. With arms full and britches still hugging both ankles, he moved like a panicked penguin. She laughed hysterically.

"Scoot over behind the wheel and drive," Gabe commanded, still ten feet from the car. "Start the engine!"

Without bothering to stop, he tumbled headfirst over the passenger's door. Catching his middle on the rubber window molding, his drawers pointed skyward like a white beacon.

"Sex-crazed hooligans!" the gruff voice shouted. "How 'bout I fill your butts full of rock salt!"

The engine roared to life and Huck tromped the accelerator, leaving the so-called Prince Charming with nothing but her missing shoe.

The next morning, Huck and Gabe kissed good-bye at the lobby elevator. "I'll see you tonight," he said, then winked, before walking out the heavy front door for his nine a.m. meeting in Texas City.

"Going up?" the elevator operator said.

"Top floor, please."

As the elevator crept upward, Huck mentally replayed the events of the previous night, now a little shocked at her own boldness. Revisiting some of the haunts from their first date had made her realize all over again how much she loved Gabe. Sometimes, she felt as though she couldn't care for him any more deeply, but with each passing day, her love continued to grow.

As the elevator door opened, Huck had an idea. Instead of grading term papers, she'd do a little shopping. Close to the wharves in an area locals called "The Strand," she'd noticed a women's boutique that advertised silk negligees from Paris.

Since last night had turned out differently than planned, she'd play it safe and surprise Gabe with a little something that evening in their own hotel room.

An hour later, Huck stepped out of a cab and joined the eager bustle of Galveston's historic commercial district. She checked her watch. Nine o'clock sharp. But instead of business as usual, people were stopped along the sidewalk, entranced by a giant orange smoke plume rising across the bay at Texas City.

Huck started to ask about the beautiful color when the plume suddenly exploded, mushrooming into a thick black cloud. The sidewalk swayed beneath her feet, throwing her down onto the hard concrete. People screamed as glass storefronts shattered. Huck tried to stand but was slammed down again as an aftershock rocked the ground.

Dazed, she sat up as even more glass and debris rained down. Billowing darkness covered the sky, suffocating the sunlight. Blood dripped from her forehead.

"Texas City's gone!" someone yelled. "Been blown off the map!"

Sirens blared as a battalion of emergency vehicles sped past from out of nowhere.

"Oh Gabe! No!" Huck cried. She finally managed to stand, but her head reeled, the

dizziness causing her to lose balance. Breaking the fall with her hands, both palms landed against razor shards, but she felt no pain.

A series of smaller explosions popped across the bay like a string of firecrackers, the rolling blackness now fueled by an inferno of towering flames. "Gabe!" Huck pleaded. "Oh please God, no. Help me. I've got to find him."

Struggling to her feet, she stumbled past several people with blank expressions. "Please help me," Huck begged anyone who would listen, but it was as if she had entered a world of zombies.

Another siren wailed as an ambulance appeared half a block away. Huck ran out into the street and waved her arms as blood dripped from her injured palms. The ambulance tried to go around her, but she blocked its path with her body. It swerved and screeched to a stop.

"Lady? Are you insane?" the driver called, leaning his head out of the window. "Move out of the way."

"My husband. Please help."

"I said move out of the way!" The engine revved and the ambulance inched forward.

"No. You can't leave me here." Huck pressed her bleeding hands against the

hood. "My husband needs me." Reaching down, she then picked up a long shard and clenched it like a knife. After climbing onto the hood, she crawled to the windshield and glared at the driver.

"Get down from there," he demanded.

"Not until you take me to my husband." She raised the shard. "Take me or I'll use this on myself."

"Danged crazy lady."

Huck pressed the point against her wrist.

"Lady, don't. Please."

Focusing on her target, she reared back the shard and closed her eyes.

"Okay!" the driver yelled. "Where is he?"

"Texas City." Huck flung the shard onto the street. "Monsanto Chemical Company."

"That's where we're headed." The driver shook his head. "I shouldn't do this, but lady . . . you got guts. Get in."

An orderly jumped out the rear door and helped Huck inside.

"Patch her up," the driver said. "I guess she's coming with us."

Fortunately, Huck's wounds were not serious and didn't require stitches. But with so many emergency vehicles clogging the road, the trip took longer than expected. In the distance, she could see a huge steel barge that had washed up on dry land.

"Please tell me what happened," Huck asked the driver, after crawling into the front seat. "It will help me find my husband."

"All we know, ma'am, is that a ship docked in the industrial slip exploded, along with some nearby oil storage tanks. The shock waves knocked two light planes right out of the sky. Before we left Galveston, there was a report that a fifteen-foot wall of water had rolled over the town."

"What about Monsanto? My husband is with another company but had a nine o'clock appointment."

"Haven't heard a word about it, ma'am." His voice trembled. "Truth is, got an older sister who works there that looks kinda like you and . . . Just haven't heard."

When they reached the outskirts of Texas City, Huck could see fires burning everywhere. Groups of people covered with a thick coating of oily soot walked aimlessly about. After they were waved through a police barricade, the destruction worsened. Some homes had been literally blown apart by the force of the explosions. Others looked as if they'd been shredded by tons of flying debris.

A little farther on, a county deputy stood at the entrance to the business district. He

held up his hand, instructing them to stop.

"All ambulances to the city auditorium," he called. "That's where they're holding the seriously wounded."

"What about Monsanto?" the driver asked.

"Might as well have been ground zero. State troopers and military personnel are still pulling out bodies. But it's off-limits to you sad wagons. Still too dangerous."

The driver nodded, then cocked his head toward Huck and the orderly. "Hold on!" With a squeal of tires, he sped past the deputy and headed toward Monsanto. "We'll find your husband, ma'am. And my sister."

Too upset to answer, Huck could only nod.

Much of the business district had been reduced to rubble. As best she could tell, ground zero was about a mile away, still engulfed in flames. When they reached the massive parking lots of the industrial area, they saw hundreds of cars slung into twisted piles of rubber and steel. A flatbed military truck passed, piled high with bodies, the stench of burned flesh almost more than Huck could bear. She gagged.

The driver coughed. "That's the Monsanto complex up ahead on the right, still

burning. What does your husband drive?"

"A blue Oldsmobile convertible. New."

"I know you said he was in a meeting, but maybe he was late."

"He's never late."

"Just the same, I'll keep my eye out." He stuck his hand out of the window. "Pretty hot out there. Don't know how much closer we can get without protective gear."

They detoured around the roofless hulk of a large blue vehicle.

At the sight of it, Huck's head spun. Was that Blue Norther? Could Gabe be somewhere close? "I think that's our car!" Huck screamed. She tried to open the door, but the driver grabbed her arm. "What are you doing? Let go of me!"

The ambulance skidded to a stop. "You're gonna get yourself killed and us too!" he yelled, then backed off. "Unless your husband drives a delivery truck, it's not him."

The next quarter of a mile was slow going. Huge hunks of steel stuck out of the ground like jagged meteors. Some cars were still burning. Others sat smoldering in giant puddles of oily seawater like wads of crumpled tinfoil. An icy sweat beaded across Huck's shoulder blades and slid down her back, chilling her entire body. The doom was closing in on her. She began to shake

336

uncontrollably.

Up ahead, an army Jeep had stopped amid the destruction. A soldier dressed in green fatigues stood at the rear holding a two-way radio. The ambulance driver pulled up alongside. "Can you tell us anything about Monsanto?"

"See that empty flatbed?" he said dryly, then gestured to the right. Thirty yards away sat a truck like the one they'd passed hauling bodies. "The corpses about to be loaded are all folks who were inside Monsanto. It's too late for an ambulance." Without another word, the soldier climbed in the Jeep and drove away.

The terrible news was more than Huck could endure. If Gabe was dead, she had to know now! After shoving open the door, she hit the ground running in the direction of the flatbed. Intense heat slapped and dizzied her mind, causing her to lose direction. After stumbling over what looked like a man's boot, she realized a leg was still attached . . . only a leg. She immediately fell to her knees and vomited. "Oh God, help me!" she sobbed. "Mister Jack, where are you?"

Regaining her composure, she continued in what she thought was the right direction. Rounding a pile of crumpled metal, she met

the ambulance driver. Directly behind him was the flatbed. Several bodies covered with a large tarpaulin lay side by side. "Gabe!" she cried. Unable to face the possible truth, she buried her face in her hands.

"He's not under there," the driver said. "All of these men have been identified as company dockworkers."

After helping Huck back to the ambulance, he handed her a canteen. "Have some water."

Huck leaned against the hood and tried to sip the warm, tasteless liquid. In the distance, she could see the part of Monsanto that was still burning. Several firemen wearing asbestos suits arced massive amounts of water onto the hellish flames. Nearby, a battered sign read, "Monsanto Parking Only." The far side of the lot was submerged under several inches of oily, debris-strewn muck. In the center of a dry area, a large sailing yacht named *Blackjack Betty* had washed ashore. A state trooper appeared from behind the splintered hull. He ran over to the ambulance. "Quick!" he shouted. "Found a man inside his car over behind that boat. Nearly missed him 'cause he was slammed up under the dashboard."

"Where is he now?" the driver yelled back.

"Pulled him out and laid him on the

ground. Thought he was dead, then he opened his eyes."

"Can we get the ambulance any closer?"

"Way too much wreckage. Grab your stretcher and come this way."

In an instant, Huck was trudging through the maze of destruction once again, this time following three men. Her knees felt as if they were going to buckle, but she had no more tears. Hoping against hope there was a slim chance that the survivor might be Gabe, even though his meeting had been the same time as the explosion. If by some miracle he was alive, he was still trapped inside the plant.

Then as they rounded the yacht's bow, she saw Blue Norther!

All the glass had been shattered, the canvas top gone, but the car was in one piece. And the man lying on the ground beside it . . . Gabe!

Huck sprinted to his side and knelt. "Oh, Gabe. I thought I'd lost you."

He opened his eyes, his voice barely audible. "I knew you'd find me. You've never lost anything, except a shoe."

"Ma'am," the orderly said. "We need to tend to his wounds and get him into the ambulance."

Huck stepped back, unable to take her

eyes off her husband. His hair and face were covered in a mixture of blood, grease, and soot. What was left of his suit had large holes burned through it.

"Pulse is strong," the orderly said. "But he's lost some blood. Right leg is broken. Looks like there's multiple abrasions from all the flying glass and some minor burns."

"Then, is he going to . . . ?" Huck tried to finish her sentence, but the words clogged in her throat.

"Looks like he's gonna be fine, ma'am," the orderly answered. "We got here in time."

"He's lucky *Blackjack Betty* went aground where she did," the trooper added, "although I can't figure why a sailboat would be docked in an industrial slip. Probably acted like a dam, protecting this small area of the parking lot from the force of the tidal wave. But with all the huge flying projectiles, that big blue car is what saved your husband's life."

In less than ten minutes, Gabe had been bandaged, given something for pain, and loaded in the ambulance. Huck remained by his side, holding his hand.

The driver started the engine. "Seen any female survivors come out of Monsanto?" he asked the trooper.

"A few. But the fire's still blocking many

of the exits."

The driver nodded, then let out the clutch.

Huck reached forward with her free hand and squeezed the driver's shoulder. "A man who once predicted my future told me to 'grab hope and never let go,'" she whispered.

"And did you?"

She gazed upon her husband, battered but alive.

"This time I did," Huck replied. "This time."

## TWENTY-ONE

As your husband
It's my passion
To buy you intimate
Paris fashion;
A negligee? A bustier?
Shout the resounding
Ditto!
But why would my wife choose
  lingerie
The French call,
"Merry widow"?

Forever, Gabe

*November 1960*
*Dallas, Texas*
The Friday after Thanksgiving was one of the busiest Christmas shopping days of the year, but Huck didn't mind the crowds. The cold, wet weather, along with all the spicy holiday aromas, gave her a feeling of cheerful coziness. She and Gabe had awakened

before daylight and driven to Dallas to shop at the most lavish department store in Texas, Neiman Marcus.

"A fellow at the office told me the store was founded on a mistake," Gabe said, then coughed sharply as they crossed the Trinity River into the city limits of Big D.

"That's hard to believe." Up ahead, Huck could see the flying red horse atop the Magnolia Oil building, a prominent landmark of the skyline that rose above the rolling Blackland Prairie. They were getting close. She pulled down the visor mirror to check her makeup. Even though she was fifty-five and Gabe was sixty, they both still looked younger than their ages. Gabe had distinguished silver highlights at his temples with only a few laugh lines, and — thanks to her beauty shop — she could still pass for a woman in her midforties.

"Fellow swears it's true," Gabe continued. "Says when the owners decided to open the store in 1907, they'd just turned down an opportunity to get in on the ground level of a new soda pop venture: Coca-Cola."

"I'm glad they said no to Coke." Huck pushed up the visor and smiled. "I like our yearly trips to Neiman's and so do you."

Their talk instantly connected her thoughts to the Texas City disaster thirteen

years earlier. When Gabe had recovered enough to ask questions, he'd inquired how she'd commandeered an ambulance. The fact that it hinged on her shopping for seductive lingerie delighted him immensely. So each November, he insisted on taking her to Neiman's to buy what he called "female finery," especially since it had been the catalyst for saving his life.

Huck argued how several additional factors at Texas City had kept him alive — a protective boat named *Blackjack Betty,* their beautiful car, and a traffic delay that caused him to still be in the parking lot at the time of the explosion. She even theorized that Mister Jack had had something to do with a pleasure yacht washing up unexpectedly out of an industrial slip . . . a boat with *jack* conveniently in its name. But Gabe had simply laughed. What he had *not* laughed about was her wish to never sell Blue Norther. They'd had it refurbished and now it was almost a classic.

Gabe coughed again. "We're here," he said, pulling up in front of the ornate downtown store. "Won't be able to check into the Adolphus Hotel until this afternoon." His cough continued. "Sorry. Must be this damp weather." He pulled a handkerchief from his suit pocket. "Why don't

you get out here, and I'll go search for an empty parking place."

"But, Gabe. I think you're catching a cold."

A concierge stepped to the curb and opened Huck's door.

"I'm okay, honey. If I'm not back for lunch, I've run off with the meter maid."

"Fine, just leave our car. She'd never love it the way I do."

"I'll be right back," Gabe called as he motored away.

Huck scampered inside. It worried her that his cough had returned, a raspy hack that would come and go. It had developed a few days after the explosion during his three-week hospital stay. Doctors said that it was due to breathing massive amounts of dust and chemical particles. They also recommended he quit smoking. He had, for the most part, except for an occasional cigarette when he was bored or under stress.

"Welcome to Neiman Marcus." A male floorwalker with slicked-back hair and an expensive three-piece suit offered a slight bow. "May I check your coat?"

"Please," Huck replied, allowing him to slide it from her shoulders. He snapped his fingers, and a young woman retrieved the coat and handed him a claim number.

"And may I direct you to a specific department?"

"No, thank you." She smiled. "I'm just waiting for my husband."

"Very well." He handed Huck the number. "Would you prefer to peruse our Thanksgiving sale items while you wait? They're conveniently located right over there." He gestured to a well-lit display near the elevators. "There's a lovely silver platter, perfect for serving next year's bird."

"What about my husband?"

"Only if he won't mind being stuffed and basted." The floorwalker briefly cackled at his attempt at vaudevillian humor, then cleared his throat. "When I see a man looking for a beautiful woman, I'll point him in your direction."

The platter was as sterling as the floorwalker's flattery. Huck slid her hand along the gleaming smooth finish. She chuckled softly. It would be a perfect complement to the silver candelabra they'd purchased on Thanksgiving Day back in 1933 at the opening of Epsom Downs.

Huck smiled at the memory of that wonderful day. Their love had only strengthened through the years. Then Gabe's voice jolted her thoughts back to Neiman's. She jumped.

"I thought I'd never find a place to park

in this Dallas traffic," Gabe said.

"You startled me," Huck said. "I was remembering when you bought our candelabra."

Gabe chuckled, then spoke with a twangy Texas drawl. "Now who'd 'a thunk a critter predicted to finish dead last would 'a won?"

Huck smiled, mimicking his speech. "Reckon it wuz the old cowboy who'd thunk it." They'd had this same conversation many times and now it was a game, even though she still believed he'd been Mister Jack.

"And who knowed that danged ole money we won would 'a been the candelabra's exact price?"

"The old cowboy knowed it," Huck replied. "But no more reminiscing. It's time to shop."

After seeing Huck to the lingerie department, Gabe sat in a comfortable lounge area and leafed through a Neiman's Christmas catalogue. Since it was the noon hour, all the shoppers had disappeared.

He chuckled. There was no telling what kind of frilly undergarments his wife would buy. She was still so beautiful, sometimes when he looked at her, his stomach ached.

He flipped a few more pages and paused. A fashion model reminded him of their

delightful housekeeper, Priscilla, who worked for them two days a week. She'd grown up without the advantages of a stable home life, but had graduated in the top quarter of her high school class back in the spring. Her plan was to work hard and save enough money to attend college. They'd offered to pay for some of her education expenses, but she'd politely declined help. And even though she'd only been with them for six months, in some ways, she was the daughter they'd never had.

Gabe glanced up from the catalogue at the sound of approaching footsteps. "You can't see it until tonight, but guess what I bought." Huck held a silver box decorated with snowflakes.

"Priscilla's Christmas gift?"

"In this department? Don't be silly. Women don't give each other lingerie unless it's for a wedding shower." She tapped on the box. "Any guesses?"

"Itchy red longhandles with a trap door in the back?"

"I'll wear them just for you." She set down the box and sat beside him. "Looking at anything interesting?"

"Don't you think this gal looks like Priscilla?" He pointed to the model.

"If she reduced. Priscilla's a little on the

plump side."

"Somewhere in this catalogue, you can order your own private airplane."

"I like our little sailboat." Huck snuggled close. "I'm tired. Let's have some lunch and see if our hotel room is ready."

Gabe turned to a place he'd marked with his finger. "Are you too tired to try on this dress?" After buying her clothes for thirty-four years, he'd become pretty good at selecting the colors and styles that enhanced her natural beauty.

"Oh, Gabe. I love the happy pink color of the full skirt. It will be perfect for dancing on New Year's Eve. And the backless black velvet bodice is so slimming."

"What about the polka dots on the skirt? Are they slimming too, or just round?" He grinned. "Want to go try it on?"

In no time, a saleslady had located the dress in Huck's size and escorted her behind a curtain to the dressing rooms. Once again, Gabe found himself waiting nearby in another "husband" lounge. He wished for a newspaper, having already skimmed through the catalogue.

"I'll come back in ten minutes, dear," Gabe heard the saleslady call. She came out from behind the curtain as he was searching his suit pockets for a stray cigarette

pack. "Your wife looks lovely in that dress. But she says you must not see it until New Year's Eve."

Gabe watched as the saleslady disappeared around the corner, then stood and gazed around the women's department. There was not a person in sight. And no one else had been in or out of the dressing area. Obviously, Huck was alone.

He chuckled.

She may not want him to see the dress, but why should he have to wait? The whole polka-dotted, black velvet, slimming thing was his idea. What would be the harm in surprising her with a quick peek? She'd be a little peeved perhaps, but would later consider it daring. Even funny.

Gabe slipped past the curtain and peered down the plush hallway of fitting rooms. It wasn't that much different from the men's department, except there were mirrors everywhere and racks full of dresses waiting to be placed back out on the floor.

He checked his watch. Eight minutes until the saleslady returned. It was silly for a man of his age and position to be acting like a schoolboy, but being married to Huck had taught him to enjoy life. Take chances. And if he was caught behind enemy lines, he'd just . . . well, he'd think of something.

Hearing movement behind a door on the right, he crept forward and opened it.

A matronly woman yelped! Luckily she was dressed.

Gabe grabbed a dress off one of the discard racks. "I'm Mr. Marcus," he said in a sophisticated voice. "This would look stunning on you!" He shoved it at the woman and closed the door.

"Why . . . thank you," came a soft voice.

"What do you think you're doing?" Huck stuck her head out of the next room. Gabe's face was redder than the horse atop the Magnolia building.

He placed his finger in front of his lips. "Trying to find you," he whispered, then handed her his billfold.

"You thought I was in *that* dressing room?" A huge grin spread across her face. "I saw a woman go in there who wouldn't appreciate . . ." Huck covered her mouth and shook with laughter. "So is she going to kill you or scream for the store detective?"

"Neither, if she likes my taste in clothes," he replied breathlessly. "I'll be waiting out front in the car . . . having a cigarette."

Huck ducked back into the dressing room. The dress fit perfectly. She changed back into her shopping clothes but, instead of leaving, plopped into a Queen Anne chair.

Her eyes moistened. What had she done to deserve a man who received more delight out of buying her a dress than most men did purchasing a new car? She dug a tissue out of her purse. Gabe's hacking cough worried her. It sounded different than it had even a month ago.

Deeper.

More severe.

"How many New Year's Eves do we have left?" she whispered.

She supposed Mister Jack knew. But would he walk though the dressing room door and reveal how many more years she had with her soul mate? No. It wasn't his way. And since only God was all-knowing, maybe Mister Jack was doing the best he could.

"Ma'am," the saleslady called. "Is everything all right?"

"For now," Huck replied.

# TWENTY-TWO

As each year passes,
Though we grow older,
Silver coin and candle holder
Stay treasures dear;
Priceless and desired.
But life holds much
Yet to be found by lovers bold;
Adventures abound!
'Cause like Blue Norther
We've just been
Re-tired!

                              Forever, Gabe

*January 1974*
*Houston, Texas*
Huck glanced out her kitchen window, hoping to see the swirl of snowflakes falling from the steel-gray afternoon clouds. The weatherman on channel 13 had said there was a fifty percent chance, but any kind of frozen precipitation in Houston, even in the

dead of winter, was about as likely as a heat wave at the North Pole.

After spooning tea leaves into a blue china teapot, she poured in boiling water. When the brew had steeped, she filled two cups, adding extra honey and lemon to Gabe's. It had been a good day, his breathing easy. Also, the tea seemed to help him breathe more freely.

She sighed.

There was no predicting what kind of day he would have. Emphysema was like that. If Gabe had only known the danger, he would have never smoked, especially after the cough he'd developed in Texas City. Since his diagnosis three years ago, he'd only suffered one really bad spell. However, unless a cure was found, his lungs would eventually lose all their elasticity and function.

But thank the good Lord, they'd been lucky so far. Progression had been slow. The only things that had changed significantly were his not being able to travel as much and limiting all strenuous activity. "It's darn frustrating how I run out of breath," he'd said one morning at breakfast. "And I'm not talking about mowing the yard!"

After placing the tea on a serving tray, she walked toward Gabe's study. The tap and ring of his old manual typewriter met her

ears. Emphysema may have slowed his body but not his mind. A day didn't pass in which he was not typing something. A grocery list. Letter. Poem.

She smiled. He'd written her hundreds of lovely poems on postcards through the years. And as soon as some of her obligations with the Texas Retired Teachers Association ended, she'd sort the cards by year and put them into albums. They'd always kept them hidden. Secret. Even from Priscilla. So if she camouflaged the albums among their collection of photographs, no one would be the wiser, at least until they were both deceased.

"Ready for tea?" Huck entered the study.

Gabe nodded, deep in thought.

Smiling, she set a cup and saucer on his desk, stood behind him, and ran her fingers through his hair. There were still a good many curls, all silver, but his sea-sky eyes remained as true as the day they'd met.

"Ah . . . that feels good." Gabe quit typing. "After a week, you have to stop."

"That's what you say now, but by then, you'll think of a reason for me to keep going." She began massaging his shoulders. "So what are you writing?"

"I was just answering Charlie's letter. Haven't communicated with him since we

met him and Chloe for breakfast at Benny's Diner, just before they moved to their retirement community. He wants to know every detail about what happened last year in La Grange with the infamous Chicken Ranch. Guess there aren't any such establishments to pick on down in Florida."

"Gabe Alexander!" She thumped his head with her finger. "That is not a very polite subject."

"Nor a polite predicate."

She thumped him again. "What if Chloe or one of their grandchildren reads your letter?"

"They'd think I was writing about poultry." He laughed. "Remember Charlie's oldest son who fought in the D-Day invasion of Normandy?"

Huck nodded.

"Well," Gabe continued, "I'd forgotten he served on the battleship *Texas*. He told Charlie that there were plans in the works to refurbish that fine old Texas gal. She was first commissioned in 1914."

"Then she probably needs a face-lift," Huck said.

They laughed.

"In a week or so," Gabe continued, "the weather is supposed to warm. What say let's take Blue Norther on a little day trip over

to where she's moored and pay our respects?"

"I like that idea." Huck stopped massaging and kissed him on the cheek. "Just don't get excited and try to join the navy."

"Not a chance. They turned me down after Pearl Harbor was hit, and I'm still mad about it."

"So did all the other branches, dear. Gulf needed you more." She picked up the tray and retreated to their private parlor. Sitting on the love seat, she sipped her tea and glanced out the window.

She could hear Gabe's typewriter again. It had been hard for him when he'd tried to reenlist and couldn't. Even though he'd served in World War I, the War Department felt that at age forty-three, he'd serve the country better staying with Gulf.

Huck sipped her tea as a familiar emptiness punched her stomach. Cutter was five years younger than Gabe, and extremely athletic, so he'd been able to enlist. After basic training, he'd excelled in flight navigation, so he shipped out to join the Eighth Air Force stationed in southern England. In 1943, his entire B-17 squadron lost their lives when they were shot down behind German lines. Since Cutter was her twin, Huck felt as if part of *her* had died. Both she and

Gabe had grieved for months. Every night of the endless war they'd held each other close, and she knew on most of those nights, Gabe felt guilty to be alive. Along with the rest of the nation, they prayed for the safety of the troops and an expedient conclusion to the madness. But Huck especially prayed for Gabe, who relived the horrors he'd suffered in the trenches. He'd awaken drenched in sweat, then shiver uncontrollably for hours. She'd wrap her arms around him and recite some of his favorite psalms. Psalms about God's protection, comfort, and strength.

Glancing out the window, Huck chose to focus her thoughts on happier times.

Still no snow.

As a child, she'd often dreamed of riding on a sled, flying down a powdery white slope. The only time it had ever snowed enough for that to happen was the winter before she'd discovered her secret glen.

Her father had rented out some of their land to a sharecropper named Colonel Blue. He wasn't a real colonel, and Blue was only a nickname, but he had been a drummer boy in the War Between the States. Huck loved to hear his exciting tales of adventure, so spent many a chilly afternoon beside a rusty pot-bellied wood stove, drinking hot-

water-tea with Blue and his wife, Stella. Since children weren't allowed to have coffee, Stella stirred cream and sugar into hot water, adding just enough coffee to give it a caramel color.

One frigid afternoon just before Christmas, she sat enraptured by one of Blue's stories. By the time he finished, large fluffy flakes were falling from the sky. In no time, the snow had piled several inches deep. With a twinkle in his eye, Blue instructed Huck and Stella to put on their coats and follow him outside. On the back porch was a little homemade sled. For the rest of the day, they all took turns sliding down a nearby hill. After the first of the year, Blue and Stella moved on. But Huck never forgot how a married couple well past retirement age had frolicked like carefree children.

That's why she loved the snow. Remembering Blue and Stella made growing old much more palatable.

Huck took a slow sip, savoring the sweet tart flavor. So much had changed since her childhood. Professional baseball could now be played indoors, and a man had actually walked on the moon. In fact, the Astrodome and NASA were only short drives from their home. And she'd never forget overhearing one of Priscilla's friends say that if man had

really stepped upon the lunar surface, on a clear night, we'd be able to look up and see his footprints without a telescope.

Priscilla.

Such a complicated woman.

And as of two months ago, a mother.

Huck shook her head at the memory. Priscilla was a mess, but they loved her like a daughter. Her child would be like a granddaughter.

Yevette Galloway.

The most beautiful baby Huck had ever seen.

Finishing her tea, she could still hear Gabe's typewriter. Over the course of their marriage, especially when they were young, they'd talked about adopting a child, but never did. And now, especially since Gabe's illness, they wished they'd pursued the idea harder. Huck's worst fear, of course, was losing him. After that was the nightmare of her ending up alone in some wretched nursing home.

Huck could feel her emotions spiraling downward. "I refuse to be discouraged," she said aloud. "Not today." Mister Jack had talked about a person playing the hand she'd been dealt. And it was clear to her that he'd always hidden a few cards up his sleeve, sliding one under the table to her

when it was most needed. Perhaps when it came to Gabe's emphysema, he'd slip her another ace.

"Sweetheart?" Gabe walked into the parlor. "Just heard the weather. All next week will be in the seventies, so we can look forward to our trip." He turned his attention toward the window. "Now would you look at that . . . Snow!"

# TWENTY-THREE

*March 1986*
*Houston, Texas*

A television in the intensive care waiting room at Hermann Hospital blared the six p.m. news. Huck checked her wristwatch. In fifteen minutes it would be time to visit Gabe again. Glancing up at the screen, she wished someone taller would turn off the noise. Sometime in her late seventies, she'd begun to shrink.

Huck yawned.

Even though ICU visiting hours were over at ten thirty, she felt it important to be there around the clock. Of course Priscilla had insisted on relieving her a little each day, but as far as Huck was concerned, dozing nights in a drafty hospital waiting room was better than no sleep at home alone in their bed. Sometimes the nurses would let her sit with him for an hour or so during the wee hours if things were quiet. Being near Gabe

was all that mattered.

A news anchor's polished baritone voice caught her attention. "This afternoon, a different kind of St. Patrick's Day event was held at Houston's Shamrock Hotel. Revelers celebrated the fortieth anniversary of its official groundbreaking with a demonstration. Instead of the traditional 'green gala,' demonstrators carried signs protesting the hotel's proposed demolition."

"Demolition?" Huck mouthed. "That will never happen." She'd been so overwhelmed with Gabe's failing health the past few months, she'd had no desire to read the papers. What she did read were his weekly postcards. Loving and witty as ever, the cards were her most cherished possessions.

Her stomach tightened.

It had been sad, almost devastating, not to receive a postcard last week, the first Friday he'd missed in sixty years of marriage. But the man was in intensive care! She could not expect him to do the impossible.

She sighed. Their lives were changing whether they liked it or not.

The biggest change happened a little over a year ago when Gabe's emphysema caused him to constantly be on oxygen. Because of the large cumbersome tanks, they'd stopped

traveling, except for a short trip or two when he'd used smaller portable units. And now most of his days were spent just trying to fill his lungs with enough air for him to walk from the dinner table to his study. Even typing required more energy than he could usually muster.

Huck glanced up at the television as the anchor handed off the Shamrock story to a field reporter. "This now famous landmark," the reporter said, "opened on St. Patrick's Day in 1949, bringing truth to the old adage: Everything *is* bigger in the Lone Star State."

*Gabe would chuckle at this report,* Huck thought. When the Shamrock was built, it had been the talk of the Bayou City for months, so they had attended all the grand opening festivities. Thousands crowded inside and out to get a firsthand look at the opulent, almost gaudy high-rise. Along with its lavishly landscaped grounds, there was a swimming pool big enough for exhibition waterskiing. Dozens of glamorous Hollywood stars attended the event with Los Angeles film executives and an army of journalists. Actress Dorothy Lamour had to cancel a live radio broadcast because of the ruckus.

The report ended and Huck checked her watch.

Ten more minutes.

She longed for that wonderful time when they were younger and Gabe was healthy. But perhaps the news report was a sign that good times were still ahead. After all, weren't shamrocks supposed to be lucky? And anyway, the doctor had said that intensive care was mainly a precaution for one night.

But during that "one night," he'd developed pneumonia and his prognosis worsened. Now the nights had multiplied into seven.

"Mrs. Alexander?" A doctor Huck didn't recognize stepped into the waiting room. "May I visit with you about your husband before you see him?"

"Where's Dr. Sloan?"

"He had an emergency and I'm covering for him. I'm Dr. Larifee."

"Oh." She'd never seen such a young-looking doctor. He hardly looked old enough to have graduated from college, much less medical school.

"May we visit?"

"Of course." She had requested to be kept apprised of Gabe's condition.

"Please come on back." Dr. Larifee led

Huck through automatic double doors into the intensive care unit, then offered her a chair in a secluded area just off the nurses' station.

"Thank you," Huck said. "But I'm tired of sitting."

"Mr. Alexander just took a turn for the worse," the doctor said, then paused and cleared his throat. "With pneumonia, sometimes it happens."

"What do you mean?"

"He's having extreme difficulty breathing and his vital signs are dropping."

"But this afternoon . . . ?" Suddenly, the intense dread Huck had felt at Texas City returned. The lightheadedness. Knees beginning to wobble. She sat anyway.

"Are you all right?"

"Just tell me," Huck managed. "I want to know the truth."

"Ma'am. Your husband is dying. He's already unconscious and probably won't make it through the night. Since he's a 'no code,' there's nothing more we can do."

"Then I must go to him." Huck stood. After sixty years with Gabe, if all she had was less than a night, there wasn't one precious moment to waste.

"Are you sure you're all right?"

*What a silly question,* Huck thought, then

marshaled all her strength. "You do your job, young man, and I'll do mine."

Walking into Gabe's room, she could immediately see that his skin had developed a grayish hue. Even though he was on oxygen, his breathing was rapid and shallow.

"I'm right here, darling," Huck said, sitting on the bed and holding his hand. She could feel tears mounting underneath her eyelids and hear the tremble in her own voice, but remained strong.

"I saw the most wonderful report on the Shamrock Hotel a few minutes ago. Remember how much fun we had at the opening? Do you recall that newspaper man from San Antonio who thought we were movie stars?" She knew she was rattling and that he probably couldn't hear her, but she kept going. A single tear escaped from one eye.

She sniffed.

"Remember, sweetheart? How we made up glitzy Hollywood names and posed by that ridiculous swimming pool so the man could take our picture?" She reached out with her free hand and stroked his thin, stubbled cheek, then stroked his hair before wrapping a silvery-white curl around her finger. "And the next day we bought a San Antonio paper? Skimmed every page until we found our photograph, laughing our-

selves silly?"

Gabe's body seemed to stiffen a little, then relax.

"I'm here," Huck said again, fighting back tears. "Right here beside you where I've always been."

A nurse stepped into the room. "Is there anything you need?"

Refusing to shift her gaze, Huck patted Gabe's arm. "All I've ever needed is right here."

Without another word, the nurse left.

Huck continued. "Have I told you lately, my sweet man . . . ?" She paused to swallow. "Told you that you were exactly who I had been searching for ever since I was a little girl? How I didn't know for sure until that first lovely night in the porch swing?" Feeling her emotion swell, she paused again, this time long enough to better gather herself. "Well, to be honest," she said finally, "I think I knew you were my soul mate even before the porch swing. I think I knew when you made that silly oyster comment the day we met."

Suddenly, Gabe opened his eyes and looked directly at Huck, then closed them again. His mouth moved, but there was no sound.

Lowering her ear to his lips, Huck lis-

tened. Nothing.

"What is it? Please tell me."

She felt Gabe's hand move ever so slightly. "I'll . . ." His voice was barely a whisper.

"Go on," Huck said, her tears free-falling onto his chest.

"I'll . . . come . . . back."

"I know," Huck whispered, "and I'll be waiting. So don't think you must linger."

She turned her head and kissed his lips, then felt a soft whoosh of air brush against hers.

Breathing in deeply, she captured the final breath of her soul mate's life.

The day after Gabe's small graveside service in Houston, Huck put on a dress that had been his latest favorite, climbed into Blue Norther, and drove north toward Huntsville. At age eighty-one, she was still in good health but leery of driving on the interstate. Most drivers on I-45 had no qualms about disobeying the speed limit, so she chose to travel the old two-lane highway, where the rule of law still existed. It would take longer, but this was a trip she felt destined to make.

When the traffic eased, Huck began to recall the horrible events of the past few days. Too numbed to cry, she'd not shed a tear since the night Gabe died. Giving him

permission to go was the hardest thing she'd ever done. But she was exhausted and tired of watching him suffer. Why make a man linger at death's door for an entire night when his hand was already grasping the knob?

Of course friends and family had soon arrived, hovering around her like flies. And as was expected, she'd done her best to put on a pleasant face, sipped iced tea, and swallowed a few bites of King Ranch Casserole, the entire time wondering how she might live another empty moment without Gabe.

Reaching the outskirts of Huntsville, Huck shifted her thoughts back to the job at hand. Since Gabe had always driven, she'd not paid much attention to specific routes, and things had changed so since she was a child. After winding through several back streets because of construction, she found a side entrance to Sam Houston's museum and historic homes.

It was a weekday and she had her pick of parking places, so she chose a secluded spot under a massive pecan tree. She turned off the engine. Luckily, no visitors were strolling about. Gabe had always kept Blue Norther in mint condition, causing admiring onlookers to ask questions about the old car everywhere they went.

The weather was breezy and warm with tiny white clouds dotting the sky. Huck opened the door, climbed out, and peered toward the location of what once had been her secret glen. After it was bulldozed some sixty-five years ago when the grounds were developed, she'd never once attempted to find the spot again.

However, today was different.

Today she needed to go back.

Moving in that direction, Huck walked gingerly along a gravel road, making sure of her footing. People her age were always falling because of carelessness, and she had no desire to be another casualty. Leaving the road, she followed a sandy path that led to some picnic tables in a wooded area. After driving for two hours, her legs and back hurt more than usual, so she sat and rested for a moment, then stood. Behind the tables lay a thick stand of pines, hardwoods, and jungly undergrowth.

*That's where I must go,* she thought, still confident of her sense of direction. But after several attempts, she could not discover a way to penetrate the dense vegetation. Determined not to give up, she scanned the area again and noticed a faint trail she'd somehow missed. Continuing on her mission, she followed the trail until it dis-

appeared.

"It's just been too many years," she said aloud. "I was foolish to try. Foolish to still believe."

Turning around, she began heading back in the opposite direction, but tripped over a root and sat down hard. A dead branch snagged the hem of her dress, tearing a huge hole.

"This was Gabe's favorite," she cried. "I didn't drive all this way to destroy what he loved."

And then like a summer thunderstorm, her pent-up tears began to pour. "I wasn't ready to lose him," she wailed. "I'm not strong enough. Don't even want to be strong enough."

Picking up a handful of pine needles, she flung them skyward. "I knew you wouldn't be here," she said angrily. "And what could you do anyway? Angels aren't God."

She wiped her face with the hem of her dress. "In case you haven't heard, Gabe's dead! I played your silly card game and lost."

With no more to say for the moment, Huck continued to sit in the dirt. In a strange way, the tantrum had made her feel better. Gabe would think the whole thing highly humorous: a woman her age plopped

atop the forest floor having a one-sided conversation with a childhood memory. A memory that was perhaps nothing more than an escaped convict.

A sudden breeze stirred the still air. Out of the corner of her eye, Huck noticed movement of a slender plant. Scooting forward, she spied something pink. A single Anacacho orchid. The most perfect blossom she'd ever seen.

Upon closer inspection, she could tell that initially there had been two orchids. Two small buds gathering nourishment from the same plant, then bursting into one. An orchid this magnificent could only be formed from two.

"Two hearts commanding devotion," Huck said as she cried.

It was at that moment she finally understood the depth of their love. A pure love, refined from a lifetime of sharing. Their marriage had joined them together into a single plant. And each year, just as the plant matured, so did their relationship, grounded in a hope that produced two beautiful blooms. When Gabe died, his bloom had not withered. Because the blossom of his love remained in Huck's heart . . .

Creating one magnificent flower.

# TWENTY-FOUR

*Bayshore Extended Care Facility, 2004*
*Mrs. Alexander*

Struggling to open her eyes, Huck felt a gentle tap upon her right shoulder. "Oh, Gabe, darling, is that you?" she mumbled. "I've been waiting all night, too excited to sleep."

"I'm so sorry to wake you, Huck." Yevette patted her lightly on the arm. "But I have another question about my mother. And I need to read you something." She paused. "Were you dreaming about Gabe?"

"Oh, Yevette." Huck adjusted the bed-covers up around her neck, then pushed a button, raising her head slightly. "What time is it, dear?"

"Nine in the morning. Have you eaten breakfast?"

"I had a bite or two, then must have dozed off." She smiled. "I don't like traveling on a full stomach."

"Traveling? I thought the beauty shop came to you?"

Huck frowned. "I don't know why the people in this wretched place think I'd rather get my hair done in bed. A lady likes to go out from time to time."

Yevette pulled up a chair and sat beside Huck. "Maybe they're just trying to give you good service."

"Humph. After today, they won't have to worry about me anymore." She smiled. "Did I tell you Gabe was coming for me?"

"When I was here a few weeks ago, you said he might join us."

"That's right, you've been gone. How was your trip? Did you win?"

"I placed well in a few races, especially up in Ruidoso. At least it paid my expenses."

"Gabe and I so enjoyed that part of New Mexico. He loved driving in the mountains. But we were always glad to get home to Houston." Huck craned her neck to see the clock on her bedside table. "Today *is* Friday, you know."

"Yes," Yevette said.

"Gabe promised he'd be back. He usually comes right before sunrise."

"Maybe he's been delayed."

"Obviously." Huck sighed. "Sometimes that man can be so frustrating. But I'm

375

dressed and ready." She slid back the covers, exposing a light pink dress with matching shoes. "That woman on the night shift was most uncooperative at five o'clock this morning."

"You mean the nurse?"

Huck ignored the comment. "I threatened to phone the police if she didn't help me get dressed." Huck motioned for Yevette to lean close. "I've phoned them once before," she whispered.

"Twice," Yevette replied.

Huck offered a slight smile. "Before you read, there's something I've been meaning to give you. In the top drawer of my dresser is a small velvet box. Would you hand it to me, please?"

Yevette stepped to the dresser, retrieved the box, and returned to her chair.

"Don't open it," Huck instructed. "Not yet."

"Yes ma'am."

"Remember Gabe's postcard poem about the two tiny shells?"

"It was one of my favorites."

"And the necklace I spoke about the day we read it?"

"You said he'd had a jeweler polish the shells and string them on a gold necklace." Yevette eyed the box.

376

"We'd not been married long when we were at the beach one weekend, and he'd secretly slipped the shells into the pocket of his bathing trunks." Huck sighed. "I never knew what romantic mischief that man was up to." She grinned at Yevette. "Now you may open it."

"It's so beautiful." Yevette picked up the necklace and held it toward the light. "But I never saw you wear it."

"I only wore it for my soul mate," Huck said, then paused until Yevette met her gaze. "And one day, I hope you'll wear it for yours."

"Thank you, I . . ." Yevette wiped away a tear, then leaned over and hugged Huck. "I will," Yevette whispered, "one day."

Huck yawned. "I'm feeling a bit woozy. Perhaps I'll take a short nap. Might your reading wait?"

Yevette nodded. "Would you like for me to lower your head and close the blinds?"

"That would be nice. Now don't let me sleep long."

As Huck slept, pleasant images of her childhood flashed through her mind. Not only specific faces, but group events such as family reunions, church socials, Christmases. At one point, she was back inside her secret glen, talking to Mister Jack.

"Huck?" Yevette's voice interrupted Huck's dreams.

"What, dear?"

"I didn't think you'd want to miss lunch. It will be delivered in a few minutes. Would you like for me to raise your head and open the blinds?"

"No. This is fine." Huck still felt a little woozy, as if she were almost floating. "I just had the most wonderful dream. I was a little girl again and all my family and friends were there. I even saw Mister Jack." She paused. "Now wasn't there something you wanted to ask?"

"There was."

"Then you must hurry with your question, dear. Gabe could walk through that door any minute."

"When he spent that week in the ICU, did my mother go and see him?"

"Priscilla looked up to Gabe like a father." Huck paused again, her words a bit breathless. "She's dead, Priscilla."

"Do you know what she and Gabe might have talked about during that time?"

"I have no idea, dear. But I do remember him telling me that she'd read him the newspaper. He so enjoyed having her read to him."

"Did she ever read anything to him out of

her Bible?"

Huck smiled. "My, how that man loved the Psalms."

"Pardon me?" Yevette said. "I couldn't hear. You must be falling back asleep. What did you say about the Psalms?"

"Gabe believes that the poetry in that book holds the meaning to life," Huck said, her words barely audible. "When he comes today, he's bringing a postcard with a new poem."

"I found a card addressed to you in Mama's Bible, Huck. On the front is a picture of the most beautiful orchid, one I've never seen. On the back is a poem written in Gabe's handwriting. I never thought about going through her Bible until last night. He must have composed it when he was in the ICU, then Mama was killed before she could deliver it." Yevette's voice trembled. "Would you like for me to read it to you?"

"That would be wonderful, dear."

The instant Yevette began reading, Huck saw Gabe. His sea-sky eyes illuminated the entire room.

```
This being Friday's final verse,
Your man could ne'er begin
    rehearse
```

The countless ways he'd hold you
Under one more starry sky.
But life is short, so he must
  wait;
(I'll stand just outside
  heaven's gate)
'Cause love which is forever
Will not die!

"Oh, my dearest Gabe," Huck said.
"You've come back shining like the sun.
And this poem is the most beautiful of all."
Then closing her eyes, Huck Alexander
slipped away into eternity's crisp blue light.

# TWENTY-FIVE

*Summer 2006*
*Adam Colby*

After reading Gabe's final postcard and thinking on it, as Yevette had asked, I called her. She was in town, so we met the following afternoon in front of the Doyle Convention Center in Texas City, near a large fountain.

"Beautiful, isn't it?" Yevette said, her eyes glued to the fountain. A statue of a giant phoenix rose out of the water. "Have any idea why we're here?"

"Not a clue," I replied, racking my brain to remember if Gabe had written any poems about a phoenix.

"Gabe almost died here," she said grimly.

"Drowned in the fountain?" I gave a half chuckle.

"Not funny. Are you aware of what happened?"

"You mean the big explosion?" I felt I'd

been tricked somewhat into making a stupid remark. "I do remember hearing talk from time to time about an industrial disaster back in the 1940s, but that's all I know."

"Let's walk," she said. "I'll continue with the Alexanders' story where I left off the last time we met. Then we'll end up back here."

She wore shorts again, but this time her hair was pulled back into a ponytail. And instead of the familiar black opal pendant, she wore a simple gold necklace with two polished seashells. The tiny shells seemed to reflect the light in her eyes.

As we strolled around the convention center, she talked about Kilgore and the death of Clark Richards. We laughed about the colorful prison rodeo, before she explained in great detail what happened right here in Texas City. Thankfully after that, their Neiman Marcus adventure gave us both a chuckle. But then she told about Gabe's emphysema, his funeral, and Huck's last visit to her secret glen. Then with a somber expression, Yevette explained how Huck died during the reading of the final postcard.

"I'm stunned," was all I could say, then noticed we were back at the fountain.

Yevette stopped walking. "Have you ever

heard any more from Haley?"

"Uh, no," I replied, not expecting the question. "She's remarried and has no desire to keep in touch."

"I'm sorry."

"Don't be. We were both at fault."

For several moments, no one spoke.

"See how that phoenix is flying up out of the fountain?" Yevette finally asked.

I studied the impressive bird and nodded.

"It symbolizes the way this city rose out of the mire of disaster. That bird is you."

Then with a slight nod, Yevette turned and began walking away.

"Are you leaving?" I wanted her to stay.

Spinning on her heel, she faced me. "That's the end of the Alexanders' story. Now you know everything."

"And I can connect the final dots," I replied, meeting her gaze. "But I don't know . . . you."

"After you figure things out, give me a call." She smiled. "Or maybe I'll call you." Turning back around, she walked toward the convention center and disappeared inside.

"I'm stuck in traffic on Buffalo Speedway!" Yevette shouted.

"What?" I asked, then shook my cell

phone, as if it would help. We either had a bad connection or she was driving with her windows down.

"Hello! Adam, can you hear me?"

"Loud, but not clear. Are you in your pickup?"

"Are you at Bering's?"

"Just outside. I thought you said it was a hardware store."

"It is. But they sell more than just hammers. So order two coffees to go."

"Coffee?"

"Don't ask why, just do it. I'll be there soon. Bye."

She *had* called me first.

I closed my phone and walked inside. The upscale store was traditional, yet trendy, and full of unique hardware, merchandise, and gifts. Sure enough, they sold coffee. I ordered and paid for two cups, instructing the girl behind the counter I wouldn't need them for a few minutes. Sitting on a stool, I thought about Yevette and chuckled.

The only reason anyone would drive around Houston in the middle of summer without AC would be because they *wanted* to get heat stroke. But she was an unusual woman.

After we met in Texas City, I was able to connect the last pieces of Huck and Gabe's

remarkable story. Suddenly, I found myself thinking less and less about Haley and more about Yevette. I'd grown so accustomed to self-pity, the oxymoronic comfort of pain, that I hardly knew how to function. Was I really beginning to accept what had happened or just forcing myself to let go? Either way, thanks to Huck and Gabe, I knew I would find the courage to move on.

When I discovered the postcards and began my quest to find the secret to a lasting marriage, I was looking for some kind of formula, a holy grail of marital bliss. After meeting Yevette, I began fitting the pieces of Huck and Gabe's life into the breadth of their story. And even though they were soul mates, they were simply two people in love, a man and a woman who — hard as they tried — couldn't always avoid The Long Division by suppressing selfishness or be in total command of their devotion. So the *secret* was no formula per se, but a culmination of things that made a marriage last. Total trust. An unbreakable bond. Completeness. Even so, I felt as though there was still one piece of the puzzle missing.

And then last night I found it. Even though I'd read Gabe's final postcard multiple times, I realized it pointed to what I'd been searching for.

The poem spoke of his love with Huck lasting forever. And because Huck had known the depth of their bond — Gabe's love remaining in her heart — she was able to live without him for eighteen additional years. But it was Huck's ultimate realization that was key for me. Something I'd already considered but now understood.

As a child, when Huck met Mister Jack, he'd advised her to grab on to *hope* and never let go. I was still not convinced that the man was anything more than a drifter. But after connecting the chain of supernatural coincidences that followed, I decided Mister Jack's wisdom was stellar. Maybe I was beginning to believe in angels too. The homeless man Gabe met in Kilgore could've been *his* guardian angel. Or perhaps angels performed double-duty with soul mates.

From the beginning, Huck's *hope* was to find a soul mate. And then it evolved into keeping that soul mate from harm, Blue Norther becoming a symbol of Gabe's safety. But when he died and her life came crashing down, she discovered a different brand of hope altogether.

As human beings, we hope for many things. Happiness. Health. Job. Children. Mate. Eternity. As we mature, we begin to recognize a mysterious force that is an

integral part of each one of us, something much more powerful than ourselves.

That force is hope, the very bedrock of our souls.

Hope has won wars, fed nations, conquered diseases. In the unquenchable human spirit, hope is the fire.

It is also different and the same for each one of us. For Huck, it was her faith in God and a gentle knowing that she would see Gabe again. For me — and I'd have to ponder more on the God part — hope was a second chance, a fresh start. The beauty is this: whatever relationship mistakes I'd made in the past, hope was where the road began anew.

The definitive puzzle piece? The power of love through hope.

I chuckled. A simple concept, really. And one that held a marriage together for sixty years.

"Sir?" The girl from behind the counter tapped me on the shoulder. "Your two coffees."

I focused my attention back into the hardware store. "Thank you," I replied as Yevette walked through the door.

"So why did you call *this* meeting?" I asked, looking around. "Are we going to build something?"

"Perhaps. Grab your coffee and follow me. Know what brand of brew this is?" she asked as we walked out into the sunny parking lot.

"What?"

"Admiration." She grinned. "Actually it's Houstonian Blend, roasted by Admiration's original company, Duncan Coffee."

"Are you implying that you 'admire' me?"

She stopped walking and looked me in the eye. Hers were as green as emeralds. She continued. "Depends on whether or not you take a drive with me."

"Where?"

"Galveston. Thought we might get some seafood."

"Mermaids? Pink champagne?"

"The answer to your first question is no, not my kind of place. The answer to your second question is only if it tastes like really fine beer."

After rounding a big SUV, I nearly spilled my coffee. Twenty feet away sat a sky-blue 1947 Oldsmobile convertible. Blue Norther.

"I don't believe it," I said, trotting over and running my hand along the gleaming finish. "I'd never even thought to ask about their car."

Yevette opened the driver's door and climbed in. "If you're waiting for a valet to

open your door, you'll be here awhile."

I hopped in the passenger's side. The entire car, inside and out, looked as if it had just rolled off the showroom floor.

"Think this old jalopy will take us where we want to go?" Yevette smiled, then started the engine.

"Hope so," I replied, then grinned at her. "I really do hope."

# READERS GUIDE

1. *Hope* is the novel's central theme. When Huck met Mister Jack at her secret glen, he instructed her to "grab hope and never let go." How does Adam describe hope in the final chapter? What role does hope play in your life?
2. In chapter 10, Adam admitted that before finding the postcards, he thought soul mates existed only in fairy tales. What do you think?
3. Adam reasoned that he and his ex-wife, Haley, had a scandalous love affair with their own selfishness. What do you think he means? Moreover, he learned that what saved Huck and Gabe from The Long Division wasn't *romance,* but rather "the willingness each of them had to continually choose each other *over* their own selfishness."

How can you imagine this kind of selflessness looking in a real relationship?

4. How did Clark's love of material possessions affect his and Huck's relationship? Even though Clark tried to violate Huck, she grieved his death. Why?

5. How would you define Gabe's idea of The Long Division? In our age of many distractions and social media, what factors might cause a married couple's "once shared passions" to separate into "single minded interests"? How can The Long Division be applied to our relationship with God?

For a more detailed *Forever Friday* Readers Group Guide, visit http://waterbrook multnomah.com/catalog.php?work=22 7694.

# ACKNOWLEDGMENTS

One's dream of breaking into fiction can be a long journey. Therefore, I'm *forever* grateful to the following people who've helped make my dream a reality.

Jodi Thomas — who convinced me I had *the gift,* then took the time to teach me the writing ropes. I'm indebted to your friendship, knowledge, and kindness. You challenged me to soar higher than I ever imagined.

Helen Bass — who knew I was destined to write long before even *I* had a clue. Thanks for your constant prayers and encouragement.

DeWanna Pace — who's masterful critiquing skills helped me discover my voice. Thanks, Dee, for your gentle patience.

Roger Otwell and David Otwell — who convinced me I could write anything, then taught me to smile on camera. Thanks, *pards,* for making me a third brother.

Cori Deyoe — my ever skillful and insightful agent who recognized this book's potential, then kept on believing. Thanks for your sound advice, friendship, and cheerfully steering me around every pothole.

Shannon Marchese — my *Editor Extraordinaire,* who believed in my voice, my manuscript, and my career. Thank you, Shannon, for your exceptional insight, professional guidance, and listening heart.

The WaterBrook team — Ken Peterson, Pamela Shoup, Amy Haddock, Beverly Rykerd, Mark Ford, Kendall Davis, and Heather Brown. I'm amazed at your incredible skills, tireless creativity, and knowledge.

Nicci Jordan Hubert and Caleb Rexius — you're masters at what you do.

My great first readers — Ginger Porter, Lisa Rutledge, Rebecca Holmes-Smart, Susie and Rick Culver, Mike and Debi Nichols, Jen Gursky, Joan Gursky, Debbie and Carroll Marriott, Harold Hurry, Suzanne Adams, Millie Otwell, Carmen Terrell, Lyn Dickerson, Bonnie Thorne, Jane Wagner, Terry Beasley, Jan Fulton, Marsha Bigham, Steve Vandiver, Brenda Alcala, Jean Pray, Sandra Dixon, Sara Dixon, Cindy Lewis, John and Susan Clark, Heather Fuller-Jones, Mary Sue Rix, George Rix, Laquitta Doak, Amy Gardner, Cathy Mi-

chael, Judy Kelln, Laura Smith, Chandler Shaw, Joleen Walsh, Nancy Sales, Nick and Becky Nichols, Paul and Rose Ferris, Lindsey Moss, Lisa French, Melissa Burns, Marty Farris, Melinda Conway, Michelle Sherrod, Linda Claytor, and Fred Blalock.

A special thanks to Dr. Darrell Bledsoe, who knows everybody east and west of the Mississippi.

Love and thanks to my family and extended family. There are too many of you to name here, but you know who you are.

My parents, Davis and Mary, who encouraged me to freely follow any career path. My mother not only instilled the joy of fiction into my soul but fed my imagination with hundreds of great books.

Our daughter, Lana, because she put up with a stay-at-home dad who always had to write, then tried his best to make a ponytail.

And finally to my wonderful wife, Dinah, who gave me the greatest gift: the freedom to succeed or fail. Without your endless encouragement, strong faith, unconditional love, and daily prayers, this book would've never happened.

Most of all, I'm grateful to God, the Author of us all!

# AUTHOR'S NOTE

*Forever Friday* is loosely based upon the lives of my great-aunt and uncle. At their estate sale, I discovered a collection of antique postcards, literally pulling the albums out of the trash heap. (They were thought to have been miscellaneous photos of people no one in the family knew.) It appeared my great-aunt had received a postcard with an original love poem every Friday for sixty years, and the collection had been kept secret. I knew I'd discovered a potentially powerful love story, but there was no conflict, no intriguing plot. So I put the albums on a shelf in my study and waited for the love-story muse to cajole me while I wrote other things. About five years later, I received a phone call from a friend whose wife of over twenty years had left him without warning. He said, "I don't believe in love anymore." I remember gazing up at the shelf that held the postcard albums and

thinking: *There lies sixty years of love. Married love.* And suddenly . . . I'd found my story.

Even though my great-uncle's poems were meaningful, they weren't the style of prose I wanted for the novel. So I penned my own, adapting a couple I'd previously written. The poem in the prologue, "Two Tiny Shells," I wrote for my wife, Dinah, shortly after our first date in Galveston. And the poem at the beginning of chapter 13, "The Morning of Our Love," was actually a song I composed for our wedding ceremony.

"So afterward," you ask, "was there really a porch-swing honeymoon?" Hmm. You'll have to ask Dinah that question!